Cracked
to
Death

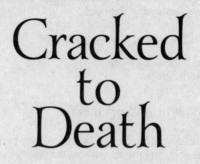

Cracked
to
Death

Cheryl
Hollon

KENSINGTON PUBLISHING CORP.

http://www.kensingtonbooks.com

KENSINGTON BOOKS are published by

Kensington Publishing Corp.
119 West 40th Street
New York, NY 10018

All Kensington Titles, Imprints, and Distributed Lines are available at special quantity discounts for bulk purchases for sales promotions, premiums, fund-raising, and educational or institutional use. Special book excerpts or customized printings can also be created to fit specific needs. For details, write or phone the office of the Kensington special sales manager: Kensington Publishing Corp., 119 West 40th Street, New York, NY 10018, attn: Special Sales Department, Phone: 1-800-221-2647.

Kensington and the K logo Reg. U.S. Pat & TM Off.

ISBN-13: 978-1-61773-764-0
ISBN-10: 1-61773-764-X
First Kensington Mass Market Edition: July 2016

eISBN-13: 978-1-61773-765-7
eISBN-10: 1-61773-765-8
First Kensington Electronic Edition: July 2016

10 9 8 7 6 5 4 3 2 1

Printed in the United States of America

Cracked
to
Death

Cheryl
Hollon

KENSINGTON PUBLISHING CORP.

http://www.kensingtonbooks.com

KENSINGTON BOOKS are published by

Kensington Publishing Corp.
119 West 40th Street
New York, NY 10018

All Kensington Titles, Imprints, and Distributed Lines are available at special quantity discounts for bulk purchases for sales promotions, premiums, fund-raising, and educational or institutional use. Special book excerpts or customized printings can also be created to fit specific needs. For details, write or phone the office of the Kensington special sales manager: Kensington Publishing Corp., 119 West 40th Street, New York, NY 10018, attn: Special Sales Department, Phone: 1-800-221-2647.

Kensington and the K logo Reg. U.S. Pat & TM Off.

ISBN-13: 978-1-61773-764-0
ISBN-10: 1-61773-764-X
First Kensington Mass Market Edition: July 2016

eISBN-13: 978-1-61773-765-7
eISBN-10: 1-61773-765-8
First Kensington Electronic Edition: July 2016

10 9 8 7 6 5 4 3 2 1

Printed in the United States of America

To Eric, Jennifer, Aaron, Beth,
Ethan, Lena,
Ricky, Mister, Pepper, Precious, Snowy

Acknowledgments

Eloyne and Bradley Erickson own Grand Central Stained Glass & Graphics, the business that continues to inspire this series. I am grateful to you in so many ways for loving the books and opening your hearts to an extremely curious student with a significant number of unusual questions.

I appreciate the wide variety of hobbies my friends enjoy and their willingness to share when I need a subject matter expert. Thank you, Sarah Weist and Gregg Bonert, for information about diving. If any details are wrong, the errors are mine alone.

Big hugs to my Gainesville support group. You provided encouragement at precisely the right time, laced with generous amounts of wine and book talk. I needed those retreat days at Joye's woodland cottage to buckle down and put billions of words on the page.

Thanks to one of my strongest cheerleaders in my hometown of Dayton, Ohio, my sister Sheila Collins. She managed to round up a motley collection of friends and relations, which impressed the Books & Company event manager at the Greene Town Center. Also in Dayton, Cheryl Whitmore and I met at a writing conference, and we, the two Cheryls, reigned supreme in our corner of the room. For years we have exchanged weekly status e-mails, which have helped me persevere in getting reluctant words into my manuscript day after day after day.

I offer my thanks to editor and inspirational writing champion Ramona DeFelice Long, who has a gentle way of telling you that your wonderful prose just might need some tiny, drastic adjustments. I check in with her sprint group on Facebook every morning for companionship and focus. What a great group with which to share the grit required to stay the course.

At Kensington, I am eternally grateful to my extraordinary editor, Mercedes Fernandez, who took a big chance on this series and who pushes me to the edge of creative sanity but doesn't let me fall. Thanks to my publicity guru, Morgan Elwell, for encouraging me to try more and more social media interactions.

Fabulous Beth Campbell and the wonderful team at BookEnds Literary Agency are a dream team to work with. They have been informative, supportive, and unfailingly encouraging in answering my approximately ten thousand questions about publishing. I'm trying to schedule a trip to meet the entire team—especially Buford.

A thank-you goes to my parents, Wendell and Marcella, for bragging about my book to every person they meet. It's embarrassing and completely adorable. Also, I offer a big sister hug to my big little brother, Mark Hollon, who has been cheering me on from the start. Thanks go, as well, to his wife, Deana, and his daughters, Alex and Ella, for an added chorus of cheers.

I am grateful to my husband, George, for putting on the mantle of writer's spouse with cheerful grace and endless humor. He is my voice of reason and plays the challenging part of devil's advocate when my monkey brain tries to take on too many tasks. For you, a hug around the neck.

Chapter 1

"Come on. Do the right thing—again," Savannah Webb muttered. She stood behind the sales counter at Webb's Glass Shop, waiting for the register to either boot up or display the blue screen of death. Relief at the sight of a normal start-up screen released the tension in her neck.

The little brass bell mounted on the front door jangled like a startled seagull.

In burst Amanda Blake, Savannah's still novice office manager, with her pudgy arms stuffed full of notebooks, pens, and teaching posters, along with two large dark green reusable grocery bags. The bulging bags, filled with empty wine and vodka bottles, hung from each of her arms, their contents clinking.

"I'm here. I'm here. I'm here," she huffed. "Like the little Whovians from the Dr. Seuss book." Tiny beads of sweat rolled down the sides of her pale face.

Savannah rushed around the counter and grabbed the heavy bags of empty bottles while Amanda staggered to the counter and unloaded the teaching supplies.

"I'm not late, am I?" A bundle of pens slipped out of her grasp, and they bounced madly across the floor like escaping mice.

"You're not late at all." Savannah shook her head as the antiquated cash register booted up to the shop's menu page.

I need to replace this system as soon as I can afford it.

"I'm not sure I've got everything." Amanda spoke between panting breaths and wiped the sweat from her face with a plump forearm.

"Amanda, you have enough materials to teach a year's worth of classes."

That's a lot of extra expense right now. Maybe I shouldn't have given her a company credit card, but up to now, she's been extremely conservative, even frugal.

"It's my first class, and I want everything perfect, absolutely perfect." Amanda turned to face Savannah. "Is my outfit okay? It may be too conservative, but I wanted to look accomplished and trustworthy. What do you think?" she said as she gave a little twirl.

Savannah's brows launched upward before she could control them. She covered her reaction with a big smile and checked out Amanda's lime-green headband holding yellow-orange, shoulder-length hair, a perfectly matching lime-green cotton shirt over a white camisole, and white stretch leggings. She sported new lime-green Converse sneakers with white laces.

Nodding slowly, she replied, "Perfect. Simply perfect." What she actually thought was that only Amanda could get away with an outfit like that. Anyone else would come off looking like a clown. "Your outfit says you're fashion forward, serious, but also artistic. Perfect."

Quickly running a hand through her black, close-cropped curls, Savannah looked down and assessed her own everyday work outfit. The white cotton button-down shirt tucked into khaki Dockers was heavy enough to afford protection while she was working with glass, but cool in the steamy heat of a west coast Florida July. A limber six feet, she towered over Amanda's plump figure. "Absolutely perfect." Savannah formed an okay sign with her index finger and thumb.

Amanda scrambled around the floor, picking up the pens, and gathered everything from the counter. "I've got to get the classroom set up before the students get here."

"You take the small stuff. I'll get the bottles." Savannah grabbed the grocery bags. They walked through the door behind the sales counter and into the classroom. "Why all the bottles? I thought the students were to bring their own."

Amanda dumped her armload of supplies onto the nearest worktable in the first row. The room was arranged into three rows, with each row containing two standing-height worktables that faced a whiteboard at the front of the room.

"I'm so nervous, I can't think properly. I kept having a recurring nightmare that no one brought any bottles, and so we couldn't have class, and then I got fired. As soon as I decided to bring these, I started sleeping." She stepped behind the instructor lectern and opened up her notebook to the first page. "Thank goodness you made me create a teaching plan." She looked up with a blinding smile. "If I get lost, I know what should come next."

Savannah placed a wine bottle and a vodka bottle on each worktable. "I'll get these, while you arrange the distribution of the handouts. We'll be done in a few minutes."

Even though it was Amanda's first teaching experience, Savannah felt confident the new class would be a success. Everyone loved Amanda's sunny disposition and eternally cheerful optimism. Students already sought her advice about the color choices among the racks of sheet glass available for sale at Webb's.

Capitalizing on a new crafting trend called upcycling, they had created a workshop to convert ordinary wine bottles into cool cheese trays, transform long-neck beer bottles into quirky spoon rests, and flatten vodka bottles into wall clocks. They touted the workshop's value for those interested in striving toward a responsible, green, zero-footprint lifestyle.

Once the bottles and handouts were distributed and the classroom was ready for teaching, Savannah stood in the doorway with her arms folded. "Don't be nervous. You're going to be terrific. You know your subject backward and forward. Plus, who wouldn't like you as their teacher?" She grabbed Amanda and gave her a bear hug. "Besides, I'll be only a quick phone call away if anything horrible comes up."

"Horrible?" Amanda's eyes opened wide, and she clutched Savannah's arm like a fledgling barn owl. "What do you mean by a phone call away?"

"I need to open up the new Twenty-Second Street warehouse studio. This is the first time Jacob will be working in the new workshop. His mother is driving him down there, but she wants to speak to me first before dropping him off. Understandable, since he doesn't like new routines."

"He is eighteen now. I was working on my own when I was sixteen."

"You weren't diagnosed with Asperger's syndrome when you were a small child. Working with my dad in the glass shop has made an incredible difference to his self-confidence, but he still hasn't learned to drive, and he still hates talking on the phone."

The warehouse studio was a new venture inspired by the growing number of glass students who had taken classes at Webb's and had graduated from beginner's status. These students needed a work space, as well as continued guidance and instruction in technique. The historical family-owned Webb's Glass Shop didn't offer the amount of space required for this, since there were only four small rooms. Customers entered the display room, which was filled with student artworks for sale, along with a sales counter. There was a supply room to the right, filled with everything an artist might need, from sheets of glass to soldering irons. In the back was a classroom large enough for six students and an instructor. At the very back end of the shop was an office, a restroom, and a rear door that opened to the alley.

In order to start Webb's Studio, Savannah had used some of her inheritance to buy a run-down warehouse. It was a risky and bold move, but one she hoped would pay off. She had found the perfect site not more than a ten-minute walk away from the shop, on the corner of Fourth Avenue South and Twenty-Second Street South.

Amanda took a deep breath and exhaled slowly. "Of course, but could you stay until all the students arrive? Pretty please." She pressed her hands together as if in prayer.

Jacob Underwood was the only carryover staff

member from when Savannah's late father owned Webb's Glass Shop. Although he had managed his Asperger's syndrome well, it had been a lucky day when Jacob discovered the joy of glasswork. Now he thrived in his role as apprentice and stained glass restoration expert. Still, an eighteen-year-old of any sort needed firm guidance and frequent reminders. She remembered her dad's frustration with her tardiness on homework when she was a senior in high school. Teens grew up at different rates.

"Nonsense. You're completely prepared—maybe too prepared." Savannah squeezed Amanda's hand and tried to sound sympathetic. "I'll stay until you start your lecture, but I've got to get to the studio. Once you get started, trust me, you won't even notice when I slip out the back."

"But . . ."

"No buts." Savannah pointed to the lesson plan. "We have a few minutes before class. Let's look at your teaching plan and review the points for—"

The front bell jangled. Savannah gave Amanda a stern, no-nonsense look. "I was saved by the bell. Now, Instructor, go greet your students."

Amanda walked into the display room and met a pair of spry elderly women.

"Rachel and Faith! I'm so glad you're taking my class." Amanda hugged them both.

They had arrived in extreme twin mode, evident not only by their identical features but also by their identical head-to-toe outfits. Both women were dressed entirely in magenta—from custom magenta glasses and oversize button-down magenta shirts, with white T-shirts underneath, to magenta capri-length trousers and magenta flats with matching bows at the toe.

"We always take Webb's classes." Rachel tipped her head back at her sister. "We wouldn't dare miss—"

Faith interrupted her sister and, in true twin form, finished her thought. "The chance to be here for your first class as an instructor."

"Did you bring some bottles?" Amanda led them into the classroom. "When you signed up for the class, you should have received an information package with instructions and a list of the materials needed for this class."

"Yes, we brought bottles, and we received the information package," they said in perfect unison.

They stared at each other for a long moment and then burst into giggles. Faith finally composed herself enough to take a look around the classroom.

"Good," she said. "We're early enough to get our regular seats. I'll sit here, against the wall, so you can be on the outside." She looked pointedly at Amanda. "Remember? Lefties need to be aware of their poking elbows."

"No need to point that out. We have always managed to suit ourselves," said Rachel.

Amanda helped them settle in and asked that they place the bottles they had brought in on top of their worktables, in addition to the two bottles Savannah had placed on top of the worktables earlier.

"I'll bet we get a lot of different types of bottles," Amanda stated excitedly. But as she watched the twins take out bottle after bottle of Belvedere Vodka, her excitement started to wane. "Whew! You have quite a lot of vodka bottles. Do you drink only Belvedere?"

"Oh, yes," Faith chirped. "We have our 'teenies' out on the deck every night. Rachel makes such divine—" Faith didn't have a chance to finish.

"Cosmopolitans are actually cocktails, dear. But apple martinis—shaken, not stirred, are a special treat for us. They're so much colder that way," Rachel said as she mimicked the motions of agitating a cocktail shaker. "We also like apple martinis. They're even sweeter. On most days, I count the mixing as my aerobic exercise of the day."

Faith giggled and patted her sister on the shoulder. "Now, Rachel, you know we love our walk around the lake!"

The ringing bell announced the arrival of the next student, who called out in a low, raspy drawl, "Hello? Anyone here?"

Savannah turned from the chatter between Amanda and the Rosenberg twins to greet a slim middle-aged woman with silver-white hair pulled into a luxurious ponytail. "Hi. I'm Savannah." She extended her hand. "Welcome to Webb's Glass Shop. Are you here for the upcycling workshop?"

"Oh yes, darlin'. That's exactly what I need." The woman transferred a bulging red canvas bag to her left hand and shook Savannah's hand with surprising firmness. "I always make my Christmas gifts for all my family and friends. Reusing my discarded bottles will be a bonus."

"Well, then, you're at the right place! I'm sorry, but I didn't catch your name."

"Oh, my stars. How rude of me. I'm SueAnn Dougherty."

"Welcome, Sue." Savannah waved her arm toward the classroom.

"SueAnn. My name is SueAnn, just like it sounds,

but it's all one word. Oh yes, with both a capital *S* and a capital *A*."

"Got it. Well, good morning, SueAnn." Savannah gave a tiny tilt of her head. "Your teacher is Amanda Blake, and she's right there in the classroom."

The door jangled again, and two lovely pale young women entered the shop, one with short brown hair and one with long amber hair. They were fresh-faced and modestly dressed in navy skirts and buttoned up white polo shirts. They smiled, and the long-haired girl spoke.

"Good morning, ma'am. Is this the place for the bottle class?"

"Yes. You must be from Roosevelt Prep School. I met with your artistic director last month to arrange for this special off-site workshop. I'm so happy it meets the curriculum for your studies." Savannah smiled and shepherded them into the classroom. "You can sit anywhere you like."

The girls exchanged hurried whispers behind discreet hands, then scooted themselves into the second row, probably because SueAnn had taken the worktable against the wall in the first row.

Amanda looked at her watch. "Okay, class. It's ten o'clock right now. Although I should be starting the class, there's still one more student left to arrive."

"Who is it?" SueAnn looked at the empty worktable beside her.

Amanda answered without looking at the student roster. "Martin Lane. He should be here already. I'll step outside and see if he's having trouble finding a parking spot," she said. Then she left the classroom and sprinted out of the shop, pulling her cell phone out of her pocket as she whizzed by.

Savannah lifted a finger to Amanda, but there was no stopping her.

Turning to the five students, Savannah grinned and raised her palms up. "It's unusual for one of our students to be late. I see you have all brought bottles you want to upcycle into something useful." She walked around to look at the bottles standing on the students' desks. "The wine bottles are great, and I see you've taken off the labels." She picked up one of Faith's vodka bottles. "The reason I specified modern vodka bottles is that the designs on them are screen printed, and they will survive the kiln temperatures. But if they're more than a few years old, the print may be dry and may flake off. It's safer to work with new bottles if you want the design to survive the heat of the kiln."

She returned to the front of the classroom. "One of the things I enjoy making with the vodka bottles are small dishes showing only the label. I'm making a bunch of them now to use as promotional giveaways to boost interest in upcycling."

SueAnn had finished wiping down her worktable with a sanitizing wipe and began emptying out her red canvas bag, which contained Van Gogh Vodka bottles in multiple sizes and varieties. Each flavor of vodka featured a different masterpiece screen printed on both the front and back sides of the bottle.

Savannah would have pegged SueAnn as a drinker of chardonnay or Southern Comfort, but with all those vodka bottles, SueAnn had to be a real lover of martinis. Perhaps after a couple of classes, she'd share some "teenies" with the twins.

The bell on the front door jangled, and Savannah heard Amanda call out, "Thanks, Vicki. That was nice of you." As Amanda walked back into the classroom with the missing student, she wiped some sweat from her face. Addressing the classroom, "The sun is steaming hot out there. Anyway, Martin's here. No need to worry. His truck wouldn't start, so his friend Vicki dropped him off."

A cute olive-skinned young man with light brown hair followed her into the classroom. He looked a bit annoyed by Amanda's explanation. He wore a faded red tank top, revealing a tattoo on his left shoulder of a pirate's chest surrounded by treasure. He also wore ragged cutoff jeans that looked like they had recently been shortened with a knife instead of a pair of scissors. The hack marks made by the knife had left a snaggletoothed fringe effect along the bottom edges of his shorts.

At least he's wearing tennis shoes, rather than the typical sandals men his age usually favor, Savannah thought. *Amanda won't have to send him home to change his shoes.*

"We're all here now." Amanda flapped the side shirttails of her oversize shirt against her chest to cool herself. "Good, good."

Savannah waited until Martin sat at the remaining worktable in the front row and placed a small brown paper bag on his work surface. She then gestured for Amanda to come and stand beside her at the front of the class. Once Amanda was next to her, it was time for introductions.

"Good morning. For those who haven't met me, I'm Savannah Webb, owner of Webb's Glass Shop, and I'm here this morning to introduce your instructor, Amanda Blake, who has worked extremely hard to create and organize this class for you. Amanda has been taking classes here at Webb's for several years and has impressed me with her patience and enthusiasm. I was so impressed that I hired her as an instructor and an office manager after knowing her for only a short time. Amanda will be in charge of Webb's Glass Shop while I work at our new location, Webb's Studio. I think you'll enjoy her professionalism and her dedication to working with glass as much as I do." She winked and waved her hand. "Amanda, it's all yours."

When Amanda moved behind the instructor's podium, her lips thinned to a tight grimace, and then she inhaled a big breath. "Welcome to our upcycling workshop. I'm glad you're all here." Then she just stood there, and the silence lengthened. As the students began to shift in their seats, awaiting instruction, Amanda gave Savannah a pleading glance.

It was a surreal moment for Savannah. She knew exactly what Amanda was going through, as it was only a few months ago that Savannah, too, had stood in front of expectant students, frozen in panic. Savannah had been prepared to instruct her first class, just as Amanda was now. But it seemed they both suffered from stage fright when the nerves hit. Savannah knew Amanda would be fine eventually, but she couldn't leave her just yet. Not when she was looking at Savannah with puppy eyes.

"Yes," said Savannah, picking up where Amanda had left off. "We're so glad you've decided to take this class. The first things we're going to cover are safety, logistics, and the rules of the glass shop. Amanda, it's right there on the first page. Right?"

Giving her head a sharp shake, Amanda opened her notebook. While she focused on the page, her shoulders dropped, and all the students could hear her exhale as she relaxed into a smile.

"Right. We have some fairly strict safety rules here because"—she held up a small printed index card—"heat burns and glass cuts. First, you must wear formfitting clothing to prevent a flapping sleeve from catching fire. You must also wear closed-toe shoes to protect your feet from a falling bottle or dropped scraps of cut glass. Notice that our first-aid kit is right over there on the back wall, by Savannah."

Savannah held her arms in a "product display" pose straight from *The Price Is Right*, and the class broke into relieved laughter. She followed it with an "Over to you" wave of her arm at Amanda.

"Thanks, Vanna." Giggling, Amanda turned to the next page in her instructor's notebook. "Next, our restroom is located in the office, through the door behind you. Last are the introductions, so let's go around the room, and each person can state their name, where they're from, and can say a few words about why they're taking this class." She put her hand on her ample chest. "I'll start. I'm your instructor, Amanda Blake, from St. Pete. I've chosen to teach this class because the subject of reusing materials, or upcycling, is close to my heart. I've been a recycling enthusiast since I was a small girl. I'm excited to merge that passion with my love of glass." She nodded to the first row. "Now it's your turn."

SueAnn rose up from her chair and stood in front of her worktable. "I'm SueAnn Dougherty. It is one word, SueAnn. Not Sue. I'm from Boston, and I'm spending a few weeks in Treasure Island, Florida. I love making folks their Christmas gifts in the summer, and I love the idea of recycling bottles and turning them into cheese trays. I can wrap up the bottle with a selection of hard cheeses, and I'm done." She sat down.

The next student began his introduction. "I'm Martin Lane from St. Pete Beach. I find all kinds of bottles and salvaged marine parts for one-of-a-kind suspended hangings. I may get a small kiln to use at home, but I wanted to try to experiment in a class first," he said in a low, husky voice as he looked directly at Amanda and winked.

Amanda tried to cover her blush with a wave to the next student in the row behind Martin.

"I'm Patty Kelner from Roosevelt Prep School in Akron, Ohio." Patty looked at the red-haired girl next to her and nudged her in the side.

"Ouch! Okay. I'll do the talking. I'm Yvonne Whittaker, also from Akron. We're cousins, not sisters." She craned her neck around to look at the twins in the back row. "We're visiting my grandparents, who live in a huge condo in downtown St. Petersburg. We're here for the summer and needed to do something to get out of their hair."

"And it also counts as school credit. That's awesome," said Patty.

Amanda looked to the third and last row and interrupted the whispering twins. "Ladies, you're next."

"You start," said Rachel.

"No, you start," Faith whispered, loud enough for all to hear.

Rachel started to protest, but Amanda broke in. "Rachel, would you start please?"

Huffing out her pursed lips, she began her introduction. "I'm Rachel Rosenberg, from right here in St. Pete, and this is my younger sister, Faith."

Faith smiled, with a little queenly nod. She glowed with the pleasure of a sibling who always got her way. "We like taking workshops here at Webb's. It doesn't matter what kind of class. Once the workshop is over, we donate our finished pieces of glasswork to charity auctions here in St. Pete."

Amanda stood a little taller behind the podium. "Thank you all for your introductions. I have only a few more housekeeping details, and we'll begin. The upcycling workshop is a full week, starting today and ending on Friday. Class is scheduled from ten a.m. to one p.m. each day. I will start with a short lecture, followed by a demonstration of the day's project. Afterward, I'll assist you in creating the day's assignment. After you've completed the assignment, you'll all work independently on variations of the day's project until the end of the day's class. I'll load up the kiln with your completed works to fire them overnight. The next day, we'll check on them first thing in the morning. For Friday's kiln work, you can pick up your works anytime we're open the following week. Now that those details are out of the way, I'd like to see the bottles you've all brought in for your upcycling projects. You first, Martin."

Rachel was quick to say, "Oh, Martin is the teacher's pet, is he? He's a tiny bit—"

"Young for you. Robbing the cradle, are we?" Faith's eyes crinkled with glee as she once again finished her sister's thought.

Amanda pressed her lips tightly together and rolled her eyes at the irrepressible twins. "Ladies, really? Let's concentrate on our lesson, shall we?"

Savannah covered her mouth with her hands to hide her chuckle. She then gave a little wave, intent on heading toward the front door, but she halted in mid-step when she noticed that Martin had removed two small deep blue bottles from his paper bag and had placed them on his worktable. "Martin, these are not modern." She picked one up and ran her finger along the seam that went from the bottom of the bottle to the bend in the neck.

SueAnn stood and leaned over to peer at the bottles. "They look like old-time medicine bottles. Does one of them still contain the liquid?"

Martin turned to SueAnn. "There were no stoppers. The liquid is long gone."

"Where did you get them?" asked Savannah.

"I found them on the beach near the Intracoastal Waterway near Treasure Island."

"On the beach?"

"Well"—he shrugged his shoulders—"sorta near the beach. I found them where I was diving."

"I don't think they're modern. They could be quite old." Savannah looked at the bottom of the bottle. "They may even be valuable."

"Exactly what I'm hoping you guys can find out. They look too unique to go into the kiln for melting into cheese trays. I was hoping you might be able to research their origins."

Savannah held the bottle up to the light. "They could be quite old. Do you mind if I talk to a couple of experts I know?"

"No. I would appreciate it," said Martin. "That's exactly what I was hoping you would say."

Savannah placed the bottle back down on the worktable. "I'll pick them up after class." As she headed to the classroom door, she looked back at the cobalt bottles. "I'm curious, wildly curious."

On her way to the rear door, her phone pinged, alerting her that she had received a text message. Savannah pulled out her phone and tapped the screen to display the text. It was from Jacob's mother.

Where r u?

"Rats!" Savannah quickly texted, **On my way**, and then bolted out the rear door of the shop.

Chapter 2

Savannah pulled into the large barely graveled parking lot of the warehouse she had recently converted into Webb's Studio. As Savannah had anticipated, Frances Underwood was pacing the small concrete pad in front of the entry door and jingling her car keys. Her son, Jacob, was leaning against his mother's silver BMW, with a backpack over his shoulder and his black and tan service dog, Suzy, snuggled in his arms. She was a bit small for a beagle, but that made her easier for Jacob to handle.

Savannah quickly climbed out of her car. "I am so sorry, Frances. I completely misjudged my time."

Frances smoothed the front of her custom-tailored navy suit. "It's not like you to be late. Even so, you should have called or texted."

"Arghhh!" Savannah palmed her forehead. "Of course I should have." She placed a hand over her heart. "I apologize. It's Amanda who has me off kilter. This morning is her first day as an instructor for a workshop. I should have anticipated she would be nervous and I would need to hang around the shop a little longer than usual."

A smile tipped the corners of Frances's precisely made-up lips. "A nervous Amanda would be a challenge. There was an incident I wanted to talk to you about, except I'm due in juvenile court in . . ." She looked at her small Rolex. "Goodness! Twenty minutes." She raised her beautiful eyebrows slightly. "It sets a bad tone if I'm late. The lawyers get unruly."

"I've had keys made, and I'll give one to Jacob so this won't be a problem in the future."

Frances gave Jacob a light peck on his cheek. "What a wonderful solution." She bent to give Suzy a good scratching behind the ears. "Suzy, take good care of him. Jacob, tell Savannah about the unfortunate incident with the nasty man." She got in her car and sped away, throwing up a few stones from the sparse gravel.

Savannah unlocked the newly painted green entrance door to Webb's Studio. The thick coat of paint covered the fact that a new door would be needed in the near future.

Another expense to be added to the list.

She stepped aside. "What's this about a man?"

But Jacob whizzed by on his way to the workshop.

He's beelining for his workbench. I'll tackle him about the situation when he's settled down to work. He'll be more comfortable.

Savannah stood for a moment and looked around at the newly painted concrete floor, the partitioned work spaces, and relished the warm glow of pride in her chest. This was her personal vision—not her father's or his father's. The planning and development of Webb's Studio were hers and hers alone.

The recent growth in the number of art galleries,

high-end gift shops, and juried art festivals had created a demand for artworks, which local artisans struggled to meet. The timing was perfect for a facility that rented out affordable work space that supported independent artists.

She wished her dad could see this. She had returned home from Seattle, where she was studying glassblowing, when her dad died unexpectedly of a heart attack about six months ago. That event had been quickly followed by the death from a heart attack of his longtime associate. Two heart attacks in one small shop had raised all sorts of alarms for Savannah. Sadly, it had turned out she was right when she helped the police investigate their murders.

The studio's layout was a glass artist's dream in terms of space, light, and comfort. Next to the door, she keyed in the code for the alarm and turned on the ancient public address system. In the background she heard the soft strains of "Für Elise." She had taken particular care to ensure that the endless loop of light classical music wouldn't repeat for several days.

Along the back wall, just beyond the partitions, a solid bank of twelve paned windows illuminated the space with gorgeous sunlight from its southern exposure. Off to the right, she had created a tiny office and a large workshop for the commissioned work she continued to receive due to her late father's excellent reputation. At the end of the wall and to the right was Jacob's large workshop. He worked more effectively in this corner, away from any noise and distraction. He was getting a reputation for his excellent restoration skills.

She poked her head in his workshop. "Hey, Jacob. Is everything all right? Do you need anything?"

Jacob looked up from the ancient seven-foot-long stained glass panel lying on their largest worktable, one with a built-in bank of fluorescent lights to illuminate the work in progress from below the clear surface of the table. Underneath the cut glass pieces, a printed template outlined the geometric design. Each small piece of glass had been placed on top of the template. The template was drawn with a unique number written on it for each tiny element of glass. Many of the pieces were missing, and some of the existing ones were covered with dirt and grime.

"No, thank you, Miss Savannah. Everything is fine." He stooped to pick up the small beagle standing by his feet. He kissed the top of the little beagle's head. "Everything is fine. Right, Suzy?"

Suzy was Jacob's service animal and was in charge of the inhaler in her service vest. He needed it in case he had a panic attack. From past experience, Savannah knew he was uncomfortable about something, or else he wouldn't have picked Suzy up.

She inhaled a deep breath and released it. "Let's try this again. I want the exact truth this time. Were there any issues when you arrived at the studio this morning?"

He looked down at his adorable dog. "It was Suzy. Suzy was not comfortable when we got out of Mom's car."

"I don't understand, Jacob. How did she behave?"

A long moment passed in silence; then he put Suzy down on the floor. Savannah was patient. She knew Jacob had something to tell her, something he found embarrassing, since there was a rosy flush around his collar that was slowly creeping up to his chin. She knew that Jacob needed to arrange the words just right. Rushing him would not help.

"There was a man."

"Okay. Where was he?"

Jacob looked down at his feet and then apparently made up his mind that showing her was better than telling her. He picked up Suzy again and left the workshop. Savannah scrambled to follow them. He walked to the front door and pointed to the corner of the warehouse closest to the street. "He was there. He was—"

"Jacob, tell me. I won't be mad. I promise."

"He was going to the bathroom on our new studio."

Savannah's shoulders dropped, and she released a tight breath of relief. She suppressed her grin and controlled her voice. "Yes, that was wrong, but there are many people who don't have homes. You didn't say anything, did you?"

Jacob shook his head. "It was disgusting, but at least he didn't pee on my side of the studio." He went back inside to his workshop.

She shook her head slowly. Jacob had been a key contributor in her investigations. His razor-sharp observation skills had been useful in her detective adventures. That kind of attention to detail gave him the potential to grow into an amazing stained glass restoration expert.

Savannah walked out of the studio and over to the corner of the building that Jacob had pointed to. Sure enough, her nose and eyes were assaulted by direct evidence of recent urination. The scraggly bushes hugging the foundation provided enough cover to shelter a behavior she wanted to discourage. She turned at the sound of a motorcycle pulling into the gravel parking lot.

She walked over to stand by the lovingly restored Indian motorcycle and waited until the driver had removed his helmet. She held his face and kissed him and enjoyed the bright look in his eyes. "Did you bring scones?"

Edward Morris laughed. Laughter came easy these days. As his British fusion pub, Queen's Head, had begun to gain traction as a Grand Central District favorite restaurant, he had become more relaxed and more confident in a financially secure future.

Savannah realized that Edward was becoming a significant part of her new life in St. Petersburg. He had been at her side through the puzzling and life-threatening investigation of her father's murder, and he continued to support her efforts to fill her dad's shoes as an influential leader in the community. She felt more and more certain that their close friendship was moving to another level.

"Hungry, as usual, I see." He dismounted with a practiced grace and was a bare two inches taller than Savannah's six feet. He unsnapped one of the leather-fringed saddlebags on his motorcycle and pulled out a brown paper bag, which he handed over. "Have you made coffee?"

"Not yet. I just got here. Amanda was a little nervous teaching her first class."

Edward fastened his helmet to the cream and tan motorcycle. "She's a natural teacher. She'll be fine. What were you looking at over by the street?"

"I've got to have those bushes cleared away. Apparently, my warehouse is the local outdoor relief station."

"Well, if you Americans would be more civic minded and would build more public toilets, it wouldn't be a problem."

Savannah punched him in the arm. "Not a solution. Try again."

Edward jokingly held his arm. "Ouch! Have you been to the gym already this morning?"

"Not to the gym. I walked over to Crescent Lake for a boot camp exercise session this morning. I had to get there at five. That's the only time it's cool enough to work out with any intensity."

Edward looked at the overgrown shrubs and patchy weeds in the parking lot. "This is untidy, but I don't know anyone who could help. I don't need a lawn service with my condo, and we have only potted plants at the pub. Nicole keeps them alive. I'll ask her when she comes in for the evening shift if she can recommend someone. As a bartender, she knows and talks to everybody."

Looking down at the thin gravel and the bare sand, Savannah chewed on her lower lip. "I'm going to have to make the outside a little more inviting if I want to increase the number of students that rent studio space. Not too much. It still needs to look a little grungy so it has some character." She shook her head. "Never mind. I'm rambling."

They went inside and headed toward the kitchen on the left side at the far end of the studio. In its checkered past, the warehouse had once housed a catering business. So there was a fully functioning kitchen, although the appliances were ancient industrial makes. The countertops were stainless steel, and once they'd been cleaned, they looked as good as new.

Savannah put the brown bag on the wooden worktable in the center of the large room. She had found ten wooden chairs for it at the local thrift shop, and now it served as a great communal dining spot.

"When are you going to paint these chairs?" Edward asked.

"Probably this weekend." She opened the top glass-fronted cabinet beside the deep stainless-steel sink and brought down two cups and took them over to the only new appliance in the kitchen, an espresso machine. "Wish me luck here. I've used this only a couple of times."

Edward sat and lounged on one of the chairs and folded his arms behind his head. "This is quite a new experience. The only one who ever makes me coffee is Nicole."

Savannah turned around to quip but instead smiled.

Coffee is vitally important to him, and he is vitally important to me. Don't blow this.

She felt small beads of perspiration form on her forehead. "She does make good coffee." Turning back to the countertop, she added, "My machine is a bit smaller than the monster you salvaged for the pub."

"Which brand are you using? My local favorite is Kahwa."

"And my favorite is the Colombian French roast from Mazzaro's Italian Market. Hush and let me concentrate." She carefully brewed two cups of espresso and added a generous dollop of steamed half-and-half to each. She finished them off with a deft shake of cocoa powder and placed the cups on the table.

Edward sipped his coffee, and his eyebrows rose over the rim of his cup. "Mmm. This is extremely good. I may have to reconsider my supplier." He lowered his cup.

Savannah felt a flush of pride rise in her chest. The practice had paid off. "I'm glad."

"Have any students signed up for studio space yet?"

"Yes, finally." She opened the brown bag and took out a cranberry scone. "Two former students, Helen Carter and Arthur Young, from my first stained glass workshop back when I first arrived from Seattle. They've already paid their monthly fee. I'm expecting them sometime this morning."

"How many students do you need to break even?"

"I need only eight, but I've got space for sixteen." They walked out into the cavernous room. "I've got eight work spaces set up. Four of them are completely ready, using existing equipment I brought over from Webb's. The remaining four need a little refurbishing work on the stuff I practically stole at an auction. I plan to add a few at a time until this space is completely filled. Then, if I clean up the loft, I could add even more."

"When are you going to move Webb's Glass Shop into this space?" They returned to sit at the table.

"I can't do it. The building for Webb's has been in my family since the nineteen twenties. It's been the center of my life since forever and has provided a generous income for a number of decades. I won't destroy the memories that live there. So the shop and the studio will remain two separate spaces."

Edward scraped back his chair and stood. "How's the huge commission piece for the big shot coming?"

"For the mayor? I'm struggling." Savannah stood as well.

They walked into her workshop, which was adjacent to her office and next door to Jacob's workshop.

"I've got it all laid out on these two large tables. I don't know what I was thinking when I agreed to such a tight deadline for a monstrous five-panel installation." The paper templates placed on the table tops outlined the intricate design, which incorporated grapevines and grapes draped along wooden trellis supports. The grape branches were heavily laden with wisteria blooms.

"When is it to be finished?"

"In about three weeks, but I need the final payment as quickly as possible, so I'm trying to finish it early. Luckily, the deposit covered all the materials."

"You'll get it done early, then. You always do what you say."

Savannah smiled. "My problem is overcommitting. Sometimes."

"Sometimes? You mean every time." Edward looked at his watch. "I've got to get back to the pub. The lunch crowd will soon be arriving. Thanks for the coffee." He leaned over to kiss her good-bye and then walked out of the studio.

The rumbling of Edward's Indian motorcycle rose and then faded, and Savannah stood in front of the commissioned pieces, enjoying the feeling of warmth he had left behind.

Her ex-boyfriend in Seattle had been controlling and demanding, and their breakup had shaken her confidence in recognizing a good relationship. She felt lucky to have Edward in her life. *Now what am I going to do? I need to commit soon or let him know I'm not interested. It seems too soon after my breakup with my Seattle boyfriend, but it's now been about six months.* When Edward's parents had visited him a few months ago, his mother had assumed they were in a relationship. *Such an adorable pair. They made me feel like I have known them forever. I'd like to be part of a family again. Is it time to step up?*

Shaking off those thoughts, she made herself another espresso and made her way over to her cozy little office. The office at the studio reflected her personality as much as the office at Webb's Glass Shop was modeled after her father. A light-giving wall-to-ceiling window had dictated the placement her height-adjusting computer desk so that it faced the window so she could see the large monitor. The bright office also contained a stained glass worktable, which stood against the opposite wall, for her small jewelry projects. She had a comfortable modern desk chair and a tall work stool, which provided her the ability to shift easily from working on paperwork to working on glasswork and back again.

As she took a seat on her work stool, she jumped into her morning routine and started checking all the tasks that needed to be completed to keep both businesses running smoothly. Trudging through invoices, orders, collections, and payments didn't take long, because she tackled this several times each day, determined not to mimic her father's approach. She remembered how he detested the piles of paper, and as a result of this loathing, many opportunities had slipped through the cracks. He hadn't minded the actual paperwork but had preferred giving his time to his students and working on complicated stained glass panels that no other glass shop could handle.

Her father's death, along with that of his assistant, had brought Edward, Amanda, and Jacob together to help her find their killer. That had led to an investigation into a death at an art festival, and this had transformed their friendship into a tighter-than-family bond.

The *tap, tap, tap* of Suzy's protective booties warned

Savannah that Jacob was on his way to her office. He peeked around the door.

"Miss Savannah, I'm ready for you to check my work."

Delighted to be distracted from her thoughts, she hopped up and followed Jacob into the large workshop. He stopped, standing barely inside the door, and lifted Suzy into a stiff embrace.

He's nervous.

"Don't worry. Your work is always perfect. But you are still learning, so that's one reason why I want to check on your work. That way if there is anything to fix, it's easier to catch it and correct it now, while the work is still in progress. The other important point is that all professionals need to get feedback from one of their peers. It's so easy to overlook an obvious flaw in your own work. Now, let me take a look, Jacob."

The restoration project had been brought to them in a five-gallon bucket by the owner of the penthouse in the Snell Arcade Building downtown. The glass pieces had provided Jacob weeks of satisfying effort as he reconstructed the original layout. He loved a good puzzle. The final panel was a traditional oblong, about seven feet long and three feet wide. It appeared to be about two hundred years old.

She ran her fingers along the cleaned pieces of glass and tried to detect which were new and which were older. It was difficult to tell. The teal color had been easy to match with a popular cathedral glass. The ruby pieces had presented a more difficult challenge.

"Well, Jacob, your idea of using the new ruby replacement pieces along the bottom edge and using the vintage glass in the main body of the panel has worked out beautifully. If I didn't know about that approach, I wouldn't be able to detect the slight color variation."

Jacob nuzzled Suzy with his chin and smiled. "Good."

Savannah stepped back and looked at the overall piece. "It's beautiful. Our client is going to be so pleased. Start soldering it together." She scratched Suzy behind the ears. "You'll soon be helping me with the five-panel commission. Well done."

She heard a car drive up on the gravel and went out through the main door. Helen, her former student, was opening the trunk to her silver car and was removing a large window–sized panel.

"Hi, Helen. Let me help you unload."

"Thanks, Savannah. Could you grab the white canvas bag and the toolbox? I'm so excited to have my own space."

Savannah grabbed the toolbox and slipped the canvas bag over her shoulder, making sure she had one hand free so she could open the door for Helen, who was stiff and was taking very measured steps as she carried her treasure to the studio.

After Helen had cleared the door, Savannah pointed toward the work spaces on the window side of the building. "There are eight work spaces, but only four of them have been completely furnished so far. So you get your pick of the first four. Sound good?"

Helen continued to walk very carefully as they made the thirty-foot journey to the first work space. She gently laid down her mounted panel on the work-table. "This is good. I'll take this one." She looked at the storage shelves, the small desk, and the full-size worktable. "This is perfect. Simple but comfortable."

"Thanks. I'll let you get settled." Savannah placed the toolbox and the canvas bag on top of the desk. "Do you remember where everything is from your first visit?"

Smiling, Helen nodded and began to unload the contents of the canvas bag.

"Great! I'll be in my office. Let me know if you need anything."

Savannah returned to her office and sat down at her computer. She opened the new Web site she had begun creating for Webb's Studio. It had an intro page and a contact page so far, and now she was trying to add a page to show the layout of each studio work space, but the hosting software wasn't exactly user-friendly.

The ring of her cell phone startled her. She glanced at the phone's screen and saw it was Amanda who was calling. She answered. "Hi there. Is anything wrong?" She looked at her watch, and it was nearly one o'clock.

Wow. Computer time is not in the same temporal plane as real time.

"Nothing's wrong . . . exactly." Amanda's voice rose. "I thought you were going to look at those old bottles Martin brought in."

"Oh yeah. I was planning on going to the shop after the class was over to take a look at them. What's the rush?"

"Martin is pushing. I don't think they should be fused." Amanda began talking even faster than her normal mile a minute. "I wasn't comfortable with putting them in the kiln, so I did some Internet searches, in case they are valuable. I used your dad's computer. You don't mind, do you?"

"No, of course not. You're the office manager now."

"Well, even though it took forever to get some answers, because of the tragically slow bandwidth speed, it appears these bottles date from the early eighteen hundreds." Amanda's voice rose even higher. "Do you have any idea what it means?"

"No. I'm not—"

"No way can they go into the kiln."

Chapter 3

Savannah touched base with Jacob and Helen to make sure they didn't have any design issues. A major selling point for the studio was that she would be available for consultation and guidance to glass artists. With time and a little training, Jacob would be a great resource for students, too. It set her apart from the other artists' lofts in the area.

Then she grabbed her backpack and keys and rushed out to her car. She opened the door to the Mini and was met with a rush of stale heat. "Damn." She hadn't put the sun shield in the window, so her car was hotter than a glass furnace. She started the car, then grabbed a small towel from the passenger seat and threw it over the steering wheel. She cranked up the air-conditioning—full fan, with maximum cold—then opened both front doors.

It took a few long minutes for the scorching heat to drop to merely Africa hot, and then she drove the half dozen or so blocks to Webb's Glass Shop. When she entered the shop through the back, Amanda was waiting for her by the large kiln in the supply room.

"At last. I want you to check out how I've loaded the kiln."

"Sure." Savannah bent over and looked down into the large fusing kiln and made a few minor adjustments to one of the recycled bottles that would flatten during the fusing cycle. "I'm adding a small block to prevent this one from rolling around. The spacing is important, but you also don't want one of the bottles to roll into anything else in the kiln. That would destroy two pieces." She stood up. "This looks good. You're getting better at using the space efficiently."

"Thanks." Amanda closed the large, heavy lid with the help of a pulley-and-cable system attached to the ceiling. "Also, thanks for programming the kiln. I need to learn how to do it soon."

"Let's look at Martin's bottles. I thought he was thinking of making them into cheese trays. Of course, that color would make beautiful trays. Where are they?"

"I left them in the classroom. After my bit of research, there was no way I was going to throw those bottles in the kiln. I asked Martin about it, and he didn't seem to want them slumped, either. He left them for me to research. Pretty strange."

"I agree, but most artists are strange—which includes you and me." Savannah winked, and they walked into the classroom, which was empty and silent now. The two deep blue bottles were standing in the center of the first worktable.

Savannah picked one up and looked at the bottom

of it. There was a small image pressed into the bottom near the edge, but it was indistinct. She rubbed her finger over the center of the bottom of the bottle. "This looks like it was mouth blown using a mold."

She held the bottle up to the light and saw the wavy shimmers typical of blown glass. "What did you find out in your online searches?"

"Mostly, I found out how difficult it is to identify vintage glass bottles." Amanda picked up the other bottle. "According to one Web site, these are typical of British bottles that were exported beginning in seventeen twenty. Then I found another site that claimed they were made after eighteen eighty."

Amanda put the bottle down and folded her arms. "Here's the rub. The bottles could be real artifacts, or they're counterfeit and not worth anything but the value of the glass itself. I thought you were going to find an expert."

"Hold your horses, Miss Blake. I'm not exactly flush with free time right now. I have a couple of ideas. I'm going to ask an old friend of mine. She's an antique dealer," said Savannah.

"Does she specialize in glass bottles?"

"No, but she will know someone who does. I'll take one of them along and see what she recommends." She put down the bottle she was holding. "Could you please wrap one of them up while I give her a call?"

Amanda grabbled one of the bottles, and they both returned to the display room. While Amanda rolled the bottle in brown paper and put it in a brown paper gift bag, Savannah picked up the phone on the counter and dialed her friend.

Her friend's phone rang only once before the

call was answered. "Good afternoon. This is Robin Jefferson Rackley at Main House Antique Center. How can I help you?"

"Hey, Robin. This is Savannah. Do you have time to look at an old bottle that one of my students brought in for flattening into a cheese tray? I think it's rare and possibly too valuable."

"Sure. I'm here all afternoon."

"Great. I'll be over later this afternoon. Thanks, Robin."

Savannah found Robin sitting on a tall chrome-and-red-leather bar stool at the Main House Antique Center's checkout counter. Located in the heart of St. Petersburg, the building housing the Antique Center, a multi-dealer antique mall, was formerly a three-bedroom home. Each participating vendor had an individual space to display antique furniture, Depression glassware, art glass, vintage pottery, retro jewelry, and more. Family owned by Robin's parents and operated for more than twenty-eight years, the little mall supported over twenty antique and collectible dealers.

Robin ran from behind the counter and wrapped Savannah in a monster hug. "What a great surprise. I haven't seen you since . . . Well, I guess the last time was about six months ago, a few weeks after your dad's funeral. That was certainly a difficult time. How are you holding up?"

Savannah took a moment to think about her answer. "I'm doing pretty well. It was a bitter shock in the beginning, but I'm really starting to rebuild my life here."

"You're the only person I know who has been involved with murder investigations. I get the deal with your father, but what about the young woman who was killed at the Spinnaker Festival? How did you get drawn into it?"

Savannah cleared her suddenly raspy throat. "Well, I didn't really have a choice. I was the only one who believed it was murder in my father's case, and I found the body of the young woman in the second case. I think it concentrates your mind wonderfully when you are the prime suspect in a murder. I had no choice but to get involved if I didn't want to be convicted."

"Good point." Robin's perfectly applied makeup and expertly groomed hair completely belied the fact she was in her midfifties. She had been friends with Savannah's mother, Dorothy, and after she died of cancer at only thirty-nine, Robin became Savannah's friend and confidante. Those flashing eyes held a spirited joy of life and a love that had sustained Savannah when in need of nurturing, non-judgmental advice.

Savannah placed the bag containing Martin's bottle on the counter. "Anyway, tell me what you think of this."

"Sure, little Vanna." Robin took the bottle out of the bag, removed the brown paper it was wrapped in, and stood it on the counter. Her brow furrowed, and she tilted her head to one side. "Yep, this is old. Ancient perhaps. There are a few reference books over in my dealer space I want to use for research. Wander around if you like. This may take some time."

Feeling a bit like she was playing hooky, Savannah enjoyed her stroll among the little nooks and crannies stuffed with each of the dealers' individual taste in wares. While browsing, she managed to appraise casually most of the furniture in her family Craftsman home and was stunned at the prices marked on some of the older pieces. She knew they were beautiful and skillfully made, but she hadn't kept up with their increasing value.

I need to review the assessment values for the furniture covered by my homeowner's insurance, she thought.

"Vanna!"

"I'm over at the front door." Savannah scurried back over to the counter.

Robin was beaming with a pink flush. "Wow. You've got a great find here." She cradled the cobalt blue bottle in her arms like a tiny infant. "I'm not an expert at all, but from what I can find in my books on collectible bottles, this is worth five hundred to twenty-five hundred dollars."

"That is very good news. I'll tell my student."

Robin placed the bottle gently on the counter and noticed the laptop on the table behind the counter. "Let me scan the online auctions now that I know that we're searching the auction sites for cobalt blue bottles. There should be a ton of pricing information."

Savannah looked over Robin's shoulder as she brought up the most popular sites and searched for vintage cobalt blue bottles. Robin's estimate was confirmed. They found bids up to twenty-five hundred dollars.

"Where did your student get the bottle?"

Savannah shook her head. "He said he found it near the Intracoastal Waterway while he was diving for salvage. It will be interesting to see his reaction when I tell him tomorrow."

Robin raised a calculating eye to the ceiling. "You know, if we can confirm that they date to the time of Gaspar the Pirate, then they could be worth many, many times that value. There are lots of rumors, but no solid confirmation, that Gaspar buried treasure in the area, but if this is even remotely possible, the value will go through the roof."

The earliest parade in Savannah's memory was the annual Gasparilla night parade through the streets of downtown St. Petersburg. It was a raucous affair, with brightly lit floats in the shape of pirate ships, populated with men and women dressed as Spanish royalty, who threw candy and beads to the crowds lining Central Avenue. The floats were each accompanied by dozens of costumed pirates firing flame-shooting pistols to celebrate Gaspar the Pirate.

"I know only about the celebrations we have. You know, the Gasparilla Day pirate invasion in Tampa, the Gasparilla race along Bayshore Boulevard, and I always went to the Gasparilla Festival of the Arts to look at the glass exhibits. I know nothing about the pirate himself."

Robin patted Savannah on the shoulder. "You poor little thing. I can't believe you've escaped all the hype over the past few years about finding one of his treasure troves. There's been a lot of hearsay that he used the Intracoastal Waterway along the Gulf of Mexico for stashing booty for years and years. That's how Treasure Island got its name."

"I knew that, but why the new interest?"

Robin's eyes brightened. "Coins dating to that era have been showing up in very quiet collector circles.

That can only mean that treasure has been found. Where there is treasure, there may also be more ordinary artifacts, like bottles."

On the drive back to Webb's, she wondered where Martin could have come across such a bottle. He had said it was on the sea floor where he was diving. It could be a cover-up story. Family heirloom? Flea market? Maybe even in a Dumpster. Martin didn't wear the look of the comfortably well off. He didn't look like he could afford the price of the upcycling class he was taking. Maybe someone had paid the fee as a gift.

Maybe you're looking too closely at this. Just because you've been involved with two homicide investigations doesn't mean that everything out of the ordinary leads to murder.

When she got to Webb's, Amanda was making the final rounds, turning off the lights and closing up the shop. When she saw Savannah enter from the back door, she flipped the light back on in the classroom and walked over to Martin's worktable.

"What did you find out?" she called out.

Savannah entered the classroom and placed the brown bag next to the unwrapped bottle on Martin's classroom worktable. "Your instincts were right. The bottle could be worth as much as twenty-five hundred."

Amanda squealed and clapped her hands. "Oh, wonderful! That would be five thousand dollars for the set. What a difference it will make to him."

"Do you know where he got them?"

"I think . . ." She hesitated for a moment and then started again. "I remember he said he found them on the sea bottom where he was diving, but he didn't say exactly where. He seemed a bit reluctant to talk about the exact site."

"Well, when he gets here tomorrow morning, we'll tell him the good news and find out how he came into possession of such valuable artifacts."

Amanda turned pale under her pearled makeup. "Okay. Well, I've got to hurry to see my mother. She's not doing so well at the nursing home, and I promised to go over right after work." She grabbed her purse and keys, then almost flew out the front door. "See you tomorrow," she called out over her shoulder.

Savannah stood in the large silence left in Amanda's wake, feeling a little confused. It wasn't like Amanda to rush away without asking tons of questions and thoroughly discussing in detail all the interesting facts she had discovered about the bottles.

Walking into each of the rooms of the glass shop, she checked that the lights were turned off. In the supply room, she walked over to the large kiln. The lid was down, but it was still attached to the rigged pulley system. Peeking inside the kiln viewing hole, she saw the bottles that the students were expecting to have slumped and fused for tomorrow's class. She bent over to look at the control panel. It was apparent that the programming was complete and that all that was left to do was to press the START button.

Savannah pressed the START button, and when she was sure the kiln's automatic programming had safely started, she keyed the shop's alarm and locked the door behind her. It was not like Amanda to forget such an obvious part of the fusing cycle. Maybe teaching the first day of class had been more stressful than Amanda expected.

Chapter 4

Monday Evening

After Savannah closed up Webb's, she hopped back in her car and noticed the box of old books on the passenger seat.

Rats! I've got an appointment with Haslam's Book Store. She checked her watch. The watch showed five minutes past her scheduled meeting time with the bookstore's owner. She took the quickest route there and sped down the alleyway behind all the businesses along Central Avenue. Savannah pulled up to the largest bookstore for new and used books in Florida. Last week she had called to arrange this meeting to determine if her grandfather's collection of motorcycle repair manuals would be of interest to the owner for the store's used book collection.

The seriously old manuals had been collecting dust in the living-room bookcases at home, and they could be rare and valuable. A little cash windfall to offset the many expected expenses of opening the studio would be welcome. She parked by the outbuilding at the back of the bookstore, climbed out of her car, and knocked on the wooden door.

It opened, and a wiry gray-haired man with a charming smile walked out into the graveled parking lot. "You must be John's girl, Savannah." He extended his hand." I'm Ray Hirst. Where are those old motorcycle manuals we talked about over the phone?"

Savannah shook his hand with a firm grip. "Hi. I'm sorry to be late." He waved a hand to indicate that it was no problem. She pointed to her Mini. "The books are right here. Should I carry them into the—"

"No, no, no!" Ray waved both hands in a stop motion. "No offense, Savannah. I'm sure you're a tidy housekeeper, but I need to examine them outside, in the air, first."

Savannah wrinkled her brow in confusion.

"Wait," Ray said as he opened the passenger door. "Just a second." He bent down to the box of books and sniffed deep and loud. He straightened up and smiled. "I needed to make sure they weren't steeped in smoke and pet odors or, even worse, moldy."

"Oh, of course. I didn't even consider that."

"These are in great shape. Where have they been?"

"In the living room, for as long as I can remember. Before that they would have been in Grandpa Roy's store. It's the same building that Webb's Glass Shop occupies now."

Ray picked out one of the manuals and opened it to the middle. "Are all the volumes in as good condition as this one?"

"Yes. Grandpa Roy was very fussy with them. Dad said he would wash his hands before picking them up to use as a reference. They were very expensive and were critical to the success of Grandpa Roy's motorcycle repair business."

"They don't make them like this anymore. In fact, they don't print these at all. The manufacturers today publish all their information digitally and post it on the Internet. It's sad." Ray shook his head slowly. "How many more do you have?" He closed the old manual and tucked it under his arm.

"There are about thirty more in the same or better condition. Are they worth anything?"

"Difficult to say." He rubbed his chin. "If you could leave these with me, I have some contacts who specialize in repair manuals. I'll have them give me an appraisal, and I'll get back to you."

Savannah smiled and propped a hand on her hip. "But do you think they're worth something?"

He returned her smile with an added twinkle. "In this condition, I think you could be looking at either no value at all versus up to several hundred each. Maybe more for the rare ones."

Savannah smiled wider. "That's exciting. It's a shame to keep them out of circulation if someone can use them to restore vintage motorcycles. That would make me happy."

Ray started to walk back to the outbuilding, which was used for storage. "I'll let you carry them, if you don't mind. I should know something in about a week."

After she carried the box of manuals for Ray, she looked across the alley at the main building.

Haslam's Book Store opened in 1933, during the Depression. It had been on the corner of Central Avenue and Twentieth Street since the early seventies. Today the third and fourth generations of the Haslam family were in charge of the new and used books stuffed on the overburdened shelves of the sprawling corner store. Savannah and her dad had spent many Saturday afternoons foraging among the crowded stacks, searching for the political thrillers he enjoyed and the science fiction series she preferred.

Savannah entered the main building. The owner's son-in-law Raymond stood at the reference desk, situated more than halfway down the main aisle of the store. As she made her way over to him, the smell of the old books stacked on the desk's surface made her feel welcome.

"Hi, Raymond. How are you?"

Raymond looked up, and his youthful face brightened into a thousand-kilowatt smile. "Savannah, I've haven't seen you in here for quite a long time, not since you left for that fancy glassblowing studio in Seattle. How are you doing with your dad's shop?"

"Reasonably well, thank you. We are still teaching lots of students, and the commission work is steady. How's the bookstore?"

"It looks like we're going to weather this latest tempest in a teapot—the ebook threat. It seems, in the long run, people still like to read and hold actual books."

"What do you mean?" Savannah asked.

"Having a staff of booksellers who can recommend what you want to read next is preferable to an artificial algorithm based on who knows what kind of voodoo. It looks like people are ready to support a bookstore that helps customers choose their next book. A book that the clerk has actually read."

"Speaking of actual books . . ." Savannah folded her arms across her chest and leaned back a bit. "I seem to remember a section on antiques and collectibles."

"Definitely. What are you looking for?"

"A student brought in a couple of curiously old

cobalt-blue bottles. My friend Robin was able to get a preliminary value for them by comparing them to similar bottles, but I would like to date them accurately. Do you have anything that might be useful?"

Raymond scratched the back of his head and looked up at the ceiling. "I recall a large red volume down the second aisle, toward the back, that provides information on vintage bottles. It includes a small section, an illustrated history about glass bottles and their origins. I remember when a young lady brought it in. It was part of an estate sale over on Snell Isle. The last living relative of the owner—a niece, I think it was. It might be helpful."

"Thanks. I'll give it a look."

Savannah browsed as she made her way toward the back of the store. She was followed discreetly by one of the two cats that lived in Haslam's. Beowulf was a ghostly brown and tan tabby with a pleasant habit of rubbing against your calves when you were looking at books. He would be deterred only if you continued to move through the store. If you stopped to browse, the toll was to pet Beowulf. Savannah reached down to give him a thorough scratching, and he rose up on his two hind feet and nipped her hand!

"Ouch!" yelped Savannah. "What's wrong? That's not nice. You're supposed to be the nice one."

Beowulf slowly walked to the back of the store and sat down near the antiques and collectibles aisle. Savannah walked over, and where she expected to see the volume Raymond had recommended, all she found was a gap in the row of books.

Beowulf looked up at Savannah and immediately began to wash his back leg with an air of concentrated innocence.

Savannah searched through the books shelved in

the adjacent section but found nothing remotely helpful. She walked back to the reference desk.

As she approached, Raymond asked, "Did you find the right section?"

"Yes, I'm sure I found the right shelf. Are you sure you remember the glass book? I can't seem to find it."

"I never forget an acquisition," he muttered. "I remember that I entered it into the store's computerized inventory. Dad doesn't like to touch anything the least bit technical, so I do all the data entry." He came out from behind the desk and made his way back to the antiques and collectibles section of the store. He looked directly at the gap in the shelf. "It was right there. Looks like it's gone. Let me check the database to see if it's been sold."

He returned to the reference desk, where he started tapping on the keyboard with amazing speed, and then he frowned. "It hasn't been sold. Either it's been misplaced within the store or someone has stolen the book!"

Chapter 5

Savannah drove down her redbrick street, still thinking about Amanda's abrupt exit from the shop and her absentminded behavior. Forgetting to turn on the kiln was an obvious indication of anxiety. Maybe Amanda needed additional positive feedback to instill confidence.

I've never been a boss, but I've got to get a lot better at it pretty fast.

The tired driveway to her parents' bungalow crunched under the tires of her smoke-gray Mini Cooper. She needed to get an estimate for repairing or replacing the driveway, but she dreaded the sticker shock. It would have to wait until the studio began to show some positive cash flow from the new glass students.

It had been a tough decision to purchase her first new car. It had seemed like such an extravagance. But losing both her parents had taught her to live wholly in the present.

I probably shouldn't have bought this car, but I love it.

No sooner had Savannah opened the car door and stepped up onto her wide front porch than "Savannah!" wafted across the street. Savannah turned to see her neighbor, Mrs. Webberly, wave a yoga-toned arm to catch her attention. "Savannah, I'm so glad you're home. Rooney's been howling nonstop while you've been gone."

As if he had heard what she said, Rooney let loose a bloodcurdling howl as he stood at the heavy oak front door.

"And there he goes again. Now you can hear exactly what he's been doing." Mrs. Webberly shrugged her shoulders. "I don't understand. I took him for a walk in the morning and in the afternoon, as well. Weimaraners are not typically needy dogs, although like any young dog, they need a certain amount of socialization. He must be upset about something."

"Thanks, Mrs. Webberly. I'm sorry he's been a pest today. I'll try to figure out what's bothering him." She smiled. "He is quite a challenge. It doesn't help that there aren't any agility meets in the summer. Those obstacle-course trials seem to keep him calm."

The agility training had also been good for their bonding. Rooney had been her father's puppy and wasn't immediately keen to put aside his grief and accept Savannah. They were a crack team now, and she expected they would win their agility competitions this fall.

She opened the door and was again confronted with a mournful howl, which slowly turned into a soft whimper. "What on earth is bothering you?" Savannah cuddled the big blue-gray dog and looked into his warm amber eyes. She gave him a vigorous rubbing that extended from behind his ears to his lean, athletic shanks. "Let's go for a short run before Edward gets here. Does that enormous wiggle mean yes?"

Savannah changed into running clothes and left the house with Rooney in tow. They started running and went on their routine two-mile neighborhood loop. He relaxed into the run after the first few blocks and returned to his normal cheerful self.

When they got back home, Savannah took a quick shower, and afterward, she slipped on a white eyelet summer dress. In the kitchen, she put on her apron, tied it in the back, and then pulled open the refrigerator door. The organic New York strip steaks had been in a thin marinade of Worcestershire sauce, olive oil, aged balsamic vinegar, and a spice mixture since last night. From the vegetable drawer, she grabbed three ears of fresh corn, along with two small sweet potatoes and a bag of fresh baby salad greens.

"Thank goodness for prepackaged greens, Rooney. I'm more a meal assembler than a real cook."

She looked at the kitchen clock. The invitation was for seven—plenty of time for a simple meal. She washed the potatoes, slathered them with olive oil, and put them in the countertop toaster oven. She stripped the silk from the corn, then dumped the ears into a steaming pot of salted and seasoned water. After placing two dinner plates and a basket of sourdough dinner rolls on top of the toaster oven to warm, Savannah put her mother's heavy iron skillet over a medium flame to preheat it.

She stood in the doorway between the kitchen and the dining room, with her hands on her hips. The table sat ready, with plain white service pieces and silver cutlery. Rooney swung his head from side to side, following her every step. With the feeble hope that feeding Rooney would dampen his interest in the unusual feast being prepared, Savannah fed him an extra portion of his favorite wet food.

"Have I done everything right?"

Rooney sat and tilted his head. His amber eyes were clear and curious.

"I hope so. You know I'm better at reservations than at actually cooking a dinner. Except for your dinner, of course. But you're too nice to complain."

His tail thumped against the wooden floor, a gesture she took as approval.

At ten minutes to seven, Savannah swirled a generous pat of butter in the skillet and waited until it had melted fully and a slight bit of foam had disappeared. The steaks sizzled and popped in the hot skillet and filled the kitchen with a savory, mouth-watering aroma. She placed the cooked corn and sweet potatoes on the warmed plates and then mixed equal shares of a local honey and grainy mustard in a small servicing dish. She carried the dinner rolls, the dressing, and the salad bowl to the table.

The doorbell rang, and Rooney barked a friendly woof. Savannah checked her lipstick in the framed wooden mirror by the front door and ran a hand through her black curls. She opened the door wide.

Edward stood there, grinning, and held a bottle of red wine, along with a white bakery box tied with curly red ribbon. "Am I too early?"

"No, not at all."

She stepped back to let him into the house. As he passed by, he planted a drive-by kiss, and then he made his way into the living room.

She smiled. "The wine opener is on the counter. You do like your steak medium rare, right?"

"Too right!" He expertly wielded the opener and poured the fragrant Médoc into the large goblets on the table. He brought them over to the stove and handed one to Savannah.

"Here's a toast to a beautiful wine, a beautiful steak, and a beautiful cook."

They clinked their glasses and then sipped with their eyes locked.

Savannah's eyes sparkled over the rim of her goblet. "Fine speech, but you're cooking breakfast."

Chapter 6

Tuesday Morning

The early morning light was teasing the birds to welcome the day as a young couple strolled down a narrow beach with their chocolate Lab, Charlie. His puppy energy was focused on catching and fetching the driftwood stick the young man threw out into the shallows of Boca Ciega Bay, the intracoastal channel that separated the main peninsula of St. Petersburg from the barrier beaches of Treasure Island.

Charlie lost interest in the stick when he got a whiff of something that captured his attention. He lifted his nose high and sniffed great gulps of salt air to find the prize. Spying a dark shape in the soft dawning light, he galloped down the beach a hundred yards to sit beside the source of the fascinating scent. He was puzzled by the reaction of his owners. They didn't seem at all happy to find the lifeless diver lying facedown at the edge of the water. Not happy at all.

* * *

"Are you the couple who found the body?" Officer Boulli's substantial bulk stood over the couple who had found a small bit of driftwood to sit on in a tiny bit of shade. Charlie was lying on the sand, panting like a steam engine. They were about twenty yards from the activity around the diver.

The young man nodded. "Yes. My wife and I were on our regular early morning walk with Charlie." He looked over at his wife, who was drip feeding water from her bottle into Charlie's lapping mouth. "We live a few houses down the street. We'd like to go home and get Charlie out of the heat."

"Okay, okay." Officer Boulli opened a tattered notebook and pulled a pen from his white uniform shirt. "Your full names?"

Standing up, the young man said, "My name is Paul Wedlake, and this is my wife, Julie. We live in the second Mediterranean Revival house over there on Park Street." He pointed to their house and waited until Officer Boulli had lifted his head and noticed which house before telling him their full home address. "We were taking Charlie out for some exercise when he found the diver."

"Did you touch anything?"

"I turned him over to see if there was any sign of life, but it was obvious he had been in the water for a long time."

Officer Boulli scribbled in his notebook. "How did you know? Are you medical specialists?"

"No, we're not medical specialists. We're certified divers and have experience in researching sea life using robotic surface and underwater vehicles." He paused and inhaled a shallow breath. "Crabs don't feed on the living." He looked down the beach toward all the activity. "Can we go home now?"

"Give me a contact number." The officer wrote it in his notebook. "Most likely, the homicide detective will be along to get statements from you." He put his pen away, pulled out a wrinkled handkerchief, and wiped his face before handing them a business card. "Until he gets your statement, don't leave your house."

Homicide detective David Parker arrived at the crime site at the same time as Coroner Sandra Grey. They both parked on red brick–lined Park Street, near an enormous, three-story Mediterranean Revival mansion.

"Good morning, David. It looks like we got the call at the same time."

"How are you?" His smile brought out the small dimple in his chin. "I haven't seen you in a while." Only Sandra could look sensuous in the white forensic coveralls. They fit her curves perfectly. He wondered if she had had them tailored for her petite form.

"That's because the city of St. Petersburg has been strangely silent on murders lately."

"It's the dog days of summer. Most of those who can afford it are now cooling themselves in the mountains of North Carolina. The rest of us are too hot to get up to much."

They followed the yellow crime-scene tape back to the narrow beach area behind the mansion's garden and screened-in pool. A portable canopy with view-blocking panels on three sides had been erected to discourage onlookers.

The tide had gone out, and the body was faceup and fully outfitted in diver's gear, with one flipper missing and no sign of a tank. Sandra knelt beside the diver's face.

"He's been struck . . . a single blow." She glanced at the hands. "It doesn't look like he put up a fight, so we might not get DNA from his fingernails."

"His diving knife is also missing from its sheath. Time of death?" Parker had been scribbling away in his notebook.

"You know I don't like to speculate on TOD prior to the autopsy."

"I do know that. I also know how much experience you have." He raised an eyebrow and smiled as winningly as he knew how.

"Okay, okay. You can turn off the charm. It looks like he died sometime after midnight and probably before two a.m. He's been in the water at least a few hours. Sufficient?"

Detective Parker nodded. "Before the body is taken away, can we look in his dive bag?"

"No problem. We can do it now." Her gloved hands untied the blue mesh bag, the size of an eight-by-ten-inch sheet of paper, from the diver's weight belt. She pulled open the top and removed a key ring and what looked like fragments of a broken deep blue bottle. She held one of the larger fragments, which appeared to be the bottom of the bottle, up toward the rising sun. "It looks odd."

Parker tipped his head so he could also take a look through the fragment. "Difficult to tell with so much grime and growth." He placed his hand on Sandra's and turned her hand ever so slightly. The new angle revealed the broken edges of the glass. "This is a recent break. You can see the clear color of the glass, without any evidence of it being underwater."

"It looks like the entire bottle is in the dive bag."

"Well . . . ," he began, then quickly released Sandra's hand, as if it had a mind of its own. "I know a young woman who knows a lot about glass. I'll give her a call and see if she can help identify the bottle."

Sandra put the key ring and the bottle fragments back in the dive bag, pulled its string tight, and placed it on top of the diver's chest. She rose and signaled for the technicians to prepare the body for transport to the morgue downtown. "I'll start the autopsy immediately. We're going to need some luck with this one, David."

"I'm going to need more than luck. Thanks." After admiring Coroner Grey's retreat, Detective Parker spotted Officer Boulli and waved him over.

"Where are the witnesses?" the detective asked.

"Oh, they're a young couple with a dog who live right in the neighborhood, so I sent them home to wait for your interview."

Detective Parker lifted his eyes to the sky and growled low. "What if they were not telling you the whole truth, Officer? What if they wanted to escape, perhaps? You certainly gave them an easy way to leave. You had better hope they are honest citizens. Now, give me the address, and you stay here and keep people out of the crime scene." Under his breath Parker continued, "And out of my way."

The walk back toward the street gave Parker the small bit of time he needed to recover from his temper. Officer Boulli could frustrate a monk, but he always managed to perform his job minimally—not in any way proficiently, but not badly enough to be dismissed or reprimanded.

The witnesses' house was indeed only two doors down from the body of the diver. Detective Parker rang the doorbell, and a fierce barking instantly followed. He could hear the owners telling their dog to quiet down. The barking instantly stopped, and then the door was immediately opened.

"Good morning." Parker showed his badge. "I'm Detective David Parker, a homicide detective from the St. Petersburg Police Department. My colleague Officer Boulli gave me your information. Are you Paul and Julie Wedlake?"

"Yes. Please come in." Julie said.

The young couple led him through the sparse but beautifully furnished house to the huge screened-in lanai, dominated by a sparkling pool with an unobstructed view of the water. The carefully placed landscaping gave the illusion of privacy. Julie waved her hand at a large sectional, with a low table the full length of the sofa, facing the water. On a short out-door kitchen counter to the side were an electric kettle, a small sink, and a selection of clear canisters filled with loose tea and ground coffee.

"Make yourself comfortable. What would you like to drink? I have regular and decaffeinated coffee, but I also have green tea and herbal tea," Julie said.

"Black coffee please. Regular would be great."

Julie nodded, deftly filled a French press with ground coffee, poured hot water into it, and brought it, along with an empty cup, over to the low table and placed them in front of Detective Parker.

"Thanks."

She grabbed her green tea from the table and sat with her hands folded around the ceramic mug. "This is an upsetting situation. I crave my comforting routines. You must be used to it."

In a low voice he said, "I hope I never get used to a violent end to life, Mrs. Wedlake. Never." He pulled out a notebook and pen from his inner suit pocket.

"Now, as clearly as possible, can you describe how you came to discover the diver?"

Back in his office, Detective Parker opened the bottom drawer of his desk and pulled out a new manila folder. With a perfectly sharpened pencil, he wrote "John Doe – Bottle" on the tab. Although most modern-day investigative information was stored on the St. Petersburg Police Department's secure server, there were still bits of paper that needed wrangling with even after they were scanned.

Sandra Grey leaned into his office, waving a few sheets of paper. "Would you like to see my preliminary autopsy report?" Without waiting, she plopped the report in the center of his desk and sat down in the nearest of the two guest chairs. "It's not complete, of course, but there's enough for you to start."

"That was fast." He scanned through the pages with a practiced eye, then looked up from the report. "He didn't drown?"

"Nope. I thought you might find it interesting."

"How? It wasn't obvious at the beach."

"Well, we were hampered by the wet suit. It covered a massive trauma to the spine. He died in a matter of seconds."

"Any indication of what type of weapon was used?"

"Sorry." She shook her head. "I've noted the ubiquitous blunt instrument, but it was the same shape as the injuries we saw on his face."

Detective Parker sat staring at the last sheet of the preliminary report.

Sandra sat forward and waved a hand slowly in front of Detective Parker's face. "Earth to Parker. Where are you?"

"I'm trying to visualize where he might have been in order to be attacked. He was wearing a complete wet suit."

She tilted her head. "It would be uncomfortable in this heat, but it offers excellent protection. A friend of mine is a frequent cave diver in the natural springs up around Ocala, Florida. She says she wouldn't even think about not having a full suit."

"So you're thinking that he considered this dive to be dangerous?"

She paused. "It was."

Chapter 7

Tuesday Morning

Savannah turned her car's radio dial to the local news station on her way to Webb's Glass Shop. She listened to the news only during the short commute from her Craftsman bungalow to work. Her goal was to keep up with the major news in the Tampa Bay area, and the time spent listening in the car was usually just enough to give the appearance to her customers and students that she was somewhat tuned in to the real world. It was certainly enough news to make her question the viability of the human race.

She turned down the alley behind the shop before she remembered that Amanda would open up Webb's today, since she was teaching in the morning, while Savannah would go and open up the studio. But who was she kidding? Since his pub was right next door, Savannah really hoped to see Edward again. His breakfast omelet with cheese and onions had been amazing, but he had returned to his condo at the crack of dawn to feed his kitten.

I won't admit it to him, though. I'll claim I wanted to

support Amanda on her second day of instruction in the new class.

She was pulling into the parking spot in the back of Webb's when the radio announcer said, "The police department is asking for any information about a missing diver. The general description is a young man of medium height, with olive skin and light brown hair. Citizens are asked to call the tip line with any information that would help the authorities identify the body that washed ashore early this morning."

Today will be a horribly bad day for some poor family.

She unlocked the back door, keyed in the alarm code, and turned on the lights throughout. Since she had taken over the shop after her dad's death, this had become a comfortable routine. It surprised her with its feeling of belonging.

Dropping her backpack on the antique oak swivel chair in her office, she did a quick cleaning in the bathroom and followed with a quick sweep of the floors to pick up any major glass shards. The cleaning service came twice a week, but she was more comfortable with a daily roundup. Glass splinters were sharp, and you could never be too careful.

Where's Amanda? She should be here by now. It's not like her to be late. I hope her mother is all right.

The next stop was the kiln in the supply room, but as she reached for the large bar across the front of it to lift the heavy lid and see the results of the overnight run, she stopped.

Nope. This is Amanda's job now, not mine. I won't spoil the pleasure of being the first one to look into a kiln she has personally prepared for firing. That's the best part of the job.

The next task in opening the shop was to fire up the cash register in the display room. She crossed her fingers and pressed the ON button. She heard the ancient computer groan with reluctance, while the protesting fan wailed a high-pitched whine for a moment, until it dropped to a humming drone. At last, the screen flashed bright with the main page of Webb's Glass Shop.

As a custom product, the register worked, but it was time to upgrade to a modern application that would handle both the shop and the studio. She sighed at the thought of what her accountant would say to yet another expense to replace a working system. Savannah thought her own arguments were good, but Burkart always had another viewpoint, one that usually required financial restraint on Savannah's part. Anyway, the upgrade would support better inventory control and therefore would result in more turnover and profit. But money had been a bit tight since the purchase of the warehouse for the studio.

The last bit of routine was to unlock the front door and turn the sign from CLOSED to OPEN. She glanced at her watch. It was already nine o'clock.

Where is Amanda? She said everything had settled down with her mother.

She pulled out her cell and dialed Amanda. It went straight to voice mail.

"Hey, Amanda. Is everything okay with your mother? Let me know what's going on."

Savannah ended the call. Amanda was probably on her way. Unfortunately, if her mother was in the hospital, there was no way to reach her. Cell phones weren't allowed in the intensive care unit.

After picking up a notepad, she walked into the supply room and started a list of glass sheets to order. She could hear Burkart's voice again reminding her of the strained budget.

By the time she had finished the entire inventory,

it was five minutes to ten and she had left two more voice messages on Amanda's cell phone.

The bell on the front door jangled, and SueAnn walked in, with Yvonne right behind. Each was carrying an armful of glass plates and bowls for today's workshop.

"Good mawnin', Savannah." SueAnn headed straight for the classroom.

"Hi, Savannah!" Yvonne smiled and shrugged her shoulders at SueAnn's abruptness. "I guess she's excited to see what comes out of our efforts today." She followed SueAnn, who was removing a spiral notebook from her bag, along with a pen.

The Rosenberg twins arrived next, with Patty between them. Rachel and Faith wore another one of their head-to-toe ensembles, this time in a vivid lilac. Patty had inadvertently played into their color scheme with a pale yellow T-shirt over green slacks. The colors assaulted Savannah's eyes, having an impact that reminded her of a birthday confetti explosion.

"I thought you told us yesterday that you were letting Amanda run Webb's." Rachel rolled her eyes at Savannah. "You do know how to delegate, don't you? Your father was miserable at it."

Savannah took a deep, calming breath. "I know how to delegate. Make that 'I'm learning how to delegate.' As soon as Amanda arrives, I'll scoot over to the studio. She texted that she's had a family emergency, but that it should be resolved by now. You know her mother's health is a constant source of concern. She's become very frail."

"Oh my. Such a trial for Amanda," said Faith. "We went to see her mother last week."

"But our visit was short, since she didn't know who we were."

Faith glared at Rachel. "Of course she didn't remember us. It was the first time we ever met her."

With a measured stare, Rachel eyed the stack of glass dishes Faith was holding. "Do you have more dishes than I do?"

"No, of course not. You're not counting properly." Faith scurried into the classroom, followed by Rachel.

Savannah walked through the classroom and stepped out the back door to see if Amanda was driving up. Nope.

Looks like I'm teaching today.

She returned to the classroom. Walking calmly up to the podium, Savannah opened the lesson plan notebook and flipped to the page marked "Day Two."

"So until Amanda arrives, I'll get us started for today." She looked over the classroom and noticed the seat next to SueAnn was still empty. "Wait. Martin's missing."

Could Martin be the unidentified diver?

"Teacher's pet," said the Rosenberg twins in perfect unison. Samantha's scowl forced them into a temporary silence.

"He's the scruffy one with the strange bottles," said Faith.

"Of course. I wanted to tell him what I found out. They could be very valuable," Savannah revealed. She looked at her watch again.

He might actually know the diver. Maybe that's why he's running late. He's probably texted Amanda to tell her that he will be delayed. Stop worrying.

"Let's not wait any longer. Today is a fun day. We're making glass flowers for your garden using plates, bowls, cups, and whatever small pieces you want to recycle. I hope you brought plenty." She ducked down to look into the storage shelves in the podium, then straightened.

Thank goodness Amanda prepared for this yesterday afternoon, she thought.

"I have a few examples for you down here." She bent down to the shelves in the podium and brought up a glass flower all in green, made from a plate, a bowl, and a tea light candle holder, then held it up.

"This is an example of drilling holes through the pieces first. Then you slip a bolt through each piece and a piece of copper tubing. Not only does this method hold them together, but the copper tubing acts as the pole to put in the ground, as well. This is an easy method, and the flower can be finished quickly. The drawback is that the length of the bolt limits how many pieces you can use. Also, some artists don't like the look of the bolt. The best trick is to cover the bolt by gluing a cover over it, like a button, an earring, or a toy china cup."

"Do you use glue?" SueAnn poised her pen over her open notebook.

Savannah handed the green flower to SueAnn and gestured for her to pass it around to the students. "Yes, I use E6000 glue for outdoor use. Another option is to use GE Silicone II clear caulk. You can use either glue or caulk, instead of drilling the pieces."

She pulled out another glass flower, created using pale pink Depression-ware dishes. It included a salad plate, a saucer, and a small dessert dish. "This is a flower I stuck together using silicone as the glue. If some of the plates are thin, that's your best bet, because drilling might shatter them." Savannah handed the glass flower over to SueAnn for passing.

Faith held up a timid hand and cleared her throat. "How do you give the flowers stems?"

Savannah pulled out a completed glass flower from the bottom of the podium. "Here's a finished flower mounted on a copper pipe. You can use aluminum pipe, rebar rods, wooden dowels, copper pipe, branches, curtain rods, or recycled railing. Basically, anything that strikes your creative fancy."

Rachel stood up in the back row. "Do you want these back?"

"Yes. Bring them up here. You can come up and look them over while you're assembling your own."

SueAnn gave Savannah a queenly wave. "Darlin', what about our glass bottles from yesterday's workshop? Are we going to get to see how they wound up?"

"Absolutely. I'll—"

The hanging bell on the front door shrieked and jangled. It was followed by a huffing and red-faced Amanda running into the classroom. "Sorry, sorry, sorry. I overslept. I didn't hear the alarm go off. I'm so embarrassed."

Although it might be difficult for a stranger to discern, Savannah noticed that Amanda wore a hodgepodge of an outfit. Her makeup was a bit streaky, and her lime earrings didn't coordinate with the peach top and pale yellow slacks. Even worse, she was wearing one brown shoe and one black shoe, which looked more like Amanda's mother's style of comfortable footwear. Amanda had an unusual style, yes, but this was extreme even for her.

"It's fine, Amanda. It eventually happens to everyone," Savannah said, using her best comforting voice. "Because everything was so well organized, I was able to cover the glass flower lecture easily." Savannah's voice dropped down to a whisper. "Next time, call or text when something unexpected comes up. It looks like we don't know what we're doing, and it's not good for our reputation."

Amanda wiped the stray wisps of hair off her forehead. "Of course. I don't know why I didn't. That's exactly what I should have done. I'm so sorry." Amanda's voice mimicked that of a small child. "Do you want to take over the teaching?"

"No. Of course not. I was about to take the class into the supply room to open the kiln. I'm so glad you're here. I didn't want you to miss opening it for your very first class. It's such great fun."

"Thanks." Amanda looked around the classroom and noticed the empty seat in the front row. "Where's Martin?"

Chapter 8

"Martin hasn't shown up." Savannah heard the sharp tone in her voice and immediately softened it. "Didn't he let you know he wouldn't be here?"

Amanda stood quietly. Her pale skin turned ashen at the neck, and this color slowly began to rise into her face. "Sure. He said last night that he might be a little late. . . . A little late for him might be an hour." Her voice rose to a high tremor. "Even so, he should be here pretty soon."

"Excuse us for a moment," Savannah said to the class and then took Amanda by the arm and led her through the door to her office. "Why don't you get a cup of coffee and calm yourself. I'll take everyone over to the kiln." She took Amanda and sat her down in the oak desk chair. After pouring a cup of coffee, she asked, "What's wrong? Is your mother ill?"

Amanda shook her head yes but didn't speak. She

sat there, looking down at the floor, the tears in her eyes ready to spill down her cheeks.

"I'll get everyone started on cleaning up their pieces, and I'll be back in a jiffy. Are you sure you're going to be okay?"

Amanda looked up. "I'll be fine in a few minutes. I'm feeling a bit disoriented. I didn't get much sleep."

"Your mom?"

"Um, yes. It's getting bad." Amanda took a drink of the coffee.

"Okay. I'll be right back."

Savannah walked back into the classroom. "Amanda's a little tired. She was up most of the night, watching over her sick mother, and she's a little distracted. She'll be fine after a hit of coffee. Meanwhile, let's go open the kiln and see what happened to our bottles last night."

There was a quick burst of chatter as everyone made their way to the supply room. Savannah stood beside the largest kiln, which was about the size and shape of a small bathtub, and raised the lid with the rigged pulley-and-cable system. She used a mountain climber's clip to secure the lid in the open position.

"I'll lift the pieces out and hand them to each of you. Once you have your piece, you need to take it over to the sink and wash the kiln paper residue off it. Also, wash the plaster mold, if you used one."

She reached into the depths of the kiln and picked out a Belvedere Vodka bottle that had been slumped in a cracker tray mold. "Which one of you is the owner of this one?" She looked at Rachel, then at Faith.

"That's mine!" Rachel pushed to the front. "I'll take it."

Savannah found another Belvedere Vodka bottle, which had been fused flat. "So this must be yours, then, Faith."

Faith smiled and took the ash-covered bottle over to the sink to wash it.

"Who has the light green bottle?" Savannah lifted a flattened bottle.

"That's mine, darlin'. I'll take it." SueAnn stepped in front of the Akron girls and took the dusty cheese tray from Savannah with pinched fingers. "I should have brought an apron. I didn't realize we'd get dirty." SueAnn held the flattened bottle away from her clothes, her fingers touching it as little as possible.

"This is not a particularly dirty craft. But you might get fairly dusty. The kiln work can be a bit messy with all the flying ash."

She'll never be comfortable with the ash.

Savannah looked at the young cousins and then gazed into the kiln. "There are only three left. Which ones are yours?"

"The clear wine bottle is mine," Patty said, pointing, "and the dark yellow one is Yvonne's."

Handing over their bottles, Savannah assumed that the remaining bottle must belong to Martin. It wasn't one of the unique cobalt blue bottles he had brought in. She picked up the flattened Van Gogh Raspberry Vodka bottle. She recognized it as one from Amanda's collection.

Savannah lifted her voice over the chattering and splashing at the sink. "When you have your pieces completely clean and dry, we'll have a little critique session, and then we'll start today's project back in the classroom."

"Miss Vanna," said SueAnn, "I allow, as we are a group of art students, that I should expect to work on various types of material. But I, I mean we, shouldn't expect to get filthy in the process. I can't abide this dust."

"But it's a natural part of the firing process, SueAnn."

"I'm positively sure it will bring on an asthma attack." She looked down at the ash-coated bottle in her hands. "I regret to inform you I have to leave."

"Oh no, SueAnn." Savannah quickly calculated the cost of a refund. "Don't worry. We'll wash the kiln pieces for you. I wouldn't want you to get sick."

SueAnn's eyes softened, and she tilted her head. "Bless your heart, Vanna." SueAnn handed the wine bottle over to Savannah, then held her hands away from her body, as if she had contracted the black death. "Doesn't that young fella, Martin, got sumthin' in there?"

"Sure he does. He used one of Amanda's backup vodka bottles. She was smart to bring them in."

Walking with her hands out to her sides like a zombie, SueAnn hurried through the classroom and into the office bathroom.

Savannah shook her head. *You meet all kinds.*

When Savannah walked back into the classroom, Amanda was standing behind the podium, with her teaching notebook open. After SueAnn returned from the bathroom, she proceeded to use three sanitizing sheets on the surface of her worktable. She bent down to examine the results and then followed this with three more. The class looked on, as if this was an avant-garde performance.

Clearing her throat and breaking the spell, Savannah touched Amanda lightly on the arm. "You look so much better. Are you okay to continue?"

"I'm good. The coffee helped like a magic tonic. I've got this."

The front door bell jangled.

"I'll get it. Carry on," Savannah said.

Savannah went to the front of the shop and found Detective Parker standing by the counter in the display room. He had placed a small brown paper bag with the flap folded on top of the counter. It was labeled EVIDENCE. Next to it was a printed list that documented the particulars of the evidence bag and also the chain of custody. Savannah knew this from her experience with her father's investigation.

"Good morning, Savannah. Is this a bad time?"

"Nope. Amanda is teaching now. That leaves me time to work on more custom commissions at the new location I've opened in the Warehouse Arts District."

"A bit risky, isn't it? You've been running Webb's for only about six months."

"It's a risk, but the volume of commissions and restorations in our glass business has outgrown this location, and there's no room to expand here. So buying the studio was my best solution."

Detective Parker nodded his head. "Well, I've got a curious object I hope you can help me identify." He opened the evidence bag and pulled out the neck and shoulder portion of a broken cobalt blue bottle.

He placed the fragment on the sales counter, then stepped back.

"A bottle? I've been hip deep in bottles lately. We're in the middle of a recycling workshop right now." She picked up the fragment and held it up to the light. "In fact, this looks like it could be a match to a set of bottles one of our students brought in yesterday. He wanted to know if it was valuable."

"Where did he get them?"

"I don't know exactly. He said it was at a beach where he was diving, but he didn't say which one."

"Is he here now?"

"No, but he texted Amanda that he should be coming in any minute. I have his contact information, if you need it. He could be a useful resource for you. Should I get it now?"

"No. E-mail it sometime today."

Savannah scrunched her brow and looked at the splotchy coating of black material that covered most of the fragment. "What's this black stuff?"

"Fingerprint powder. We didn't find any prints, so you can wash it off if you need to."

"Hmmm. That might help." She held the fragment up to the light again. "This appears to be part of the neck." She felt along the shoulder of the bottle, where the neck joined the body of the bottle. "I can't tell much. It's been underwater for a long time. I need to clean it off to get an opinion about it. Is the rest of the bottle in here?" She leaned over to look inside the evidence bag.

"We think all the pieces are there, but I haven't a clue." He tipped the bag, and the remaining fragments spilled out on the counter, along with some dried sea debris. "Would you be able to clean the pieces up and reconstruct the bottle so it could be identified?"

Fingering the pile of glass fragments, she replied, "It doesn't look like there are many small pieces." She looked up quickly. "Are you hiring me as a consultant for this?" She held her breath. A consulting fee right now would help her financial situation. "How much does it pay?"

"If you think you can get to it quickly, I can request express services. That should work out to about seventy-five dollars per hour." He glanced at the pile of glass fragments. "In order to qualify for express status, I'll need an answer within the next twenty-four hours."

"Absolutely. Why? What's happened? Is this about the body I heard about on the news this morning?"

"It is. We're trying everything to identify the victim. He had this bottle in a small mesh bag tied to his weight belt. Can you help?"

"Absolutely. I'll ask Martin to get in touch when he shows up. They must know each other. I'll start on it right away."

"Keep track of your hours. Let me know the moment you have any information."

"No problem. See you later."

"Bye."

The bell rang as he left Webb's. Savannah placed the bottle fragments back in the bag and took it with her back to the classroom. Amanda was leading the students through today's craft project. Savannah eyed her carefully. Her color was back, and her voice was calm and confident. As an afterthought, she grabbed the brown gift bag containing the wrapped bottle, and she also tucked into the bag the other bottle Martin had brought in, so that she now had both of

Martin's bottles to use as comparisons to the evidence bottle. Moving quickly through the classroom, she waved so long to Amanda and went out the back door.

An unpleasant thought played havoc in her mind. Could Martin be the diver on the news? No, it couldn't be. He'd texted Amanda. Where did that idea come from? She pushed the thought away.

In her workshop at the new studio, Savannah laid out the bottle fragments and then spread them out. The volume of fragments looked about right for a small bottle. She aligned a few of the larger fragments to see if they fit together. After several dozen attempts, two fragments finally mated perfectly. She smiled. *Yes!*

This consulting fee was going to be a slam dunk and a complete plus in her financial plan. Maybe her accountant would even smile at this month's meeting.

She placed the fragments in a plastic bin and took them over to the washing-up station. The sea growth and debris was stubborn to remove, but a stiff brush driven by elbow grease was free and readily available. She began to hum while cleaning.

A knock on the front door interrupted her song.

"It's open," she yelled, then regretted it immediately. That was rude, and she could hear her mother saying, "Were you raised in a barn?" when she was a little girl and made mistakes with her manners.

She perched the plastic bin on one hip, walked to the door, and opened it with her free hand. "Welcome to Webb's Studio."

Standing in the bright sun, holding a two-by-two-foot stained glass mounting board, was Arthur Young, a student from the first class she had taught after her father's death. Unchanged from that first class, he was deeply tanned and had brown hair and brown eyes. That he still dressed in a plain golf shirt with khaki trousers didn't surprise her one bit.

"Arthur, it's so good to see you. Come in. I've got your space ready for you."

They walked over to the work space at the end of the row.

"It is close to the facilities?"

Savannah nodded. "It's the closest one in the building. I was concerned I wouldn't be able to rent this particular one because it is so close. Do you mind—"

"Nope. In fact, I'm blatantly outspoken about it. I have Crohn's. It is an inflammatory bowel disease that causes my intestines to become inflamed. Part of it is physical, and another part is phychological. My doctor prescribed some supereffective pills for the medical issues, and I've found that if I know where the facilities are, I'm a lot calmer mentally."

"So, this is a win-win for you, then?"

"Yep."

He gingerly laid his mounting board on the surface of the worktable and turned a complete circle to look at the small desk, the shelves, and the wall of windows. "This is grand. I'm going to love this."

"How's your wife? Her name is Nancy, right?"

"She's great, but not thrilled about my taking this studio space. She's disappointed I can't play in the orchestra anymore. At least not until I get the symptoms under control. She adored being a musician's wife."

"Wow. What a big adjustment."

"She's rallied. This disease has given her a crusade

to champion, with me as the poster child. But honestly, I need somewhere to be alone and do something with my hands."

Savannah felt her grin grow into a wide smile. "I'm glad. Make yourself at home and have a good wander around the studio. I'll be back in a second."

She walked to her workshop, put the bin down on her worktable, and fished a labeled key out of her desk drawer. She found Arthur and handed him his key to the front door.

"Here's your key, so you can come and go as you please. If you have any questions, I'll be in my office or my workshop, right down there." She pointed to her office.

She left him so that he could settle in, picked up the plastic bin again, and finished cleaning each glass fragment. When they were clean, they shone that beautiful cobalt blue. She placed them in a row at the top of her work surface. The reconstruction took quite a bit of focus. She started at the bottle's bottom and used ordinary white school glue so the bottle could be dismantled if needed.

In less than an hour, the bottle stood on her worktable, next to the two bottles that belonged to Martin. She picked it up and felt all the seams. It was an exact match.

Oh no. Martin is a diver. Is this his?

A rock-sized chill formed in her chest. She looked at her watch. It was after two in the afternoon. Amanda's class would be over by now. She called the shop.

"Webb's Glass Shop. How may I help you?"

"Amanda, did Martin ever show up for your class today?"

"No. I gave him another call to see if he was quitting the class. His cell went straight to voice mail."

"Okay. I wanted to talk to him about the bottles. Let me know if you hear from him."

Savannah didn't like the path her sense of logic took as she connected the broken bottle with the discovery of the unidentified diver. She dialed Detective Parker. He picked up on the third ring and gave a terse hello.

"Detective Parker, I've reassembled the broken bottle. It is a perfect match to the bottles my student brought to class. Have you identified the diver yet?"

"No. His fingerprints were not in the system, and there are no missing person reports that match. We're hoping we get credible information from the tip line. But so far, nothing is checking out."

"I have an uneasy suspicion your unidentified diver might be my absent glass student. Does the diver have a tattoo of a pirate's treasure chest on his left shoulder?"

"Let me look at the autopsy report. Hang on for a second." She could hear a shuffling of papers. "Here it is. Pirate's treasure chest tattoo on the left shoulder."

Savannah felt the bottom of her stomach sink. "Oh no. It's got to be him. This is horrible. His name is Martin Lane."

"Excellent. That's a tremendous help. When did you see him last?"

"He attended the first class yesterday, so I saw him only at the start of the day, which was a little after ten. He had two bottles with him that look just like the broken one you gave me to restore. As I said, I've got it pieced together now, and it looks exactly like the two bottles Martin brought to Webb's yesterday."

"Good. I'm going to need all the information you

have on his registration form. E-mail it to me as soon as you can."

"Sure. I'll send it right after this call. Do you want me to continue my research into the origins of the shattered bottle?"

There was a short pause. "Yes, definitely. We need to know everything."

Chapter 9

The run-down trailer park looked like it was killing time until a developer bought the land for a multi-story condominium. The location was too far away from the gulf beaches to tempt an investor for at least another decade.

After pulling down the one-way crushed-shell road, Officer Boulli parked the unmarked cruiser beside Martin's moss-stained travel trailer. Both he and Detective Parker stepped out of the cruiser. A small window air conditioner had been fit into a hole cut on the door side of the trailer. It looked like the only thing keeping it in the raggedy opening was the aging layers of duct tape circling the crusty aluminum supports on the wheezing unit.

Beside the tiny concrete patio that supported the metal trailer steps, a stack of pale gray driftwood was piled about four feet high. Next to the driftwood were separate mounds of large shells and bottles. The last collection was composed of a rusty boat engine, a lawn mower, and tractor and marine specialty parts, all jumbled together.

Officer Boulli put on gloves, then unlocked the trailer door, using a key on the key ring found in Martin's dive bag. He and Detective Parker slowly entered the eight-foot-wide trailer. It smelled faintly of bacon combined with sea life and art glue.

The layout was a central kitchen with booth seating in the front and a small bedroom in the back. Opposite the kitchen was a tiny bathroom. The cast-iron frying pan with a congealed layer of bacon grease on the stove explained the predominant odor. The sink was clean, and there was a plate, a cup, a fork, and a spatula drying in a small dish drainer. Half of the dining table served as a work area and was piled high with small driftwood twigs, polished seashells, copper wire, encrusted marine parts, and bits of sea glass, which were being assembled into wind-driven sculptures.

"It looks like he dived for salvage parts to use in his mechanical wind machines." Detective Parker looked at a completed piece that was hanging from a hook in the ceiling. "This is quite good. I wouldn't be surprised if this fetched a few hundred dollars at a gallery. Have we determined if his work is with any of the local shops?"

"Not yet." Officer Boulli took out his notebook and scribbled a line. "I'll check it out."

"Check to see if he had a Web site or if he was selling online," said Parker.

On the other side of the table was an open laptop connected to a charger and a pad of paper, along with some library books arranged in a stack. Parker bent over and peered at the titles on the spines.

"It looks like he was researching the early history

of Tampa Bay," he said. Several sheets had been roughly torn from the pad of paper, exposing a blank page. "If we can find the torn-out sheets, that might help us. They could be in his vehicle."

"A BOLO was ordered right after he was identified."

"Make sure that the computer forensics technician gets the laptop." Boulli opened the tiny refridgerator. "Not much here."

Detective Parker walked back to the tiny bedroom, where he found a made bed and a phone-charger cord on the nightstand. "His phone must be in his vehicle. There's enough stuff here for forensics to process. You had better give them a call."

Boulli's phone rang while he was dialing forensics. "Officer Boulli."

Detective Parker watched while Officer Boulli listened for a few seconds.

"Thanks," Boulli said. "That was headquarters. A traffic officer found Martin's vehicle, with his cell phone inside, not far from here."

"Tell them we'll be there in a few minutes." Detective Parker looked inside the bedroom dresser, went into the bathroom and peeked in the cabinet, and shrugged. "Nothing more for us here. Let's leave this for the forensics team."

It took them only a few minutes to find the address on the west edge of St. Petersburg. Martin Lane's vehicle was a beat-up white Toyota two-passenger truck. It was the only vehicle in a boat launch parking lot less than a mile from where his body was found. There were signs of rust showing at the bottom of the cab doors and along the bottom of the truck-bed door. The vehicle also looked recently washed.

The doors were locked. Detective Parker took out

a flashlight and peered into the driver's side window. The inside of the truck showed its age by way of the wear and tear in the upholstery, but everything was tidy. On the bench-style seat was a folded white T-shirt on top of a pair of worn cutoff jeans. On the floor of the passenger side was a beach towel with part of a Superman logo showing. It looked placed rather than tossed. A clamshell phone lay on top of the towel.

"He's probably got a 'pay as you go' phone plan. It's the cheapest you can get." Officer Boulli sniffed. "What a loser."

"Loser? I don't see Martin as a loser. Strapped for money maybe, given how Spartanly the trailer was furnished and how little food he had. He might have been recovering from an addiction of some kind, but he had a talent for making things with his hands. His craft brought in cash and apparently made people happy. You would do well if that was your legacy at such a young age." Parker switched off the flashlight. "Hand me the keys. Let's look inside before the forensics van gets here."

Officer Boulli tightened his lips into a thin line. "The keys?"

"Yes. You opened his trailer with them. Where are they?"

Patting all his pockets, Officer Boulli came up with the cruiser's keys, his personal keys, but no victim's keys. "I'll go back and get them. I think I left them in the trailer."

"You think?"

"I'm sure. I'm sure I left them on the table."

Detective Parker released a small sigh. "Perfect. That means the trailer is unlocked. Yet another mistake, Officer." Parker shook his head slowly. "I'll look around here. Did you call forensics yet?"

"Ugh. I forgot to call them after headquarters called us with the information on the car." Officer Boulli pulled out his phone. "Calling right now," he yelled over his shoulder, moving as quickly as he could to the cruiser.

The bed of the small white truck looked worn, and there were shadows of rust encroaching from around the wheel wells. The sand, pebbles, and shell debris embedded in the tire grooves looked recent, as opposed to being a long buildup. There were three large pieces of driftwood tangled together, along with a remnant of netting and two horseshoe crab carcasses, inside the truck bed.

If he had been hauling his beach and snorkeling finds in the truck, Martin had been pretty regular about washing out the mess.

Interrupting Parker's thoughts, Office Boulli came trotting over, with a drenched shirt and rivers of sweat dripping off his hair and face. "Here are the keys," he panted, then grabbed his side. "Ugh! I've got cramps."

Detective Parker took the keys and pulled out his handkerchief to wipe them dry. "You passed the annual physical?"

Face red, Officer Boulli kept taking in deep breaths but nodded all the same.

"Really?" Parker made a mental note to research the results.

On the passenger side, Parker unlocked the door and pushed the button to the glove compartment. There was a white business-sized envelope with "REG" written in green ink, two hotel pens, and a red spiral notebook inside the glove compartment.

He straightened up and beckoned for Officer Boulli, who was several yards away, standing in the shade of a palm tree. "You know, sometimes it's not about what is here, but about what is missing, that tells us the most about the crime and the victim. What do you think is missing?"

Officer Boulli leaned into the cab and made a dramatic pretense of looking around. He straightened up and shook his head. "I don't get what you mean. There's hardly anything here at all."

"My point exactly. This guy was searching the bottom of the gulf for salvage parts and other items to use in his mechanical artworks."

Officer Boulli shrugged his bulky shoulders. "So?"

"I don't believe he was searching blindly. He must have had a plan of some sort. He probably didn't have a GPS. Even the least expensive one would be several hundred dollars. But I truly don't understand why there are no drawings, sketches, or marine charts of any sort. That's not right."

Chapter 10

"Most workshops hit their routine by the second day, but this one is already at the third day, and there's no routine." Savannah sipped the warm mocha latte Edward had brought over to Webb's from Queen's Head. She snagged the last cranberry scone and spread it with his private supply of butter shipped by his parents from a London shop. "Other than the predictably outlandish outfits worn by the Rosenberg twins, there is no routine. This is not a comfortable feeling."

"I didn't know you looked for it," Edward said.

"Well, I didn't know I was looking for it until it didn't happen." She popped the last morsel of the cranberry scone into her mouth and wiped the edges of her lips with her thumb and index finger. "It's like remembering an itch you don't have anymore. You sorta miss it."

"Sounds daft to me." Edward began to gather the breakfast cups and saucers on a black, round tray. "I've got to get back to the pub. I'll ring you up later."

He bent down to kiss the top of her head. "Try not to think about your itches."

It was only a few minutes after Edward's departure when she heard the bell on the front door ring, followed by Amanda's voice calling out, "Savannah? I'm here. Nothing to worry about. I'm here."

Walking into the classroom, Savannah felt her heart sink when she got a look at Amanda. "What's wrong? Has your mother taken a turn for the worse?"

Amanda's eyes were puffy and red rimmed. Although her outfit was wildly eclectic, it was clear to Savannah that the effect had not been achieved by Amanda's usual meticulous planning but more by donning the first things she had laid her hands on this morning.

Clasping Amanda by the shoulders, she said, "What's wrong? Is it your mom? Has she had a relapse with the pneumonia?"

"I'm sorry." Reaching into her enormous patchwork hobo purse, Amanda found a tissue and blew a loud trumpet and snuffled a sob. "Mom's not breathing well. They're watching her closely, and they'll call if she gets worse. I'll be all right. Just give me a few minutes to get my head clear." She trudged on into the office and ducked into the bathroom.

Shaking her head, Savannah stood behind the instructor's podium and opened the lesson plan to "Day 3" and reviewed the teaching points. It was possible that Amanda wasn't capable emotionally of teaching. Perhaps it was too much to ask.

It must be her mother. Although she's been dealing with those issues for the past few months. It might be something else. Maybe she's unnerved by Martin's death.

Amanda emerged from the office with more color in her face and a freshly applied bold streak of color on her generous lips. "Sorry. I'm trying to cope with my mother's progressing dementia. Occasionally, it hits hard. Yesterday was a particularly bad visit."

Savannah nodded. "I'm sorry. Didn't she remember you? That must hurt."

"No. Actually, it was quite the opposite. It was one of those days where she thinks clearly and knows exactly where she is and why." Amanda took a sobbing breath and put a hand on her chest. "She wanted me to pack up her things and take her back home immediately."

"I'm so sorry." Savannah tucked Amanda into her arms and held her until the shuddering stopped. "You must feel so helpless."

Amanda moved back and reached into her bag for another tissue. "Thanks. That's the frustrating part. When she's truly herself, I can't enjoy it, because of her awareness of her present circumstances. When she thinks she's away on a vacation trip, she's not herself." She blew her nose. "Thanks for understanding."

Amanda looked down at the open lesson plan. "Did you think I might not be able to teach today's class?"

Savannah waved a hand at the notebook. "I was reviewing today's lesson, just in case."

Throwing her shoulders back to stand straight, Amanda cleared her throat and said, "I've already studied the lesson. It's called 'Glass Menagerie,' for the animals we're going to make out of bottle pieces. I'm good." She looked at Savannah with a steely glint in her eye. "I've got this."

"Okay, but I have to tell you something. I've got some bad news." Savannah put her hand on Amanda's shoulder.

"What is it? Is it about Martin?" Her voice lifted into a shrill squeak.

"Yes. You remember that Detective Parker brought a broken bottle over for me to help identify? After I reconstructed it, I thought it was a match with the ones Martin brought into class on Monday."

Savannah saw Amanda's whole body stiffen.

"I'm afraid the unidentified diver the police found yesterday was Martin."

Amanda turned to Savannah and whispered, "I was expecting it."

Savannah crinkled her brow. "Why would you think that? He's a new student, right? We just met him for the first time yesterday. It isn't that unusual for a student to miss a class."

"I'm not sure why, but when he didn't show up yesterday, it made me nervous."

"But we've had students drop out of class before. I don't get it."

"I don't know. I think my mother's health condition has me all out of sorts. It's nothing to be worried about."

Savannah rubbed Amanda's arms. "I'm sorry. He seemed like such a nice young man. Anyway, I'll be working with Detective Parker as a consultant to help identify any leads that may be connected to the bottles. By the way, they're at the studio now. I needed them for comparison."

Amanda's head drooped. "I can't get it in my mind that Martin's gone."

Savannah patted her on the back. "Amanda, are you going to be all right? You need to get ready for class. Everyone will be here in—"

Just then the bell jangled as the front door opened, announcing the noisy entrance of the Rosenberg twins.

At the sight of the twins, Savannah let out a chuckle, which she lamely tried to hide with a cough. After composing herself, she greeted the twins. "Good morning, ladies." They were dressed in matching orange today. The cartoon image of a huge pumpkin turning into Cinderella's coach caused Savannah to hold her breath until the urge to laugh went away.

"Did you see the morning paper?" said Rachel. "They have identified the body—"

"Of that diver who washed up on the beach," Faith said, finishing for her.

"Not on the beach. It was in the Intracoastal, down by Park Street," Rachel said, correcting Faith.

Faith nodded her head. "Oh yes, pardon me. Right near all the fancy houses. Did you all see it in the paper?"

Rachel handed two papers to Savannah. "I thought you might like to have these. I know you're an online reader—"

"But it's nice to have a real paper sometimes." Faith patted Savannah on the forearm.

"Why two papers? You live in the same house," Savannah said.

Faith looked pointedly at Rachel. "Some things just can't—"

"Be shared." Rachel returned the hard stare.

Amanda, who had made a sudden appearance, was just staring at the twins.

Addressing the twins, Savannah said, "I didn't see the paper, but yes, the diver was our student Martin

Lane. I'll tell the class when everyone arrives. I would appreciate it if you could keep this to yourselves until we've made the announcement."

Amanda turned without speaking and quickly ducked into the classroom.

She must be extremely upset. I've never seen her speechless.

"I must say, there always seems to be a crime connected with each of your classes." Rachel's tone was church-lady stern as she looked over the top of her glasses. "I'm beginning to have grave concerns about your associations, young lady."

"I know." Faith clapped her hands in joy. "Your classes have been full of the most excitement we've seen in years. You must surely admit that Savannah's murder investigations have livened up our evening conversations. You have to admit that, Rachel."

Rachel lifted her head up and walked toward the classroom. "We don't have to seek out notoriety, Faith. It's not Christian."

Faith's eyes flashed her satisfaction. "She's embarrassed by her curiosity." She looked at Savannah. "I think it does us both a world of good." She followed Rachel into the classroom.

As soon as the rest of the students had arrived and settled nicely, Savannah motioned for Amanda to stand next to her at the front of the classroom.

"Excuse me. I have a sad announcement. It's already in the paper, but I want to tell you that the unidentified diver turns out to be our missing student, Martin Lane. I thought he was a nice young man, and out of respect, would you please join me in a moment of silence in honor of a young life cut short?" Savannah rested her folded hands on the podium and bowed her head for the minute of silence. Then she raised her head. "We'll provide memorial information as soon we get the details." She waved her hand at Amanda. "Thank you, and let me turn you back over to Amanda."

Savannah waited until Amanda was teaching comfortably before she decided it was okay to head over to the studio. But she reminded herself to call Amanda immediately after class was over to make sure everything went smoothly.

When she reached the studio, she parked her car next to the two other cars in the lot. She grabbed her backpack, then opened the door and went inside to find both Arthur and Helen in their work spaces, laboring away on their projects. Arthur looked up and waved hello. Helen was oblivious to whatever might be occurring outside of her tightly controlled space.

Savannah sat on the stool in front of her worktable and looked at the two bottles Martin Lane had brought to class. When they were placed beside the reconstructed bottle from Martin's dive bag, it was obvious that the color of all three was nearly identical.

"That one is different."

"Yikes!" Savannah jumped off the stool. "Jacob, you scared me!"

Jacob's eyes blinked shut, and he picked up Suzy.

Savannah laughed. "Oh, no. I'm sorry, Jacob. It's okay. I was startled and didn't mean to yell. I shouldn't have yelled."

Jacob nodded in his teenage disapproving way. "The broken bottle is the same as this one." He pointed to one of Martin's bottles. "But this one isn't made the same way." He pointed to the second of

Martin's bottles. "It's a copy." He pointed to a unique pattern in the originals. "This joining fault has been repeated."

Savannah pulled a large magnifying glass from a drawer in her worktable and wiped off the thin coating of dust on it with a soft cloth. "You're right. It looks like it's a tolerably good molded copy." She lowered the magnifier and shook her head slowly. "You can't duplicate the process exactly when you are mouth blowing glass vessels. The manufacturing process is unique to each bottle."

"It's a copy." Jacob returned to his large workshop.

Why would Martin have this? Why would he have them at all?

Savannah grabbed her phone from her backpack and speed dialed Detective Parker. He picked up right away. "Detective Parker."

"Hi, it's Savannah. As I reported, I've got the blue bottle reassembled, and I also have the two bottles Martin brought to our workshop on Monday sitting in front of me. Two of the bottles, including the one I reconstructed, are quite old and authentic . . . probably dating to about seventeen hundred or thereabouts, but oddly enough, the third bottle appears to be a copy."

"How does that help?"

"I don't know yet, but I think there's something here that could be important to the investigation. The copy may be a factor in why Martin was killed. Can I contact a vintage glass expert for more information? I think it will help."

"How many hours have you logged so far?"

"Not more than two hours."

"Hmmm."

Savannah was holding her breath. Ten hours of

consulting at seventy-five dollars per hour could make the difference between red and black in her bank balance this month. It would certainly please her grumpy accountant, Burkart.

"Fine. Maybe you can identify more leads. They're quite scarce right now. You're authorized for a total of eight hours. I've e-mailed you a generic consultant form. Make sure you fill it out and send it back right away. It's your key to getting paid. Keep me informed."

The dial tone on her cell told her how poorly the investigation was progressing. Detective Parker was normally polite and positive when he talked about a case with her.

Anxious to prove her value as quickly as possible, Savannah punched in the cell number for Robin. She picked up after two rings.

"Hi there. I'm currently working as a consultant for Detective Parker on the diver case. Could you use your contacts to round up an academically qualified expert in ancient glass?"

"Sure. I'm guessing you need one immediately."

"Sooner if you can."

Robin laughed large. "Right. I'll get back to you within the hour."

If I can come up with a plausible motive and lead in the case, maybe he'll use me as a consultant on a regular basis. It certainly pays well, Savannah thought.

Chapter 11

In the studio office, Savannah's concentration broke when her cell phone rang with the tune she reserved for friends. "Hey, Robin. What's up?"

"I've been researching a little wider afield for a glass bottle expert, and I've found one for you. Fortunately, she's downtown, at the St. Petersburg Museum of History. Her name is Dr. Ruth Smithfield."

"That's absolutely fantastic!"

"What are friends for? You certainly don't want to destroy a valuable artifact in the name of upcycling. Anyway, I talked to her already this morning. She's at the museum all day today and would be happy to talk to you."

"I appreciate this."

"Fine. Let's meet for an early dinner. That's your payment. I want to know everything you discover about these bottles."

Savannah laughed. "Cheap date you are. How about a late lunch at the Three Birds Tavern on Fourth

Street? It's not too far away for either of us. Also, I'm hungry for their prizewinning Kenz Salad."

Savannah walked through the front door of the museum, passing the bronze statue of a newsboy selling an edition of the *Evening Independent* newspaper. She walked up to the information/ticket sales counter to the left of the door. It was staffed by a young woman, who lifted her gaze from an open chemistry book.

"I have an appointment with Dr. Ruth Smithfield." Savannah handed over one of her new business cards advertising Webb's Glass Shop on one side and Webb's Studio on the other.

The attendant examined the card. "Sure. I'll call and let her know you're here." She picked up the handset of her complex-looking telephone console and punched a few buttons. She waited for a short time but got no answer. After placing the handset back on the console, she addressed Savannah. "Look, I know she's back there, but sometimes she gets so focused, she doesn't hear the phone ring. I'll go back and tell her you're here. I'll be right back."

Before the clerk could move, Dr. Smithfield emerged from the plain door behind the counter and walked around to greet Savannah with an outstretched hand. "Sorry. I heard the phone, but I was putting away a delicate artifact and couldn't stop. It's nice to meet you, Miss Webb. Welcome to the St. Petersburg Museum of History."

Savannah smiled and gave Dr. Smithfield's hand a shake with a firm grip. "Thank you for taking the time to help me find out more information about these bottles, Dr. Smithfield." She lifted up a small brown bag holding all three securely wrapped bottles.

"Oh, we can spare the formalities since you're a friend of Robin's. Call me Ruth. Now let's take these bottles back to my office so I can get them under some magnification."

Savannah followed Ruth to a small office that was stacked to the ceiling with plastic see-through bins crammed with objects apparently waiting for exhibit space. As she walked into Ruth's office, Savannah immediately felt a touch of claustrophobia, but as she looked closer, she appreciated the meticulous order. Each object within each bin was numbered, and the bins were labeled with coded identifiers.

On the back wall stood a tall lab table that was clear of any items. It was the only bare surface in the office. On the left side of the table sat a modern microscope, its display screen mounted on the wall.

"I gave up my lab chair this year. I was becoming too sedentary. I hope you don't mind standing," Ruth said.

"Not at all. I stand most of the day, when I'm either working on glass or teaching."

"Great. So, what do you have for me?"

"This." Savannah handed over the brown bag. "I own Webb's Glass Shop on Central Avenue. Robin recommended you as an expert on vintage glass. I'm working as a consultant for the St. Petersburg Police, and I need to know more about these bottles. The young man who had them washed ashore yesterday morning. It appears certain that he was murdered. These bottles may be the only lead related to the circumstances surrounding his death. The police might be able to trace his killer based on their provenance."

Ruth looked up from the brown bag, her eyes lit with interest. "This is a first for me. Mostly, I work with antique dealers or estate executors. Who was killed?"

"A young man who had signed up for my upcycling glass workshop. His name is Martin Lane. There was an article this morning in the *Tampa Bay Times* about his death."

"Well, let's see what we have." Ruth placed the bag on the table and removed one of the bottles. She shoved the bag to the back of the table and slowly unwrapped the bottle on the clear space in front of her. She looked at the cobalt blue bottle for several minutes, turning her head in one direction and then another. "Interesting," she mumbled to herself. "This is interesting."

"Interesting how?"

Ruth jumped and turned to Savannah. "Crap! I forgot you were here. I get lost so easily in some things."

"So . . ."

"There are conflicting indications in the features that would conclusively identify the age of this bottle. I think the next best step is to contact a colleague of mine in Bristol, England, to get his take on these details. Bristol is the original location for glass made with cobalt oxide. That's where this looks like it was made. Do you mind?"

"No, of course not. I hope he can answer quickly. Before you contact him, can you look at one of the other bottles I have? Perhaps he can help with that one, as well."

Ruth rewrapped the first bottle exactly as it was, using the fold lines in the brown paper as a guide, set it along the back of her table, and then reached into the brown bag for the next bottle.

Savannah wondered if she would spot the indications that this bottle was a copy, like Jacob had.

Ruth unwrapped the second bottle. "Hmmm. This is a copy of the first bottle." She looked over her shoulder. "It's an excellent replica, but a replica all the same. The color is pretty good, but not quite as clear or deep blue. It also appears that the mold used was flawed. Probably not cured properly, or there were contaminants in the molten glass. Those are the most common problems." Ruth straightened up and started to rewrap the copy. "Not very interesting, since it was probably made within the past few years."

"I need to know as much as you can tell me about both the original and the copy. It may be a factor in Martin's death."

Ruth looked a little disappointed. "As you wish. I do have many things requiring my attention, but I understand your desire to know as much as possible. My other projects are not based upon current events, nor are they connected to modern crimes."

She unwrapped the copy bottle again and ran her fingers slowly along its seams and joins. Then she placed the bottle underneath the microscope. "I don't think this was made quite so long ago." She looked over at Savannah. "By that I mean less than five years. There's no real sign of age or wearing down of the seams with use. If it had been stored safely, it would have been protected."

"Are there any clues about where it was made?"

"There are some possible indications of where it was manufactured. The making of this cobalt color is dependent on the purity of the cobalt oxide mixed with the lead crystal. It's possible that my friend in

Bristol could identify the source. It's also possible that it's a common formula in wide use. No real help."

"There's one last bottle. It was found with Martin, and it was broken. I managed to piece it back together temporarily. Can you help?"

"Let's see." Ruth took the last bottle out of the bag, unwrapped it, and ran her fingers over the surfaces. She smiled. "Nice job."

Savannah felt extraordinarily pleased. Though she had known Ruth for only a short time, she valued this woman's opinions.

Ruth placed the reconstructed bottle underneath her microscope, and its image appeared on the monitor.

"This is an old bottle. It appears to be an original Bristol blue, like the first bottle."

"That's what I suspected. Can you estimate the age of the bottles?"

"Well, opinions vary, of course, but it is generally agreed that the manufacture of Bristol blue glass started in the late seventeen hundreds. There must have been some experimentation before then, but these appear to be early production bottles. May I keep them for consultation with my colleague?"

"Unfortunately, I don't have permission to let the evidence bottle out of my sight, but let me find out what might be possible. It will probably be some routine set of forms for the police. As a result, I need to keep that one with me. The other two bottles are a different matter. I can leave them with you."

"I don't need the copy. Just the vintage bottle, please."

After she gave Dr. Smithfield her contact details,

Savannah stopped by the little craft beer joint next door. It was called Hops and Props, after the wide selection of craft beers on tap, as well as the giant wooden airplane propeller mounted on the back wall. She ordered a Beach Blonde Ale, along with a plate of hummus and pita chips. She took her snack outside, to a seat overlooking the bay, then checked her watch. Amanda's workshop was over for the day, and she had planned to check in on her. It was also time to think about how to proceed. Maybe the next step was to find out where Martin had discovered the bottles. That could be helpful to Detective Parker. She was definitely out of ideas, but her friends would be able to help. They were never short of suggestions.

She texted Amanda and invited her over to the studio for a brainstorming session focused on the blue bottles. Amanda texted back a smiley face.

Savannah sat back and admired the view, enjoyed her favorite brew, and recalled the delights of last night. She called Edward.

"Hi, Poppet," Edward said as he answered.

"Poppet?"

"British term of endearment. You need to get used to that."

"Yes, I do. Can you come over to the studio in about an hour? I'm struggling to come up with ideas for my consultancy efforts for Detective Parker. Can you help us with not only your ideas but some treats, too?"

"Now I know why I'm included in your adventures. It's really just for the scones. Right?"

"Yes. You've solved the case of the unexpected invitations. It's for your cooking."

They both laughed until they were breathless.

She recovered first. "Anyway, please help me make sure this first consultation is more than perfect. I'm going to go the extra mile."

"Sure, love. See you soon."

She continued to smile and counted herself a very lucky woman.

Chapter 12

"This conference room is much nicer than the office at Webb's Glass Shop." Jacob walked over to the far end of the conference table and stood behind one of the six worn dining-room chairs Savannah had salvaged for peanuts at the local thrift shop. He was holding Suzy.

"I think so, too." Savannah looked around the large room. In addition to the long, well-used table, she had found a giant used whiteboard at an office furniture consignment shop, along with a good-sized corkboard for the large wall opposite the bank of windows. Savannah straightened the stack of pictures she had printed from her phone archive and placed them facedown at the head of the table. "We have more room here at the studio. This is going to work out well."

"Can Suzy have a chair?"

"Absolutely. I didn't know she liked being on a chair."

"She doesn't like it very much, but she's getting used to not being in my lap quite so much."

Savannah nodded. *He is trying to grow up, but he also knows he needs Suzy's help.*

Jacob placed Suzy in the chair next to him and sat down at the end of the table.

Amanda arrived with a plate of cranberry scones, and Edward followed with a pitcher of iced tea and some plastic cups.

"Iced tea?" Savannah grabbed the first cup Edward poured. "Are you getting acclimated?"

"Sad as it may be." Edward poured cups for the others and himself. "I'm finding that day after day of ninety-degree heat and ninety-five percent humidity lends itself to a demand for cool beverages." He smiled. "Yes, I'm slowly turning into a Southerner, but at least it is not the dreaded sweet tea. Not yet."

He sat down to Savannah's right, and Amanda sat to her left, leaving Jacob at the end. He grinned and petted Suzy who sat in the chair next to Edward.

After everyone had settled, Savannah cleared her throat. "I've called you together to beg for your help with my first official police job. Detective Parker has asked for my help in providing information about the bottles Martin Lane brought into Amanda's workshop. It also includes the broken bottle that was discovered with his body. This time I'm working as a consultant."

"That's new, isn't it?" Edward mumbled through a bite of scone.

"Yes, and it comes at a perfect time."

"What do you mean?" asked Jacob.

Savannah pressed her lips together. She shouldn't be bringing up financial uncertainty with Jacob. He didn't like change, and moving his work area from the glass shop to the studio had been more than enough. Bringing up the financial strain she felt would cause him even more stress on top of the move. She would avoid the topic with Jacob for now. She turned to look directly at him and lowered her voice. "It's helpful to have a few extra commissions so soon after opening the studio."

Savannah addressed the group. "We're always such a great group when we brainstorm together. I wanted to get it going again. If you're willing to help me. Are you?"

"Yes, Miss Savannah." Jacob nodded his head. "My mother says analysis puzzles are excellent therapy for me."

Edward grabbed the pitcher and poured another glass of iced tea. "Brilliant, Jacob's spot on. We're a good team, and if it helps bring in a little cash, even better." He looked at Jacob and Amanda, and then at Savannah. "So, we're willing. Now, how can we help?"

"Good. My friend Robin, the one who owns the antique mall and salvages discarded furniture, recommended that I take the bottles downtown, to Dr. Ruth Smithfield, for her expert opinion. I met with her today, and she thinks two of the bottles were manufactured in the late seventeen hundreds in Bristol, England. She's contacting a glass expert over there to see if he can verify her opinion."

"Bristol?" Edward perked up. "I have some friends that live near there, in Redland. They might also be helpful if you need local confirmation."

"I don't think so, but thanks." Savannah looked over at Amanda, who was being quiet and very not like Amanda. "What's wrong, Amanda? Is this because Martin was one of your first students?"

Amanda looked down into her lap and shook her head. "No, I'm fine. I've been trying to do too much this week, and now I'm paying the price for it." She rubbed her eyes and then suppressed a yawn. "Worse, I'm not sleeping terribly well."

Standing, Savannah reached over and rubbed Amanda's arm. "Sorry. I hope your mom gets better soon. It is a great worry when someone is chronically ill." Savannah walked over to the corkboard and plucked out a tack. "Amanda, you had better move to the other side of the table so you don't get a crick in your neck. That wouldn't help your sleeping problems at all."

Amanda sat for a long moment and then sighed deeply. "Thanks." She moved slowly around the large table and sat between Edward and Suzy. Suzy looked at her from across the table with her sympathetic big brown eyes. Amanda responded with a tiny smile.

Savannah continued. "I think another way to be helpful is to find out more about Martin." She tacked an eight-by-ten color picture of Martin onto the corkboard. "Since we have this corkboard handy, I want to pin images as we go to help us make connections for more leads. I found this photo on the Internet, from one of his craft shows." The picture showed Martin behind a table, along with a young woman, selling his artworks to passersby. "This looks like it was taken in stealth by one of his customers at the Saturday Morning Market downtown."

She then pinned to the corkboard images of each of the three bottles involved. "This first bottle is one of the two that Martin brought to class. It is most likely an original Bristol blue artifact made in the late seventeen hundreds. As I said, I've got Dr. Ruth Smithfield tracking down a friend in Bristol. So let's get these labeled up here." She stepped over to the whiteboard and grabbed a marker from the shelf. "Let's label this one Bottle number one." She wrote that on the first picture, and then on the second picture she wrote "Bottle #2." "This is the copy bottle that he brought to the class." On the final picture, she wrote "Bottle #3." "Last, we have a picture of the bottle that was found with his body. This is the one that Jacob noticed was also a copy."

"What about trying to figure out where Martin found the bottles?" asked Edward.

Savannah pointed at him. "Great thinking. I think we should start with a few calls to the local salvage ship captains." She stepped back, with the marker poised in her hand. "Also, I think we need to know a bit more about Martin."

Jacob raised his hand. "Miss Savannah, I thought Detective Parker wanted you to investigate only the bottles."

Savannah could feel the flush rising from her neck. "That's perfectly correct, but Martin brought those bottles in for some reason. I would like to know why, so I'm willing to go the extra mile—or even two."

"But won't Detective Parker get annoyed?" Edward raised his eyebrows. "He's not likely to be tolerant of interference in an active case. You've been warned before."

"I know, I know, but this is only a little stretch. Martin was a student in our workshop, so I have already e-mailed the information from his registration. I won't be stretching my authority by much." She took another look at the picture of Martin. "Amanda, I think you can get us a good start on his background. You can look up his address from his application, right?"

Amanda looked up at Savannah with a weary expression. She pressed her lips together tightly. "Yes, of course."

"I know you're busy with your mother, but would you mind doing the social media crawl to find out about his connections and how he was selling his creations? You won't need to go anywhere if you can do that on your smartphone. I think the more we know about his crafting business, the better we'll look in reporting our findings. Good?"

Amanda nodded.

Edward frowned and placed a hand on Amanda's shoulder. "If you're uncomfortable with taking time away from your mother, you'll have to say it out loud. You know Savannah gets manic when she's on the hunt."

"No. It's not too much trouble." Amanda's voice went soft. "I can do this in my sleep. And since I'm not sleeping, this is perfect."

"What else can we do?" said Edward.

Savannah looked at the group around the table. "I'm going to meet my friend Robin for some catch-up, and maybe she'll have some more ideas about the bottles. I haven't checked the library yet for books on old glass. When I went to Haslam's for their used books, their only volume was gone—either it had been sold or it was missing—but there are other used bookstores in town."

Savannah put her hands on her hips. "I think that's plenty for now. I want to do a thorough job, but I don't want to featherbed the task. I'll let you know when we'll need to meet again, but for now I think this is fine. Thanks a bunch."

Three Birds Tavern was nearly empty after its usual midweek lunch frenzy but before the happy hour crowd arrived. The hostess greeted Savannah by name and led her to a small black wrought-iron table overlooking the patio where the musicians played in the evenings. Savannah had barely managed to order her usual appetizer when Robin approached and flopped down into the opposite chair.

"Hey, girl. I've got some great news." Robin plopped her enormous electric-blue purse on the edge of the table and looked at Savannah with barely suppressed excitement. "Those bottles could actually be part of Gaspar the pirate's long-lost treasure."

"What? No way!"

"Absolutely possible. Shush!" Robin covered her mouth when the server brought them a large bowl of hot sweet potato fries, accompanied by a side serving of cinnamon-flavored honey butter.

Robin ordered a glass of pinot grigio and a Caesar salad, while Savannah ordered the house specialty, the Kenz Salad, and a Blue Point Brewing Company Toasted Lager draft.

As soon as the server left, Robin leaned over the table. "I'm dying to tell you about those lovely blue bottles. It's so exciting." She leaned back, dipped a fry into the honey butter, and waved it at Savannah. "I'm convinced, absolutely convinced, that they are part of Gaspar's buried treasure. It's in the right location." She gulped down the fry and grabbed a few more.

"But treasure hunters have been searching for it for decades—longer even."

"I know. Honestly, why do you think that community is called Treasure Island?"

"Yes, yes. I've heard the stories since I was a small child. Hang on," Savannah whispered while their server placed their drinks and salads on the table.

When she started to clear the bowl of fries, Robin waved her hand. "No, way. Leave those lovely beasties right there. They're delicious."

"And addictive." Savannah grabbed one of the last few.

After the server had gone, Robin continued. "I'm telling you, Savannah. This is the big one."

"But—"

"No, I feel certain that the bottles are from one of his buried treasure sites."

"Well, I agree that it's certainly a strong possibility." Savannah sat back in her chair. "What are the odds that after all these years one of his treasure troves would be found by a starving artist?"

"Apparently, for Martin, the odds were one hundred percent. Luck is luck."

"But, on the other hand"—Savannah lowered her voice—"it would be a very powerful motive for murder."

Chapter 13

Amanda drove her mother's ancient Cadillac back to Webb's Glass Shop, unlocked the front door, and turned the hanging sign over from CLOSED to OPEN. She felt a huge weight pressing down on her heart because her friends knew nothing about her relationship with Martin. She should have told them when she had the chance. It didn't make sense, but she appeared to be keeping secrets from the sheer habit of it. *Despicable.* What remained of her heart seemed like a deep hollow, and she had a sense that a possible future had been severed.

She went back to the office and logged into the computer system. Although the system was old, it still worked like a champ. She logged in to her social accounts and started the slog to find connections that might prove helpful to the investigation into Martin's bottles.

Although they had texted almost obsessively, she knew he hadn't frequented the popular social sites and shared anything personal. He had regularly posted a link to a Web site he used for selling his driftwood creations, but the entries had been scheduled in advance. She followed the link and, starting with last month, began searching through the comments participants had left when he posted pictures of his creations.

Most of the comments were complimentary, and Martin answered questions about the components he used and where he had found them. One poster, however, was consistently caustic and accused Martin of using unsavory methods for acquiring the more esoteric parts that were skewing his work toward the steampunk crowd.

Not sure how this could be relevant, Amanda continued to gather a list of unpleasant interactions. She noticed one of them in particular increased in venom as she neared the current date. That Martin didn't respond to the attacks seemed both strange and sensible. He had ordinarily been quick to try to align fate to his will. Maybe Martin knew that nothing would thwart a troll's attacks. The most vitriolic postings originated from someone with the user name Anonymous. And all postings from Anonymous had stopped abruptly on the day of Martin's death.

She leaned back in the creaky old chair, then stood and paced the small office. The next bit of research would entail a bit of hacking in order to identify the troll that had plagued Martin for no apparent reason.

She looked at her watch. It was closing time for the shop, so she went from room to room, turning off the cash register, locking the front door, checking on the status of the kiln, and turning off all the lights, except for the ones near the street-side windows.

Back in the office, she settled down to the tricky challenge of identifying Martin's troll before she needed to visit her mother. There was always the pressure to make time to go to the home and visit her mother every day, if at all possible. Sometimes, her mother didn't know her, but the staff knew she was apt to visit her mother at all times of the night and day. Amanda was convinced that the staff gave extra care and attention to her mother because of the frequency and irregularity of her visits. It also made Amanda feel better.

After following multiple threads of information, Amanda finally tracked the owner of the vicious comments to an identifier pointing to a business Web site. She followed the address to a salvage and dive operator who advertised private excursions into the Gulf of Mexico at half-day and full-day rates. The name of the business was Collins Salvage and Diving. It took another series of selective searches to track down the registered owner of the business. The owner was Captain Larry Collins.

She had begun to consider the impact of her discovery when she was startled by a loud knock on the front door. She frowned. The sign was turned to CLOSED, and no one should be trying to get into the shop after hours.

"Ridiculous," she huffed. "We're closed."

She peeked around the office door to see who might be trying to get in. It was Detective Parker. He was standing in front of the door, with a very determined and no-nonsense look on his face.

He knows about Martin and me!

She hurried to open the door and stepped back. She stepped back so quickly, she lost her balance and had to grab the door quickly to keep from falling. As Detective Parker walked into the shop, Amanda thought he had gotten taller since she saw him last. She cleared her throat.

"What on earth brings you here? It's after hours."

Detective Parker looked down at Amanda, and the silence grew long and loud.

Amanda repeatedly wrung her hands in a folding motion. "I know. I know. You found Martin's phone, didn't you? I knew you would. You know, don't you? You know about us, right?"

"Since you knew I would find the phone, why didn't you call and save us both this aggravation?"

"I thought there was a possibility the phone was lost. It was possible, you know. Martin was ridiculously careless with his phone. It was a cheap flip phone with the tiniest call plan ever."

"We would have gotten the phone records regardless. Even without the physical phone. It merely takes a little longer."

Amanda covered her face with both hands. "I know. I—"

"I know for certain you know," Detective Parker interrupted. "What I don't understand is why you didn't contact me as soon as Savannah suggested to us that the diver's body was that of Martin Lane."

"I was afraid you would arrest me."

"Not without reasonable evidence."

"But I don't know that. I've been involved in two separate investigations where a completely innocent person was suspected of murder. That's twice! Twice!" She halted for a moment to press her ample chest with her hands. "Then the other thing is I need to be with my mother every day. She needs me every day. She would get frightened and maybe the staff would neglect her and maybe she would fall and . . ."

Amanda lowered her hands and looked at the floor. "What do you want?"

"It's not a big problem. You only need to come down to the station to make a statement about your relationship with Martin and answer our questions about his actions. I also need to know where you were the night Martin was killed."

"It's a big problem." Amanda looked up at Detective Parker. "You see, I was with my mom at the nursing home that night. I used to work there before I got my job with Webb's Glass Shop, and I still have a key. All the staff know me, and I usually help them out when I visit Mom. But her memory isn't good, and no one knows I was with her that night, so I don't have an alibi." She bit her fingernail. "No alibi."

"We'll do our job and check with the staff. You might not have seen someone who saw you. But if we can't verify that you were definitely elsewhere, I'll have to bring you in for questioning."

Amanda felt her heart in her throat.

Chapter 14

Savannah opened her front door and stepped out onto the porch as Edward drove up to her street on his rumbling Indian motorcycle. It was a collector's delight, refreshed but not diminished; it gleamed from care and polish. He drove up to the curb, dismounted, and pulled off his helmet.

"I've remembered something." He hopped up the steps, then kissed her lightly. He took her hand and led her over to sit on the porch swing and put a strong arm around her shoulders. "I should have spotted this when you pinned up Martin's picture on the corkboard. Last Monday Martin and some friends were at Queen's Head to celebrate something big. He wore a loud Tampa Bay Buccaneers football jersey for some reason."

"Celebrate what?" Savannah reached for his hand and held it softly.

"I don't know. But evidently, we were the first stop

on a bar crawl through the Grand Central District.
It's possible they revealed the reason for the celebration at one of the other stops."

"We should definitely check it out. Maybe the
reason for the celebration is connected to his death.
In any case, we might be able to discover some friends
who knew him. Do you know where they went?"

"I know they went to 3 Daughters Brewing after
Queen's Head." He tilted his head. "Are you up for a
scavenger hunt?"

Savannah smiled wide. "Yep. Let me lock up and
call Mrs. Webberly to tell her I'll be gone for a while."

"Won't she mind?"

"Oh no. Quite the opposite. She loves walking
Rooney around the neighborhood. It's an official
excuse to catch up on gossip and admire everyone's
flowers." She walked over to the door. "Hang on for a
second. I'll be right back."

In a few minutes, Savannah returned with her
backpack over her shoulder. She turned to lock
the front door. "Okay, let's start with 3 Daughters
Brewing, or do you think we should park at Queen's
Head?"

"3 Daughters Brewing will do."

Savannah clicked the unlock button on her key fob
to open the doors of her Mini Cooper. "Let's go."

It took barely ten minutes to complete the drive
down to 3 Daughters Brewing. The brewery was fairly
crowded with regulars and a few tourists. They latched
on to two chairs at the bar, and Edward caught the eye
of the bartender.

"A Beach Blonde Ale and a Bimini Twist IPA,
please."

As the bartender drew their beers, Edward asked,
"I'm trying to track down a mate of mine who had a

bar crawl on Monday night. Do you remember them? One of the guys was wearing a maroon-and-gray-striped Buccaneers football shirt with a pirate skull on a flag."

"Sure do. Monday is a quiet night here, and they practically took up the whole table." She nodded toward the large table behind them. "They were celebrating a valuable find of some kind."

Savannah looked at Edward and raised her eyebrows. "Interesting." Her eyes were bright with repressed excitement. "Maybe it was something about the bottles."

The bartender placed their cool pints in front of them. "Would you care to start a tab?"

"No. We'll pay up." Edward handed over a twenty.

They each took a long pull from their beer. When the bartender returned with Edward's change, Savannah asked, "Do you know where the party went after they left here?"

She sighed and put her hands on her hips. "I think they were planning to go to Urban Brew and BBQ next. It looked like they were walking to all the bars, because there was a lot of discussion about how far it was from here."

Savannah nodded her head. "Thanks. You've been helpful. Did you get any other hints about what they were celebrating?"

"I don't know, but they certainly had fun with their theme."

"Theme?" Edward crinkled his brow.

"Sure. They kept singing, 'It's a pirate's life for me,' and one of the guys brought out bandanas for them to wear with eye patches."

"Weird." Savannah drank the last of her beer and noticed Edward's was gone, as well.

"Not really." The bartender wiped down the bar.

"A lot of sports fans identify with Gaspar the Pirate as a symbol of rebellion."

"Thanks," said Savannah as she rose to her feet. She hooked her arm with Edward's when he stood. "Let's get out of here. They may have been more talkative as the evening wore on."

Edward placed his hand over Savannah's, and they walked out onto Twenty-Second Street North, heading for Urban Brew and BBQ. "I haven't been here long. What's this pirate business?"

"You'll understand when business perks up during Gasparilla."

She could see that Edward was puzzled.

"It's based on the legend of Gaspar the Pirate, who supposedly used the Tampa Bay area as a base of operations for hiding his loot and recuperating between voyages."

Savannah thought it was foolishly pleasant to enjoy the fact that Edward seemed pleased to hold her arm so elegantly. *I could get used to this. He has seriously nice manners, and he doesn't appear to be ashamed of them.*

Edward held open the tiny door to Urban Brew and BBQ, and they stepped inside. It was an eclectic place filled with hand-built high-top square tables that had been placed by the street-facing windows and along the left wall of the small taproom. A server asked if they wanted to be seated on the back deck, and they both nodded yes.

The picnic benches on the deck were long and encouraged a sense of community, as the space was shared with other customers. Savannah turned to Edward. "Let's sit in the middle. We might learn more by talking to our neighbors on either side."

"Good plan." They sat as close to the middle of the space as they could get.

As soon as they were settled, the server handed them a paper menu. "Our list of craft brews is on the blackboard. We're running a Wednesday special on Six Ten Magpie, a rye pale ale. It's a two for one until we run dry."

Savannah quickly scanned the blackboard. "We'll take the special."

After the server placed two beer coasters in front of them, nodded, and left, Savannah looked at Edward. "Gosh, I didn't even ask if you like rye beer. Do you?"

"Luckily for you, I do. But this isn't about the beer." Edward smiled a wry grin. "It is strangely pleasant to have decisions made for me."

She shrugged. "I'm used to being decisive."

"And you know a lot about beer."

"That I do. Here they are."

The server placed two glistening amber pints on the coasters. "Would you like to order something from the food menu?"

Savannah looked up at the server. "Nope, just the beer. But I would like to ask you about a group that came by here on Monday night. They were celebrating an event of some sort, and I was wondering if you remember them."

"Sure. Monday is usually quiet. Why do you want to know?"

Savannah leaned back, and Edward quickly said, "I own Queen's Head Pub, and we're thinking of offering a similar beer crawl to event planners. So, Savannah and I are asking the bars on their route how the event worked."

Edward stole a glance at Savannah, who rolled her eyes.

"Like I said, it was a quiet night, so they were a nice

surprise. It would have been nice to know beforehand, as they tapped us out of a popular local beer. We're having a hard time getting more, and with the weekend coming, we'll disappoint some regulars."

"Could you gather what the celebration was about?" asked Savannah.

"It was strange. The beer they ran us out of is called Gaspar's Tropical Ale, and they kept toasting to him." The server shrugged his shoulders.

"The pirate?" asked Savannah.

"Yeah. It's a good ale. There was also a lot of talk about some sort of bottles. Oh, and when they left, they starting singing that bottles of beer song, only they changed the words. So instead they were singing, 'A hundred bottles of beer on the beach.'"

Savannah looked over at Edward and hid a huge smile behind her hand. Trying to keep the excitement out of her voice, Savannah asked, "How many were there? Did you catch any names?"

"Nope. They paid in cash. Well, one of them paid for the whole group. There were about six of them."

"Do you know where they went next?" said Edward.

"They said their next stop was the Amsterdam, but groups like theirs are not reliable. They could have gone anywhere." The server smiled and then returned to the kitchen.

"How far is it to walk there?" Savannah held her glass up to the light, sipped her beer, and followed that with a long pull.

"Not too far." Edward pulled out his phone and tapped the map icon. "It looks like a fifteen-minute walk. Are you up for it?"

"I sure am!" They left their drinks, laid enough cash on the table, and started the walk down Central Avenue, toward the waterfront.

"Why do you think they were celebrating?" Edward asked.

"I think they had discovered a cache of these bottles and then had determined they were valuable. It's strange that Martin would bring them to class if he already knew they were valuable. Was he trying to get validation?"

"Maybe he didn't find out until that afternoon— that would be enough time. The class lets out at one. Maybe he didn't trust his friends."

They finally made it down to the Amsterdam. It was packed to the gills.

"What's going on here?" Savannah managed to squeeze in and stand inside the door. "It's Wednesday night, for Pete's sake."

"You don't follow sports. The Tampa Bay Rays game has let out. They must be running a special event of some sort." He looked around at the sea of noisy baseball fans dressed in royal blue and white team logo wear. "Of course, this might be the natural overflow from Ferg's across the street."

"I haven't been here before, but I hear they carry a draft Trappist ale." Savannah grabbed Edward's hand and wove her way around the customers to the bar. "Too bad this crowd is here. I would have liked to try it." Catching the eye of the frazzled bartender, Savannah pulled out a twenty-dollar bill and waved it.

She had his attention immediately. Leaning closer to be heard over the din, she said, "We need to know who came in here on a bar crawl late Monday night." She held up the twenty. "It's yours if you can tell me."

A big smile flashed across the young man's face. "No problem. It was a group led by two guys. They're regulars here and have been stopping here near closing time for several weeks. So most nights they were the last ones here, and I got to talk with them a little. They were divers. The one guy was Martin. I don't know his last name. He sometimes showed up with a girlfriend." He snatched the bill. "The other always paid, and the name on the credit card was Larry Collins."

Chapter 15

Savannah opened the back door of Webb's Glass Shop to find Amanda tapping away at the old office computer. "Morning, Amanda. You're here early." Savannah plopped her backpack down and sat in the small side chair. Amanda was dressed in various shades of lavender—definitely on purpose. Savannah looked over Amanda's shoulder at the screen. "Any luck yet with Martin's social media?"

"I need to tell you something." Amanda turned around in the desk chair. "I've been hiding things from you."

"What do you mean?" Savannah narrowed her eyes.

"Detective Parker came by the shop yesterday to question me about Martin's death."

"You? Whatever for?"

Amanda looked down at the floor.

"Stop stalling and tell me what's going on."

Amanda's lips quivered. "I knew Martin before he showed up for the class. Detective Parker found our text messages on Martin's phone. He asked for an alibi, but I don't have one."

"There's nothing wrong with knowing a student. This isn't like a university. We're not professors with the power to give good grades. We can have friendships with our students." She patted Amanda on the shoulder. "You must be upset. I'm so sorry."

"It's been a shock." Amanda turned back to the computer and sat quietly for a few moments. She cleared her throat. "Regrettably, Martin used the Internet only for e-mails and limited them to one account. There are tons and tons of images of him with his steampunk creations, but there's nothing personal posted at all."

Savannah wrinkled her brow. "I thought when you used social media, you were supposed to try to make a meaningful connection with your prospective buyers on a personal level."

"That's the theory. Isn't that what we should be doing?" Amanda looked back over her shoulder. "Webb's has to start from square one, with a company Web site as the highest priority."

"Yes, yes, I know you're right. We need to start soon."

"Savannah, you've been saying that forever."

"Next week."

There are so many things yet to be done for the studio. The parking lot, clearing the shrubbery, preparing more student work spaces. So many things.

"There are no classes next week, so we can start then. I promise." Savannah crossed her heart. "Now, what about his friends?"

"Well, it appears that he had a partner in selling the artworks. She apparently handled the promotional stuff and all the preparation tasks for getting the work ready for sale."

"Do you know who it is?"

"It looks like it might be another artist. Look here." Amanda clicked on an image of one of Martin's art pieces. "This one is a joint effort with another artist named Vicki Lilith. He complained about her a lot. She was the one who dropped him off on Monday. He was trying to figure out how to split up their partnership, but I think there was more to it than merely her skills at online selling."

"Do you mean they were . . ."

"Yes." Amanda nodded her head. "I think they were lovers, and he was trying to extract himself from her clutches. He referred to her as a drama queen, and a lot of outward stress came with her creative designer skills."

How long could she keep her relationship with Edward a secret? How did he feel about her? *A single overnight does not a relationship make. It's too early*, Savannah thought.

"What about their shared sales?"

"According to his e-mails, that was the biggest problem. She apparently was demanding a percentage from the sale of his recently created works. Vicki claimed their joint work had influenced his solo pieces so much so that she should get a percentage of his future sales."

"I'll bet that went over like a lead balloon. Do you have any contact information?"

Amanda clicked on a few more links. "Yes. Her cell phone number is here on her Web site. Hmmm . . ."

"What do you mean by hmmm?"

"I'm looking at some of the pieces she's advertising here." She leaned into the screen to peer closer. "These belong to Martin. He sent her photographs of them for her to post in the online store. She's selling them as her own." Amanda stood up and placed her hands on her hips. "This is wrong . . . just wrong!"

Savannah leaned over to the screen. "You think she took them after finding out he was the diver on the beach?"

"No, I think she knew he was dead, and she cleaned out his trailer." Amanda reached for the landline and dialed Vicki's number. "Let's find out now."

The phone was immediately answered. "Hello. Vicki's Treasures. May I help you?"

Amanda put her hand over the telephone receiver. "How do I get this on speaker? I want you to hear this."

Savannah raised her shoulders in a shrug. "The phone at Webb's is too old for that feature," she whispered. "Let's call back on a cell."

"Uh, sorry. Wrong number." Amanda replaced the handset and dialed the number again on her cell.

"Hello. Vicki's Treasures. May I help you?"

"Hi, Vicki. My name is Amanda." She pressed the speaker button on her cell and placed the phone on the surface of the old rolltop desk. "You know, Martin's instructor at the glass shop."

"Martin didn't have an instructor. He didn't need one. I would know. He was my business partner."

"Yes, I know. My name is Amanda Blake. Surely, he told you that he was taking an upcycling glass class from me at Webb's Glass Shop. You drove him here on Monday."

"Oh, you're *that* Amanda. I remember him talking

about you. He did talk a lot, you know. It was a typical Martin trait."

"He wasn't like that at all. He promised to announce our relationship right after the workshop."

Savannah waved at Amanda, as if to say "Get on with it."

"He did tell me he was learning some new techniques that would change the look of his new creations," said Vicki.

"Oh?" said Amanda. "Did he mean he didn't want to work in partnership with you anymore?"

"No, that was never the case. He'd been getting lots of new clients through our partnership. He hated social media promotion. He wouldn't change direction over a few new techniques. We were a good team, and he was on the brink of making lots of money on commissions."

"I don't recall him talking about the partnership in that way. But regardless, I wanted to ask you about Martin's family. The owner of the glass shop I work for has been consulting with the police about the bottle that Martin had in his dive bag. She thinks his family might know more about it, so I want to get in touch with them. He also left some items here at the shop, and I would like to return them to his family."

"The only family I ever heard him admit to was a sister he never spoke to."

"Do you have her name or an address?"

"I think her name is Tracy. That's right. Tracy Patterson. She works at the University of South Florida in Tampa."

"Thanks. By the way, I've looked at your online store, and it looks like some of the items posted there were uniquely Martin's. Have you taken more than just his designs? Are you selling his—"

The sound of the dial tone indicated that Vicki had ended the call.

Savannah leaned back in the small chair. "I think this deserves another line of investigation." She stood up and grabbed her backpack. "I'll bet anything that Detective Parker is already working on the sister. Anyway, you might be able to find out more about Vicki. Since she used social media so much, you should have more success."

"Good. I don't understand her. She always takes things differently than what I would expect. Anyway, I'm good to track down whatever I can dig up on that minx."

Savannah scrunched her forehead. *That seems a little harsh.* "Come over to the studio after class. I'll round up Edward, and we'll discuss what we've all found out and our next steps."

Chapter 16

Parker relished the early morning hours. This quiet time before the throng arrived was when he reviewed complicated issues and sorted them down to a list of tasks. Tasks that could be dealt with quickly by investigators to make progress on a case. The routine was simple. Get coffee and sit with a yellow pad in the conference room. Make notes.

Before Parker wrote a single word on his yellow pad, the phone rang. It was Officer Williams.

"Sir, there's a lady who has come in about the dead diver case. Shall I send her in to you, or would you prefer for me to handle this?" She cleared her throat. "It's an artist friend of the victim."

"I'll take it. Send her through."

In a few minutes a sturdy young woman with short red hair marched into the coference room. "Are you Detective Parker? Are you in charge of Martin's murder?"

Parker looked up. "The Martin Lane case? Yes, I'm the investigating officer, miss. What is your name?"

"I want to report harassment by your consultant."

"Interesting. Give me your name. Last name first, please."

"She called me this morning and threatened to charge me with murder. She was being perfectly ridiculous. I was Martin's partner—in business and in his bed."

Parker raised his eyebrows and noted the shrill edge to her voice. He tried to maintain a low, calm tone. "Ma'am, if you sincerely want to report this, you are required to give me your name and the name of the consultant."

"Oh," she said, then stopped talking.

Parker stood and raised his voice. "Ma'am, if you want to file a complaint, you must give me your name."

"Her name is Amanda Blake. She works as an instructor at Webb's Glass Shop. I think she killed Martin. She had the nerve to accuse me of stealing Martin's artworks to sell online. That's a lie. Martin and I had an agreement. I inspired his work and gave it a fresh spin. That's when his pieces began to sell. Sold like hotcakes."

"Ma'am—"

"I don't believe her when she says Martin was trying to dissolve our partnership. Martin wouldn't have done that to me. She was jealous of my influence. I was Martin's muse, not her. You need to arrest her for Martin's murder. She killed him. I want to make this an anonymous complaint, but you need to take action." She quickly turned and left the conference room.

He looked down at his yellow lined pad. He had written, "Amanda as consultant?" Knowing that Amanda was indeed connected to Martin Lane, since there was plenty of evidence of their texts in Martin's phone records, he dialed the extension for Officer Williams.

Parker was thrilled with this new recruit, Officer Joy Williams. She was a breath of fresh air compared to the officer she would hopefully replace in a few days. A small, trim young woman with long dark hair, she was Officer Boulli's opposite in every way. Her parents had fled Cuba during the intellectual exodus a few months before she was born. Boulli was being transferred to Jacksonville. It was a win for everyone.

"Officer Williams, have the complete phone records been extracted from Martin Lane's cell phone? The one we found in his truck? I know we have a copy of the texts, but what about the full record?"

"I'll check. One moment."

Parker could tell she had tucked the phone receiver between her ear and shoulder. The fast clicking of her keyboard was a skill he envied. He was a "one finger on each hand" typist. More and more data was shared on secure servers, and he was beginning to feel like a Luddite, asking for hard copies of critical reports.

"It's been posted to the investigation folder. Would you like for me to print a copy for you?"

Blessing her thoughtfulness and acknowledging that she was a quick study, he said, "Yes, please. Put it on my desk. Thanks. And could you check the visitors' log for this morning? I would like to identify our reluctant visitor. She had to show ID to get up here. I think we may have another person of interest."

He picked up the yellow pad and his coffee cup. After pouring his third cup of the morning, he walked into his office, sat, and eyed the stack of morning reports piled on top of his basket labeled IN.

Much more caffeine would be needed for him to trudge through the reports that were piling up.

No sooner had he gotten comfortable than Williams flew in and placed the phone records in his hand.

"Thanks. Very fast." He smiled. He flipped to the back of the stapled list of Martin's calls. At the bottom of the page, in her neat hand, was a small note. "Most frequent number called is registered to Amanda Blake. The next two most frequent numbers called are registered to Vicki Lilith and Larry Collins."

Williams smiled and quickly left Parker's office.

Parker nodded. As he flipped through the preceding pages, the records indicated that Amanda and Martin had been calling each other five or six times a day for a little over three weeks. He also noted the next two most popular numbers on Martin's cell. One was a local number Martin had called every morning, at around 1:00 a.m. That was Collins. Definitely worth investigating, so he took a yellow highlighter and ran it over those calls. The next one was called at random times throughout the month. He highlighted that one, as well. *Must be Lilith*, he thought.

Finally, Officer Williams entered at a trot and presented Parker with a copy of all the texts Martin had sent and received over the week prior to his death. As Parker scanned the messages, he could see her reading them upside down. A dusky flush began to work its way up from her neck to her hairline.

Parker chuckled. "I'm guessing you know what all these text shortcuts mean. True?"

Officer Williams nodded. "Yes. Would you like for me to explain them?"

"You could confirm that I'm interpreting them correctly, how's that?"

She took a deep breath, aware of the fact that she had implied that her new boss was unaware of the insular language of texting—more specifically, sexting. The flush began to lighten by the time she had translated the tenth acronym into explicitly graphic language.

"Good enough. I certainly get the gist." Detective Parker adjusted his collar. "Would you interpret from these texts that the couple was in an intimate relationship?"

She nodded her agreement. "Oh yes, sir. They were definitely lovers in the first stages of a relationship."

"I don't even want to know how you know that."

She grinned and handed him a yellow sticky note. "Yes, sir. Here's the name of this morning's visitor."

"Vicki Lilith," he read. "Okay, she appears to be Martin's partner and knew him well. I would like you to arrange an interview with her and see what you can add to our investigation. Are you good?"

Her cocoa-brown eyes lit up. "Yes, sir. I'd be happy to set it up."

"Good. Meanwhile, I'm going to personally investigate her complaint about Amanda Blake." He stood.

"Yes, sir."

"I'm sure our visitor would be pleased with an immediate response. If you have any questions or need assistance of any kind, give me a call."

"Yes, sir."

"Officer Williams, I would expect you to need some advice, and it would be a good indication of your potential if you took advantage of the vast experience of your peers and superiors."

"Thank you, sir. I'll keep that in mind."

"Excellent, Officer Williams. Report to me when you return."

"Yes, sir."

"Officer Williams, a few 'Yes, sirs' indicate respect. Dozens of 'Yes, sirs' get annoying."

"Yes—" Officer Williams quickly cut herself off. She didn't want to be annoying.

Chapter 17

Savannah kicked the bottom of the studio door with her toe, trying to attract the attention of anyone inside. Her arms were full with a stack of pizzas from Cappy's Pizza, and the bottom box was seeping hot grease on her bare arms. "Hey, guys! Can you let me in?" She kicked the door with her toe a little harder.

The door opened, and Edward stepped aside. "Looks like you need a doorbell of some sort. Do you want me to install one?"

"What a great idea. Thanks."

She set the stack of four pizza boxes in the center of the conference table and arranged them side by side, with their lids flipped open. She also lined up paper plates and napkins at the end of the conference table. Amanda and Jacob gathered around to see what kind of pizza was on offer.

"Let's get Arthur and Helen to join us. I think Pizza Thursday is a good idea for the clients of this place. What do you think?" Savannah said.

"Good marketing tool." Edward grabbed a large slice of pepperoni and bit off the tip.

Amanda piped up. "I'll get them."

Savannah spied the sweating pitcher wrapped in a bar towel, along with the red plastic cups. "Thanks for bringing the iced tea, Edward. It's so nice."

Arthur and Helen joined them, and soon everyone was munching and chatting about current projects, plans for new works, local eateries, and upcoming craft shows. Savannah felt a deep, satisfying warmth in her chest. This was exactly the kind of supportive environment she had dreamed of providing to amateur glass artists. The studio provided a creative space for beginners to grow into professionals.

After everyone had had their fill of pizza, Arthur and Helen returned to their work spaces. Jacob and Edward cleared the boxes, paper plates, and napkins, and took them to the Dumpster outside, and then the posse settled back in their positions around the conference table.

Savannah cleared her throat. "Let's share what we know. First, I have gotten quite a bit of information about the bottles. It's clear that they're old and could be worth somewhere around twenty-five hundred to three thousand dollars each, in good condition. Robin believes that if they can be traced to Gaspar the Pirate's treasure, the value will increase to ten times that, at a minimum."

Edward whistled. "That's a lot of dosh."

Savannah looked directly at Amanda. "Do you want to tell everyone what you told me earlier?"

Amanda looked down at the conference-room table. "I knew Martin as a friend before the class. Detective Parker stopped by to ask me some questions because he found the texts that Martin and I had exchanged. I know I should have told you sooner, but the more time passed by, the harder it became for me to admit this."

Edward leaned toward Amanda. "Why? What kept you from telling us?"

Amanda paused for a few seconds. "I just don't know. I'm—"

"Sometimes"—Jacob scratched Suzy behind the ear—"your inside voice gives you bad advice."

Savannah relaxed back into her seat. "Okay. In your own time, Amanda. We'll listen when you're ready. For now let me tell everyone about our call this morning."

Savannah cleared her throat. "Martin had a business partner helping him with the marketing of his new line of fantastical artworks. Her name is Vicki Lilith, and we discovered her through the Web site she and Martin shared for online sales." She glanced at Amanda, who nodded for her to continue. "So we called her up, and, wow, did we get an earful. She apparently has been over to Martin's trailer and has put all his recent pieces up for sale on her site, without waiting for any kind of permission from his family." Savannah tilted her head. "Anyway, she did tell us, accidentally, I believe, that Martin has an estranged sister in Tampa. I think we should talk to her."

"I'm free, now that I'm done the social media search." Amanda walked over to the corkboard and pinned up a picture of Martin's artwork and a picture of Vicki. She looked at Savannah. "I got the one of Vicki from their marketing Web site. I thought we might want a picture of her." She turned around and looked at each of them. "I still haven't told you everything. There's more about me and Martin."

"Okay. We're here for you. Go ahead," Savannah said.

Amanda pulled a tissue from her pocket and dabbed at her eyes. "I'm so disgusted with myself that I haven't been completely honest with you guys about Martin."

"What do you mean?" said Edward.

"I've known Martin for over a month. I can't believe it's been such a short time, because we hit it off so well." She looked down and folded her hands into a tight grasp. "We met online, on one of those dating sites."

"What? You were dating Martin? Isn't he quite a bit younger?" Savannah asked.

Amanda looked around the table. "See! You're doing it, as well. Judging me! You have to understand. I am seriously lonely." She looked down and rubbed her hands. "Between the hours I work here and the erratic times I spend with my mother, I don't have a chance to casually hang out with people. I thought a dating Web site would be perfect."

Savannah looked at Edward. "Amanda, we're not judging. We know how difficult things have been for you."

Edward nodded and placed an arm around Amanda's shoulders. "You should have let us know. We wouldn't have talked you out of it, but we could have given you some support. You didn't have to deal with Martin's death alone."

Leaning her head into Edward's hug, Amanda replied, "I know that. I should have let you guys know."

"Let's focus our forces a bit differently." Savannah looked over the group. "Edward and I have to talk to Martin's neighbors and also track down Captain Collins." She noted Amanda's puzzled look. "Captain Collins was part of the celebration pub crawl on

Monday night. Edward and I stopped by his place once, but we haven't connected with him since."

Edward nodded in agreement. "We still have Jacob in reserve, in case we need any additional help."

Jacob nodded down at the end of the conference table. "I'm good at analytical tasks and synergetic thinking." He lifted Suzy from her conference chair and started out the door. "While I'm waiting, I have work to do on this restoration project," he said over his shoulder.

"Do you think he's upset?" Savannah watched Jacob return to the large workshop.

"He might not understand what Amanda is saying. Let him absorb it in his own way," said Edward. "Now, where were we?"

Amanda returned to her seat. "I think I should be the one to talk to Martin's sister." She rummaged in her large hobo purse for another tissue. As she pressed it in the corner of her eyes, she said, "I've been such a fool. I don't deserve you guys."

Savannah turned toward Amanda. "Don't be silly. We're going to clear things up."

"No, it's not that." Amanda placed her hands on top of the conference table. The dark wood accentuated the pale coloring of her arms. "It's something way worse. There's just one more thing I haven't told you."

Savannah raised her eyes at the trembling tone of Amanda's voice. "What is way worse?" Savannah nodded to Edward. He quickly refilled Amanda's cup with iced tea and set it down in front of her.

Amanda grabbed the cup like a life preserver and quickly downed the cool drink. "It *is* worse." She lifted her eyes to Savannah. "You see, I knew Martin from before the workshop. About a month before the workshop."

"You just told us that—"

"Let me finish in my own way." Amanda's voice was stronger now, and she straightened her shoulders. "I mean, we were secretly engaged."

"What! Good grief, Amanda." Savannah stood up so quickly, her chair fell back and crashed to the floor. "How do you expect us to investigate properly if you don't tell me everything about you and Martin? Why don't you tie my hands and then blindfold me? That's pretty much what you're doing." Savannah folded her arms and looked at Amanda, her anger clearly showing.

Edward quietly picked up the chair, placed it behind Savannah, and she plopped down into a seated position.

Amanda bowed her head. "I know. I know. I'm being stupid."

"Tell us everything. I mean everything," Savannah muttered.

"Well, Martin and I were, well, intimate, I guess you could say, pretty quickly after we met. I was afraid I had jumped into his bed too quickly, but that wasn't the way it turned out. He felt we had a future, and on Saturday night he asked me to marry him."

"What?" Savannah gasped.

"Yeah, I know. I've been keeping all this hidden. Anyway, I accepted, but then I started having second thoughts about how quickly everything was going."

"Understandable." Savannah recalled feeling the complete opposite about her ex-boyfriend back in

Seattle. He hadn't seemed to want to move forward in their relationship at all. It had ultimately been the cause of their breakup. "How did you handle it?"

"Not well at all. On Sunday he suggested we meet his sister."

"Tracy? The one that Vicki said he didn't talk to?"

Amanda nodded her head. "Yes, that's right. He wanted to make a big effort to mend their differences. It's kinda sad that they didn't forgive each other before he died."

Savannah shook her head slowly. "I don't understand why she was willing to go along with a secret engagement and why she's still keeping it a secret."

"I'm not sure how much longer she will keep it quiet. Our visit was not a happy event. In fact, she and Martin fought like cats and dogs. It was horrible, and I called off the engagement as soon as we left. I'm sure she doesn't want it known any more than I do."

"This gives an entirely different focus to our investigation. We now need to concentrate fully on finding the killer."

Amanda nodded and lowered her head.

Savannah plopped down in her chair at the conference table. "So, that's why you've been so emotional the past two days. I thought it was the pressure of the workshop, combined with your mother's condition." She lowered her head to touch the surface of the table. "Ugh! I'm such an idiot. Some boss I'm turning out to be."

"Uh-uh." Amanda's voice strengthened to its normal timber. "This is not your fault at all. I won't have that." She looked around the table. "You've been the best friend I've ever known."

Savannah straightened up and sat tall. "This changes everything. Detective Parker doesn't know about this. Or does he?"

Amanda pulled a tissue from her pocket. "That's why he came to see me at the shop, and I didn't tell him anything, but he knows we were in a relationship, because they found Martin's phone. We texted a lot. I mean a lot." She snuffled into the tissue. "I was going to delete them from my cell, but I couldn't do it."

Jacob returned with Suzy in his arms. "I don't understand. What's wrong?"

"Crikey." Edward slapped his forehead. "It means that Amanda will be questioned closely about Monday night."

"I agree," Savannah said. "The next time Detective Parker sees us, it will be to question Amanda." She pressed her lips into a fine line. "Here's the ultimate question. Amanda, where were you on Monday night?"

"I was with my mother until about two a.m. But I'm sure no one saw me."

"That's not good, not good at all." Savannah folded her arms. "You have to tell us more about you and Martin."

Amanda sniffed and blew her nose. She looked over at Jacob, who was still holding Suzy. "It's not a pretty story. I'm ashamed of the way I've behaved."

Jacob tilted his head. "Did you kill Martin?"

"Jacob!" Savannah screeched. "That's a horrible—"

Edward interrupted, "That's exactly what Detective Parker will ask." He looked at Savannah. "She had better be prepared for his questions. This is good practice."

"He's right." Amanda put away her tissue and

folded her hands on the table. "I desperately want to find out what happened to Martin."

Savannah softened her voice. "Of course you do. The best way is to tell us everything."

Amanda nodded and exhaled a deep breath. "I'd signed up for a dating service with an emphasis on common interests, and Martin was a match for location, plus an interest in glass art. We arranged to meet for coffee, and we clicked."

"When was this?" Edward asked.

"Let's see." Amanda looked up at the ceiling. "I think it was a little over three, no, maybe four, weeks ago. Then, after coffee, we went to the Chihuly Collection. I have a season pass, so it was literally half price for Martin. He doesn't . . . didn't have much money." She sniffed and pulled the frayed tissue from her pocket.

"Wait a tick. You're going to need more." Edward fled the room and returned with a box of tissues from Savannah's office and placed it in front of Amanda.

"Thanks." She pulled several tissues out of the box and wiped beneath her eyes carefully to avoid smudging her makeup. "After that we walked down the street and got some ice cream. We must have sat at one of the tables in front of Kilwins for hours. We had so many things in common—art, movies, even books. It was a great afternoon." She sat quietly, lost in thought for a long minute.

Savannah tapped her fingers on the conference table. "I'm sorry to keep prodding, but what happened next?"

Startled, Amanda continued. "That's when we started texting a lot, and then I invited him over for a meal." She looked at Savannah. "I'm an excellent cook. He was very surprised."

Edward and Savannah exchanged a knowing look.

Savannah said, "Is that when it became more serious?"

"Everything moved very fast after that." Amanda spoke quickly. "It was the next morning when I realized that I hadn't told anyone about him. But at the time, it seemed to me that if I told anyone about him, then I might lose him. It's happened before. Mother was always fiercely protective, and she was so ill. Then, the longer things went on, the more difficult it became to say anything."

"How did Martin feel about the secrecy?" Edward asked.

Amanda looked down and let her fingers follow the grain patterns in the conference table. "He seemed oddly pleased that no one knew about us." She looked up at Savannah, with tears ready to spill. "I was going to tell you after the workshop was over on Friday." She looked around at everyone. "Honestly, it was getting very hard to keep it a secret after so many weeks."

Savannah stood and paced around the room. "This changes everything. Without an alibi, you're going to be at the top of Parker's suspect list. We need to get in front of this very quickly."

Edward piped up. "I don't see how we can prevent an investigation."

"I'm not suggesting that we prevent an investigation. Far from it. I think we need to conduct an investigation that will clear Amanda before Parker decides to arrest her."

"Arrest her!" Jacob said. "But Amanda says she didn't do it."

Edward reached for the iced tea pitcher and filled his cup. "The police are frequently told that by each suspect. Parker is going to wonder why Amanda didn't tell him immediately that she knew Martin extremely well. I agree with Savannah. We need to pull this together quickly. What's first?"

"We need to find out a lot more about Martin, and our best resource is you." Savannah pointed at Amanda. "First, where did he live?"

"He lived in a very small travel trailer near the Intracoastal Waterway." Amanda flushed pink and ducked her head. "I've been there a few times, but no one saw me. It was always very late, and he made sure that none of his neighbors were around."

"Good." Savannah rubbed her hands together. "Let's go talk to the neighbors and see if Martin's neighbors are a lot more curious than he thought. Edward and I will handle this."

"Martin was involved in salvage diving," Amanda said. "It was one of the few things we disagreed about. He wanted me to get certified for scuba diving, but I'm too afraid of the water. He even took me on one of his salvage trips to watch. I still didn't like it."

"What boat? That could be a lead," Savannah said.

"I didn't look at the boat's name, but the owner was Captain Larry Collins of John's Pass Marina. You know, the same Collins that was on the pub crawl."

Savannah looked over at Edward. "We can check that out after we see where Martin lived." She gazed at Amanda. "Amanda, I know this will be difficult for you, but you are the best at social media. Could you see what you can find out before all of Martin's sites get removed?"

Amanda sniffed and nodded yes.

"What about me and Suzy?"

"Sorry, Jacob. Nothing for you as yet, but it's early." Then Savannah stood back, with her arms folded across her chest. "Okay, posse, we're officially on the hunt."

Savannah looked over at Edward and gave a tiny shrug of her shoulders. "Okay, let's start at the top. I haven't heard anything from Dr. Smithfield yet, so I'll give her a reminder call right after this."

"Then what?" Amanda asked.

"Next is a trip out to Martin's trailer to talk to his neighbors for me and Edward, and we need to track down Captain Collins. Can you do that this afternoon?"

"Absolutely." Edward poured himself another iced tea. "I need to stop by Queen's Head for a few minutes, and then I'm free until this evening."

"Great. I'll pick you up in, say"—she looked down at her watch—"thirty minutes?"

"Perfect." He gathered the glasses and the pitcher and waited until Amanda had left the conference room and Jacob returned to his workshop. He gave Savannah a kiss on the cheek. "Perfect."

Edward left on his motorcycle, and Amanda walked back to Webb's Glass Shop, leaving Savannah to go to her office and dial Dr. Smithfield.

"Good afternoon. Dr. Smithfield speaking."

"Hi. This is Savannah. I wanted to ask if you have heard from your colleague in Bristol about the bottles."

"I did get some clarifying questions from him, but nothing definitive yet. I may need to send an actual bottle over there, even a fragment would be helpful."

"Send them over to Bristol?"

"Yes. He hasn't asked for them, but I think we should be prepared for that eventuality."

"Wow. I don't know if it's possible. The shattered bottle is part of the evidence collected at the scene of Martin's death. So I'll ask Detective Parker. He's in charge of the investigation. I'll let you know. I'll try to get back to you this afternoon."

"Perfect. It would be good to be prepared with an answer. I expect I'll hear some news early tomorrow morning."

"Thanks, Dr. Smithfield," Savannah said, ending the call.

Next, Savannah dialed Detective Parker's cell phone. She hoped it wouldn't make her too late for Edward and try his patience.

That's something I don't know. What kind of patience does he have?

"Detective Parker, Homicide."

"Hi. This is Savannah. I have a question about the cracked bottle you gave me to investigate."

"Sure, but quickly. I'm on my way to the morgue."

"Okay. I've contacted a source who believes the bottle was manufactured in Bristol, England, in the late seventeenth century. Her own contact may actually need to have the bottle in hand to confirm it originated from that area. Would it be possible to send it over to him?"

"Yes, it's possible, but administratively, very complicated. We would send it to New Scotland Yard, who would deliver it to the specialist. Do you think it will be necessary?"

"She's not sure yet but wanted to start the process, in case her colleague needs the bottle for confirmation."

"Understood. I'll—" A distant female voice could be heard through Savannah's phone. "I'll research the process, but I sincerely hope we don't have to go there. Sorry, but I've got to go. Thanks."

Savannah heard the dial tone and hung up her desk phone.

Her watch indicating she was late, Savannah grabbed her backpack and threw it in the backseat of her Mini.

Time to find out if he's patient.

Chapter 18

Savannah drove down to Queen's Head. Edward was pacing out in front of the pub, but he smiled wide when she pulled into the narrow parking lane.

Edward climbed into the car. As he settled into the passenger's seat, Savannah apologized. "I'm sorry. I was talking to Dr. Smithfield."

"No worries." Edward raised his eyebrows. "Any word?"

"Nothing yet." *Hmmm. He does have lots of patience, then.* "She heard from the guy in Bristol, and she asked if it was possible to send over a fragment or even an entire bottle for his analysis."

"And . . ."

"Then I called Detective Parker to start the process." She grinned. "It's the first time I've ever heard anyone in real life use the name New Scotland Yard in a conversation."

"Real life, as opposed to TV life?"

"Yes. Chills!" She held her hand out and faked a tremor.

Edward took her hand and kissed it. "The strangest things make you happy."

Savannah glanced at the handsome, confident, funny man holding her hand. Unbidden, a shocking thought struck her—this was the happiest she had been in the few months since her father died. It felt very, very good.

After a few wrong turns and several attempts, while giggling, to teach Edward the mapping program on his phone, she pulled up to Martin's tiny trailer. They got out of the Mini, and Savannah noticed a twitch in the curtain of the somewhat larger trailer across the sandy gravel and dirt road. She noted the baby stroller and the toy-strewn yard, then turned to Edward.

"Why don't you go ask the park management about Martin's payment patterns, and I'll tackle the stay-at-home mom?"

"Don't have too much fun!" Edward walked toward the front of the park.

A petite, dark-haired beauty who couldn't have been over twenty years old quickly answered Savannah's knock on the trailer door. "We don't want whatever you're selling."

"No, I'm not selling anything." Savannah held out her hand. "My name is Savannah Webb, and I'm a consultant with the St. Petersburg Police Department. I'm investigating Martin Lane's death. I would like to talk with you for a few minutes."

She felt a little uncomfortable stretching the truth, but if it helped to get people to trust her, she was going to use every tiny edge.

The young woman stood quietly for a long moment. "Sure, I liked Martin, but I hated all the diving stuff. I kept telling him to be careful."

She backed up into the small space behind her to let Savannah into a clean living room furnished with only a worn love seat and a sagging, comfortable chair, which faced a flat-screen TV on the same wall as the door. The smell of chili bubbling away on the two-burner stovetop caused Savannah's mouth to water.

"Thanks, Miss . . ." Savannah had to bend her head to keep from hitting the ceiling and slumped over a bit.

"Just call me Ashley. Here. Sit in the easy chair." She smiled easily. "You're a little tall for our camper." She cleared away some of the toys and tossed them into a wooden picnic basket shoved against the wall under the flat screen. Then she sat on the love seat.

"How long did you know Martin?" Savannah sat, then dug a pen and a notepad out of her backpack and placed it on the floor beside the chair.

"We've been here only about a month. He was already here when we pulled into this lot. He was home at the time and helped us get set up. He was nice about helping out like that. Always helpful."

"Did he have many visitors?"

"Not very many. Mostly girlfriends."

As in plural. Maybe not as shy as Amanda thinks.

"Do you know their names?" Savannah asked.

"No. They never stayed around. He was pretty private."

"What did they look like?"

"Oh, the one who was here last had wild hair. I loved it. The yellow orange was perfect for her pale face and figure. She was a bit heavy but carried it very well—sexy even."

Savannah frowned at the perfect description of Amanda. "When was this visit?"

"I'm not sure."

"Please try to remember."

"I think it was Monday night, but it might have been Sunday. My husband works at the Walmart on the night shift restocking team. All nights seem alike to me."

"Thanks, Ashley. Here's my number." She handed her card over. "Call me if you think of anything else. It sounds like Martin will be missed around here."

"Yes, especially by the old man next door to him. Martin was always over there helping him out. Leroy has a hard time taking the trash up to the community recycling containers. Martin always took it up for him. I'll be watching out for him now." Ashley looked closely at the card. "This says you own a glass shop."

"Yes, I do. I've been consulting with the police department for only a very short time. I haven't had a chance to order professional cards."

"Oh, well." Ashley stood and stepped toward the door. "Come back if you need more information. I'm going to miss Martin."

Savannah ducked her way out of the little trailer. She had walked over to stand by the Mini when she heard the cry of a baby, followed by Ashley cooing. "Good girl. What a good nap. Do you want a snack? Let's get a new diaper first."

She leaned against the Mini while she waited for Edward. The heat beat down with a vengeance, and the welcome cooling of a quick rain shower remained unfulfilled. The cloying humidity sapped at her will and caused rivulets of sweat to trickle down her back. She was about to get in the Mini and turn the

air-conditioning on full blast when the door opened
out on the trailer next door.

A wizened, white-haired man leaned out. "Would
you like to get out of the heat? I have some fresh
iced tea."

Savannah turned to him. "Absolutely. It's brutal
out here." She walked through the open doorway
into a trailer home that was twice as big as Ashley's.
"Wow. This is bigger than it looks from the outside."
She didn't have to bend over to get in the door—
there were at least six inches of clearance.

The old man used a beautiful wooden cane with a
silver fish mounted on the top to get around. He
made his way to the kitchen counter and handed her
a glass of tea packed full of ice in the traditional
Florida way. "Sit yourself down over there. There's a
little table for your drink."

She did as she was bid and gulped down more than
half the tea. "Thanks. This is perfect."

"So, did Ashley give you the answers you were looking for?" He sat slowly in a well-used brown leather
recliner covered with a fleece throw.

"How did you—"

"We're a very close little community here at
Happy Campers. It's a way of life here. We all look
out for each other. So, did she?"

She stalled by taking another sip of her tea. "Not
really. She said she couldn't remember who had been
to see Martin on Monday night."

"I'm Leroy, by the way. And you are?"

"Savannah Webb. I'm a consultant with the police."

He nodded. "Martin was a nice young man. He
had a lot of crazy ideas about getting rich quick, but
he had a big heart. I'm going to miss him."

"Did he have friends?" Savannah dug out her

notepad and pen. "Ashley said he didn't have many visitors."

"Well, Ashley is very busy with her beautiful new baby, and her husband is a hard worker but high maintenance, as well. She's always got dinner on the table at five thirty sharp. It's made from scratch, too—none of that prepackaged stuff for them. I'm as likely to throw a frozen dinner in the microwave and call it done."

"Martin's friends?" she said, reminding him of her question.

"Oh, yes. He used to get a lot of visits from a girl who was quite loud. We always knew when she was here." He leaned over and whispered in a soft voice, "There's no privacy in these little tin boxes. She loved his fantastical conglomerations. He sold them on the Interweb somehow. I don't know anything about such things."

"When was she here last?"

"Oh, I hadn't seen her in a few days, and then she stopped by on Tuesday, while he was gone."

"Did she have a key?"

"Nope, but she knew exactly where he hid it and let herself in as bold as a brass monkey."

Savannah looked up from her notepad. "Where is the key?" Modifying her tone, she said, "I would like to see if there are more bottles. It could be important to the investigation. The police have already been here and gotten their evidence. It's not taped off."

He clamped his mouth tight. Then, after a pause, he said, "I don't know about this. If you work with the police, why do you need a key from me?"

"Please?" She used her kindest tone. "I'm actually just a consultant, and this is my first case. I want to do everything I can to find out what happened to

Martin. I'm looking for something else that's related, but not something that the police would recognize. I'm trying to identify the origin of some bottles he found. I'm a glass expert."

"I don't see any harm. It's in a little magnetic box underneath the trailer, on the other side of the wooden steps. It's painted the same color as the trailer, so you need to know where to look."

"Thanks, Leroy. I appreciate it."

"Don't you want to know about his girlfriend?"

"Certainly. Ashley mentioned her. When was she here last?"

Leroy furrowed his brow and looked over at the calendar hanging on the wall beside his chair. "Let's see. It was on a Monday night, because that's bingo night up at the recreation center. I won the second jackpot."

"When did you see her?"

"Well, it was before I left, so it had to be before six thirty. It takes me quite a while to walk over to the center, but I like talking to everyone before the game begins, so I leave pretty early. That detective asked me all these same questions."

"Of course, but I'm being extra thorough. One last question and then I'll get out of your hair. How long did she stay?"

"Oh, I couldn't say. I'm usually so tired after bingo, I can barely walk all the way back to my door. I didn't notice anything. Sorry, miss."

Savannah put her head in both hands and shook it. *Exactly what I thought. Why didn't Amanda tell me she visited Martin on Monday evening?*

Chapter 19

Thursday Afternoon

Savannah poked through the piles of driftwood, shell, and bottles on the little entry patio, but came up with nothing of interest. She had just opened the door to Martin's trailer when Edward arrived back from the park office.

"What are you doing?" His voice was firm, and he lowered his chin.

Savannah stood very tall. "The neighbor told me where the key was hidden. He didn't see any harm in my looking around. Do you?"

Edward shook his head. "No. It's a good idea. Maybe we'll turn up a clue Detective Parker has missed."

"Not likely, but maybe I can offer some expertise on some of the glass still here."

"But wouldn't Parker have already given you that evidence?"

Savannah smiled and put her hand over her heart. "It's possible he might not recognize something vital to a craftsman. Besides, it won't hurt to look. Right?"

Edward glanced around uneasily and then nodded his head.

They walked into the tiny front room, where the dinette sat underneath a set of windows that wrapped around the end of the trailer.

"This is where he worked on his creations." Savannah pointed to the side of the table with craft supplies and tools arranged neatly.

"And this looks like where his laptop was. The police must have taken it away for analysis." Edward walked to the back end and poked his head into the bathroom. "He was pretty neat for a guy."

"It also appears he didn't have much." Savannah opened and closed the small kitchen cabinets and drawers. "That makes it easier. Oh, what did the park manager say about Martin?"

"He said Martin was a nice guy. Didn't cause trouble. Paid in cash right on time each month. The model of a perfect tenant."

Savannah followed Edward back to the tiny bedroom. The bed was made. It looked like the bedspread and curtains were leftovers from a bankrupt motel chain, but everything was neat and tidy. Looking at Edward, she said, "This is not making sense to me. Where did he store all his marine cleaning material?" She moved back into the small hallway and looked under the bed. "Nothing. Is there a shed out back?"

Edward shrugged his shoulders.

They closed and locked the trailer and circled around the back, but there was nothing behind the trailer except the electrical hookup post. Savannah stood with her hands on her hips. "There must be a storage area somewhere. There would be a lot of work involved in cleaning up his salvage items. I'll bet the rules of the park would prevent that."

"I don't think he could afford a storage unit, but it's something Amanda might know."

"Well, Amanda doesn't seem to be telling us all she knows about Martin. Leroy, Martin's neighbor, told me she was here with Martin on Monday night." Savannah started for the Mini.

"Why didn't she say so?" Edward opened the car door for Savannah.

"You don't have to do that. I'll get spoiled." She smiled up at him. "It is nice, though."

"I think we need to find this captain to get more answers." Edward sat in the passenger's seat. "Buckle up."

Savannah pressed her lips together to hold in a reply about not being a child, then relaxed and clipped the belt. *He's right. Sometimes I do forget to buckle up. That's observant and thoughtful.* She smiled.

"Where was Captain Collins's business?" She pulled out from in front of Martin's trailer and headed down the dusty road. "Wasn't it in an industrial park near here?"

Edward reached into the side pocket of his trousers and pulled out his phone. "Let me punch in a search." He tapped the smartphone. "Here it is. It's called Collins Salvage and Diving. The address is supposed to be near the trailer park."

"Oh, that's up the street."

"Grrrrr. I'm still not used to the number grid here. I can't tell you how many times I've gone to three places in a row that are *not* where I wanted to be."

Savannah smiled. "It's the exact opposite of New York City in terms of the grid. St. Pete has streets that go north–south, while the avenues go east–west. Central Avenue is the dividing line between north and south, and Beach Drive downtown is the dividing line between east and west." She looked over to see Edward rolling his eyes. "It's simple, really."

"Grrrr. You were born here."

"Choose one to memorize. Streets go north–south, divided by Beach Drive. Simple!"

"Okay, okay." He peered at the road signs, matching them to the map on his cell. "I should have written this on a slip of paper." He scowled at the screen. "We should be getting close now." He looked back at her. "You were right. That north-south thing of yours does help."

Savannah shrugged and turned into a small, run-down industrial park. There was a large sign at the entrance, which listed all the businesses within the park. She looked at the names of the businesses, and Collins Salvage and Diving was listed near the bottom. "This is it."

The industrial park looked more like a junkyard than anything else, with three rows of low cement-block buildings running the length of the property. Each building had been built with large garage doors facing out. It looked a lot like a storage rental property, but instead, it was outfitted for small business rentals. Savannah pulled up to the far left side and began driving along that side of the long building, passing a vitamin discount store, an antique furniture refinisher . . . in other words, everything under the sun.

After searching the central bank of businesses, they found Captain Collins's business near the back.

It was spread over the final three bays in the building, and all three garage doors were up. Inside the first bay were storage racks crammed with diving suits, belts, masks, flippers, and everything needed for renting dive equipment. The second bay held diving tanks and the compressors used to refill them.

Finally, they found a thin, deeply tanned, and scruffy man in the third bay, bent over a lump of something and scrubbing it with a small wire brush. He was barefoot and clad in cutoffs, a tattered T-shirt, and a grass-woven hat aged to a brittle beige. The bay appeared to be a sorting area, with large tables down the middle and floor-to-ceiling storage racks around the walls, which were filled with marine artifacts.

Savannah parked the Mini across from the open bays so as to not block the limited thruway for the other businesses. At the sound of the closing car doors, the man looked up from his work, wiped his hands on his shorts, and walked toward them.

"Can I help you?"

"We're trying to find Captain Collins." Savannah offered her hand for shaking. "I'm Savannah Webb, and this is Edward Morris."

"I'm Captain Collins." He shook their hands, Edward's first. "Do you want to sign up for a salvage dive?"

Edward quickly looked at Savannah and gave a tiny nod. "Sure. That would be great." He exaggerated his British accent. "We heard you offered a fantastic experience diving for treasure."

"My specialty." He led them over to the table. "Here's a few of the artifacts we salvaged on this morning's tour." He picked up a heavily barnacle-crusted propeller blade. "A young woman from

Montreal found this on her first dive. I'm cleaning it up a bit so it won't smell up her suitcase."

Savannah leaned over the propeller. "Is it valuable?"

"Only in the sense that it will be a memento of an enjoyable dive. She said she'll keep this on her desk to remind her of her first trip to Florida."

"Do we need to be certified divers?" Savannah asked.

"No. We can go to places you can explore by snorkeling. When would you like to schedule a trip? I still have a few openings for tomorrow morning."

"Well, sweetie, do you think we might want to try our hand at this?"

Edward's eyes opened wide, but he recovered quickly. "If this is what you want to do, love, I'll play along."

"We heard a local artist has been making fabulous creations by using items he found on salvage dives. Do you know him? His name is Martin Lane," Savannah said.

"I have lots of customers who enjoy the sport of diving for artifacts, and many of them use their finds in lots of interesting ways. Would you like to sign up for the sunrise cruise in the morning? I still have a couple of seats available."

"Well, no. We're not interested in diving, actually." Savannah coughed into her hand and then looked the captain straight in the eye. "We're here to find out more about Martin Lane. I'm a consultant who is helping the St. Petersburg Police investigate his death, and we heard you frequently took him diving."

Collins sucked in a quick breath. "You tried to trick me. I don't know anything about Martin's death. You need to leave." He backed away and quickly pulled the garage door down over the salvage bay and locked it. "You need to leave now, before I call the police and report you for harassment." He turned to face them and put his hands on his hips. "Leave. Right. Now."

Chapter 20

Thursday Afternoon

Savannah dropped Edward off at Queen's Head and parked behind Webb's Glass Shop. She entered through the back door.

"Amanda, I'm back. Where are you?"

"I'm here in the supply room, loading the kiln."

"Good job." Savannah peered into the large, deep fusing kiln. "It looks great. You've got enough kiln paper. You've placed blocks against the pieces so that nothing rolls during the fuse. You've even got a two-layer deal going with some small pieces." She raised her head to look at Amanda. "Perfect. You've graduated to journeyman—no longer an amateur."

Amanda's face flushed. "Thanks. That means a lot to me. I love this job."

"You're good at this. I'm grateful to have you."

As Amanda lowered the large lid on the kiln, Savannah asked, "What did you find out about Martin's sister?"

After pressing the START button on the control panel, Amanda stood. "Oh, I wrote it all down in the

office. Let's sit down for a minute. I'm bushed. I had
no clue teaching could be so draining. Really, why
didn't you warn me? Oh, wait . . ." She laughed. "You
did warn me."

When they arrived in the back office, Amanda
picked up from the center of the desk a manila folder
with "Martin's Sister" written on the tab. Savannah
grinned at the childlike script, with hearts for dotting
all the i's and curlicues for crossing the t's.

Savannah sank into the creaky oak office chair and
opened the folder. On yellow ruled paper, Amanda
had compiled the information she had gleaned from
her research. Martin's sister lived in Tampa, near her
job at the University of South Florida, where she was
an associate professor of marine biology. A printout
from USF's staff Web site included a picture of Tracy
Patterson and a brief description of her teaching
qualifications. The family resemblance to Martin was
strong. Amanda had researched the course catalog
and had noted that Tracy taught a lab on Thursday
nights.

"Very thorough. I think we need to talk to her. Do
you have any idea why Tracy and Martin didn't talk to
each other?"

Amanda flushed at her pale neck. "I don't have a
clue. I'm as surprised as anyone that he had any
family at all. He always said he was alone in the
world."

Savannah stood up. "Well, anyway, we need to see
her face-to-face. I'd like to pay her a visit right now.
Are you able to come with me? If you need to see
your mom instead, I'm good with that."

"Mom's doing better physically, but she's in a
phase where she doesn't know who I am. It helps me
to stay away for a few days. I can go."

* * *

It took about twenty minutes to close up Webb's and get on the road to Tampa. When they pulled onto I-275 to cross the bridge over Tampa Bay, Amanda looked over. "It looks like we've timed this perfectly to be stuck in the rush-hour traffic."

The traffic inched along at about twenty miles an hour. Savannah moved over into the rightmost lane. "It's been a long time since I drove over to USF, but let's take North Dale Mabry to Fletcher and bypass all this. It will only get worse when we get to the I-Four turnoff. Agreed?"

"Yep."

Nearly forty-five minutes later, Savannah pulled into a university parking spot clearly marked for visitors. They found the building that housed the biological sciences and the office number that was listed in the catalog. The door was closed, but there was a row of chairs in the hallway, with a student obviously waiting to talk to Professor Patterson.

As one, Savannah and Amanda sat down and tried to look like students. It was a failure. Compared to the waiting student, who was wearing shorts, sandals, and a tank top, they appeared to be modestly covered up like religious initiates.

Savannah whispered, "When did tiny, short shorts come back into style?"

"Forever ago. You've been buried in glassmaking."

"I guess I have."

They had barely settled when the office door opened to release a tall young man, who headed down the hallway at a fast clip. Without waiting to be called, the student waiting to see Professor Patterson slipped through the open door and closed it behind her. They got the briefest glimpse of the cluttered office, which had a couple of chairs ready for student counseling.

"This seems to be a practiced ritual," Savannah whispered. "What time does class actually start?"

Amanda opened the manila folder and flipped through the research material. "We have about forty-five minutes."

"Be ready when this student leaves."

They sat quietly for a few minutes, and when the door opened, they barely let the student squeeze by before entering Professor Patterson's office. Amanda sat against the wall near the door, and Savannah sat in the chair in front of the piled-up desk. In fact, everything had piles of papers and stacks of books on it, and only a space large enough for a table was clear in front of Professor Patterson.

The professor wore a starched white lab coat over black polyester trousers and sensible black tie-up shoes. Her salt-and-pepper hair was cut in a short chop, and her reading glasses hung in a ring on a small chain around her thin neck.

The professor wrinkled her brows at them. "What are you doing here? You're not students."

Savannah leaned forward. "We're not students. My name is Savannah Webb, and this is Amanda Blake. We're here to—"

"Sorry, ladies. I don't need any more interns or lab assistants. You're a bit too late for this semester, but I'll happily give you an application for this fall." She turned in her chair toward the large table behind her and snatched two application forms from a neat stack next to the wall.

"No. We're not here for enrollment." Savannah waved her hand to prevent Professor Patterson from handing the forms to her. "Let me explain. I'm a consultant for the St. Petersburg Police Department, and I need information about your brother, Martin Lane."

"My brother? We don't see each other. I haven't seen him face-to-face in years. Not since our parents' funeral. What's this about?"

Amanda cleared her throat. "How long ago?"

Professor Patterson leaned back in her chair and looked at the ceiling. "Let me think. That was the year I was accepted as a doctoral candidate here at USF. I used my inheritance to pay off my student loans and buy a condo near the university. Why do you want to know this?"

Savannah hesitated. "Do you know where Martin is now?"

"No. I told you. We haven't seen each other in more than three years. Look, I need to know why you're here. What is your connection with the police?"

Oh no. She doesn't know about Martin's death. How can that be? Why hasn't Parker been here?

"Have you heard anything from the St. Petersburg Police Department?"

"No, but I was out of touch for the past few days at a yoga retreat, and I came straight to campus for my student consults an hour ago. I haven't even checked my messages yet. What are you trying to say?"

Realizing there was no way they could not tell her, Savannah cleared her throat and spoke in a low, soft tone. "Professor Patterson, I'm very sad to tell you that your brother, Martin, was found washed ashore Tuesday morning. It appears he was murdered."

There was a long silence. Professor Patterson sat behind the desk with her eyes down, looking at the cleared spot on the surface before her. Finally, she lifted her head. "You're right. That is incredibly sad."

Savannah waited for some sort of emotional reaction, but the professor sat quietly for a few more moments and then looked at both of them in turn. "Do you have any questions? I need to prepare for my class."

Amanda and Savannah looked at each other with eyebrows raised at the complete lack of emotion.

Savannah recovered and replied, "Yes, please. Could you tell us if there are any other relations?"

"No close relations. Our parents were killed in a boating accident when we were living in Key West. That was about twenty years ago. My mother's aunt raised us, but she died last year, and she was a childless widow." Professor Patterson recited these facts as a well-rehearsed spiel. "I left to study for my master's degree here in Tampa as soon as I graduated from college, and I've been here since."

"So you're his only relation?" Savannah asked.

"I've been on my own for a long time now."

"Did you know that he was a talented artist?" Amanda asked, piping up. "He made some amazing works out of found materials from the beaches and from salvage diving."

"It doesn't sound lucrative to me. Did he have a house or property? I'll have to deal with it all again. I did my parents' place with my aunt. This time I'll be alone."

"Um, not that we know of," said Savannah. "But I'm sure the investigating detective will want to get in touch with you. His name is Detective Parker."

Professor Patterson wrinkled her brow. "Oh, great. He should have been here already. This will cause more interruptions. I'll have to reschedule my Ph.D.

dissertation defense. Well, anyway, I want to thank you for letting me know. We were not close, but it is sad to know I have no family now. I should have made an effort." She stood up. "If you'll excuse me now. I have a class to teach in a few minutes, and I have to review the lecture before it starts." She came out from behind her desk and gestured with her arm that they needed to leave.

As soon as Savannah and Amanda were out in the hallway, the door closed behind them with a sharp click, and then they heard the lock turn.

Amanda puffed out a pent-up breath. "That's the coldest woman I have ever met."

Chapter 21

Thursday Evening

Savannah dropped Amanda off at Webb's and drove on home. She was exhausted and a little disturbed by Professor Patterson's chilly reaction to the news of Martin's murder. They didn't get even a normal question, like "Who killed him?" from her. What kind of childhood could explain such distance? Could it even be explained?

Rooney chased all those thoughts out of her head with an enthusiastic welcome. Although he was no longer puppy sized, given his actions, it was clear he thought he was a cuddly bundle. Savannah went straight to the kitchen and fixed his dinner and threw in a frozen dinner for herself.

While Rooney was wolfing down his meal, Savannah called Detective Parker's office from the wall-mounted kitchen phone.

He answered immediately. "Hi, Savannah. This is late for you to be calling."

"Even so, it appears you're still there to take my call."

"Fair point. Do you have a result from your glass expert?"

"Well, not so much results as I have a discovery to report. Martin Lane had a sister. She lives in Tampa and works as a professor at the University of South Florida."

"Interesting. His public records don't show any relations. Well done. A sister, you say?"

"Yes. Her name is Professor Tracy Patterson. Amanda and I went to see her about Martin, and she didn't know he had died. I thought it was strange, since the discovery of his identity was all over the news yesterday."

There was silence on the phone.

"Parker, are you there?"

"I'm going over my notes. Hold on a second." There was another long pause. "Did Amanda behave differently with Professor Patterson?"

"What do you mean?"

"What I mean is . . ." He hesitated a moment. "Did you feel Amanda may have already known Professor Patterson?"

"No. She seemed surprised that Martin had a sister."

"Are you certain?"

"Of course I'm certain. Amanda is my good friend. I know her. What are you suggesting?"

"Evidence is beginning to pile up that proves that you don't know Amanda as well as you think. Has she been absent more than usual in the past month?"

"Well, her mother's been sick lately. So she's been taking time to make sure everything is being taken care of at the nursing home. Amanda knows that being around the place frequently means that her mother gets better care. That's pretty normal, though."

"What about mood swings? Anything out of the ordinary?"

"Mood swings? Honestly, this is Amanda we're talking about. The most cheerful person on the planet."

"Right, but she might be more involved in this case than you know."

"Are you trying to tell me Amanda is a suspect?"

Detective Parker's voice softened. "I am suggesting that you be careful."

Before she could respond, the dial tone interrupted. After looking at the receiver for a moment, Savannah hung up the phone.

Why would he suggest that Amanda wasn't her friend? she wondered.

Rooney nudged her knee and looked up at her with pleading amber eyes. It was time for their evening run, but that was the last thing Savannah felt like doing.

"Okay, Rooney. Let me eat, and we'll go."

She plopped down on the living-room couch to eat her meal and watch a bit of the news. Rooney stretched out his lean gray frame on the floor in front of her, put his head on his paws, and huffed. The reporter on the news stood in front of a large Mediterranean Revival mansion near the site where Martin's body was discovered.

"Why do they do that?"

Rooney's head came up.

"This whole crime scene has been bagged, tagged, and cataloged thoroughly. Everything has been taken away. There's nothing there at all."

"There have been no new developments in the case of the murdered diver who washed up behind this house on Tuesday morning. Sources close to Detective Parker, who is leading the case, indicate several persons of interest are being investigated, and he expects an important development soon. More news at eleven," the reporter finished.

Savannah clicked off the television, finished off the frozen meal, and cleared up the small mess in the kitchen. After changing into running clothes, she took Rooney out for some exercise. The first few blocks of any run were slow, since Rooney needed to smell all the new smells in his front yard and then relieve himself on each new sample.

Finally getting syncopated for a good run, Savannah realized the calming rhythm stimulated far too many thoughts in her head. Detective Parker's comments had her rethinking Amanda's strange behavior over the past few weeks. It looked suspicious to her now. There had been quite a few more visits to her mom than normal. During the same time frame, Savannah had been busy with buying the warehouse building, applying for all the permits, hiring the contractors for the electrical and plumbing improvements. It had been a distracting month.

Why was she letting Parker's insinuations get to her? Was he trying to glean more information from her before tackling Amanda? If that was his plan, it wasn't going to work. He wouldn't be able to erode her loyalty to a close friend who had seen her through many difficult times. Times when she had needed a friend and Amanda had been there.

The run finished, Savannah headed back home.

Once there she gave Rooney his organic treat and started her bedtime routine. No matter how many times she pounded the pillow, turned over, and tried to relax, sleep didn't arrive until about 2:00 a.m. Over and over, she kept rehearsing the questions she had for Amanda the next morning.

Lots of questions.

Chapter 22

Friday Morning

Savannah unlocked the back door of Webb's Glass Shop, stepped into the office, and dropped her backpack on the floor beside the old oak desk. She briefly thought about moving the desk over to the studio but quickly ditched the idea. Her great-grandfather's desk had been here as long as she could remember, and ever since her father's death, stability had been important to her. The desk was part of the fabric of the shop and wouldn't be moving anywhere.

The bell over the front door jingled. Amanda was struggling with multiple bags full of glass materials for today's final lesson in the workshop.

"Hey! Let me help." Savannah rushed over and relieved Amanda of several plastic bags and led the way into the classroom. They piled everything on the two student worktables in the first row.

Amanda mimed a thank-you through her huffing and puffing and sat on the nearest student work stool, fanning her flushed face with her hand. "Whew! It's already Africa hot out there. I can't wait until

October. Guess what I found on an online auction site last night?"

Savannah slouched onto the next work stool. "No clue."

"Oh, come on. It's no fun if you don't guess. Please?"

"No. I didn't sleep much last night." Savannah combed through her short curls with a quick hand. "Just tell me."

"Spoilsport. I found a site that offered a bottle just like Martin's up for bid."

"Is it like one of the bottles he brought into class?"

"It looks like it."

"That's a great lead. Who's selling them?"

"I've got only the seller's online moniker so far, but I was thinking if we ordered the bottle, we might get the whole deal."

"Deal?"

"Have you had any coffee yet?"

Savannah sighed and held her head. "No, I haven't. Being both sleep deprived and caffeine deprived is not a good thing. So you're suggesting we bid on the bottle. When does the auction end?"

"The bidding stops at noon on Monday but—"

"Noon on Monday? That's too long. Anything could happen."

Amanda cocked her head sideways. "We could use the 'buy it now' feature and pay the asking price. If we pull the trigger now, we might get more details on the seller within a few minutes, if he's monitoring the sale."

"Good idea but—" Savannah ran her monthly budget numbers through her head. It would be stretching an already tight budget. She nodded her head slightly. "Let's do it. Use my business credit card. Great idea."

They moved into the office and Amanda sat at the desk. With a few clicks at the computer, Amanda bought the bottle. She leaned back in the antique oak swivel chair. It squeaked a little louder than normal. "I'll leave my e-mail window open and turn up the volume for the incoming mail beep."

Savannah eyed the distance to the lectern in the classroom through the open door. "Yep, you should be able to hear—"

Beep!

"Already?" said Amanda. She turned to the computer and clicked open her new message. "It looks like he has an e-mail account specifically for the online auctions." She scrolled down through the message. "Wait, wait. He's asking for an address for mailing out the bottle."

"Perfect." Savannah leaned over Amanda's shoulder. "Give him the shop address. It matches the one on the credit card, anyway."

Amanda punched in a return e-mail, clicked on the SEND key, and relaxed back into the chair again. "If he's hovering, this will take only a minute."

"Ha!" Amanda leaned forward to peer into the screen again. "He's asking if you want to pick it up and look at his other items up for auction."

"Of course we want to pick it up, but also ask him to confirm the provenance of the bottle. Is it from José Gaspar's hidden treasure?"

The keys clicked a staccato beat and were followed by a mouse click. "Boy, he's hovering, all right. He says he has proof of the bottle's provenance back to Gaspar the Pirate. That's followed by the address where we can pick it up."

Savannah looked at the screen. "Why is it familiar?" She wrinkled her brow. "Of course. It's the industrial park Edward and I visited yesterday. So this auction belongs to Captain Larry Collins? We didn't see any sign of blue bottles."

"I'm thinking he uses the online auction to attract gullible buyers for his Gaspar the Pirate bottle copies. He must have made the copy of the bottle Martin brought in here. Because you and Edward wandered in off the street, he didn't offer one to you. He hadn't vetted you with a credit card and an address."

"I think you're right, but it means that you and Jacob will have to go and pick up the bottle. He's already seen Edward and me, so we're out of the picture for a new lead."

"I can do it after class today. Work up a list of questions, and I'll pick up Jacob and work this lead for all its worth."

Savannah said, "Speaking of questions, when I talked to Detective Parker last night to tell him about Professor Patterson, he had more questions about you than about Martin's sister."

"Last night?"

"Yes. I told you I was going to tell him what we learned. He insinuated that maybe there might be more information closer to home."

Amanda stood up, and the color drained out of her face. "What did he mean?"

"Precisely. What *did* he mean?"

"What did he ask?"

"He suggested that perhaps you knew a lot more about Martin than you have shared so far."

"Savannah! Please!" Amanda stretched herself so that she was as tall as possible. "I'm the innocent one here. Detective Parker is trying to get more information out of you by accusing me—and it appears to be working."

"Calm down. You haven't been quite yourself for some time now."

Amanda stood even straighter. "You know my mother has been critically ill. You know what that does to me. I can't believe you believe him."

"I didn't say I believed him. I merely told you what he hinted."

"I'm going to be sick." Amanda bolted into the bathroom and slammed the door.

"Amanda, don't be upset," Savannah pleaded in front of the bathroom door.

"Go away," came from inside, followed by retching sounds.

Savannah hung her head. *What a mess!* She had raised her hand to knock on the bathroom door when she heard a loud knock on the front door.

When she looked through the shop, she could see it was Parker's new officer, persistently rapping on the glass with one hand and holding a folded piece of paper with the other.

After she dug the keys out of her backpack, Savannah walked quickly through the entire shop to the front and unlocked the door. "Good morning, Officer. What's the problem?"

Officer Williams looked up at Savannah. "I have a search warrant to serve to Amanda Blake. Is she here?"

"Search warrant? For Amanda?"

"Yes, Amanda Blake. She is here, isn't she? She wasn't at her home." Officer Williams turned and pointed to the vintage Cadillac parked next to the shop. "That is her car, isn't it?"

"Yes, of course." Savannah stepped back so Officer Williams could enter the shop. "Sorry, sorry. Amanda is ill . . . really more like upset. It'll be a few minutes before she is ready to come out."

"Thank you, ma'am, but I need to give this to her right now."

"Sure. Let's go back to the office, and you can give it to her when she comes out of the restroom. She might be a few minutes."

"I'll wait."

Savannah led the way back to the office. They stood there, listening to the sound of running water from the sink in the bathroom.

"Have a seat." Savannah waved a hand at the side chair, while she sat down with a plop on the oak swivel chair in front of the desk. "I'm sure she'll be out in a minute."

"No, thanks. I'll stand."

The silence between them was strained, and the young officer fiddled with the warrant and constantly adjusted her new uniform.

Finally, Officer Williams cocked her head. "The sound of the water running in there hasn't changed at all. Are you sure she's in there?"

"Yes. I saw her go inside and heard her throwing up."

Officer Williams approached the bathroom and gave a sharp rap on the door. "Amanda Blake. This is Officer Joy Williams. Please come out immediately."

Silence.

Officer Williams followed with another rap on the bathroom door. "Amanda Blake? Are you in there?"

She grabbed the door handle and pulled the door open wide.

The bathroom was empty, with the water still running in the sink.

"What!" Officer Williams flew out the back door just in time to see Amanda's old Cadillac turn down the street.

Officer Williams used the radio clipped to her uniform. She held the PRESS TO TALK button. "This is Officer Williams reporting that Amanda Blake has fled from Webb's Glass Shop. I was unable to serve the warrant."

The radio speaker crackled a message. "Officer Williams, this is Detective Parker. Meet me at the nursing home where Amanda's mother is living. We've got a warrant to search there, as well."

Officer Williams released the PTT button and clipped the radio back to her uniform. "Amanda shouldn't have run away. Detective Parker is going to be angry—very angry."

Chapter 23

Friday Morning

Detective Parker stood in the bright sunshine at the entrance to the Abbey Rehabilitation and Nursing Center, waiting for Officer Williams to arrive. She had reported that Amanda Blake had slipped through the back door of Webb's Glass Shop. He would continue with the plan to serve a search warrant to Amanda's mother.

He waited patiently while Officer Williams parked her patrol car and walked up to him with the warrant in her hand. "I'm so sorry. I should have brought another officer with me to watch the back door."

"Good lesson, then." Parker took the warrant and opened the front door for Williams. She forced a smile on her face and walked through the door.

Parker looked for and quickly found the administrator's office near the reception lounge and entered the small office, which obviously hadn't been decorated since the seventies. The modular desk was suffering from delamination, and the bottom edges and the small piles of sawdust bore witness to the internal disintegration of the desk.

A woman in her midfifties, dressed in a black skirt, a white blouse, and a sparkly chain holding a red sweater in place across her shoulders, stood up to greet them. "Good morning. Have you come by to visit someone?"

Parker handed her one of his cards. "Yes, ma'am. I'm Detective David Parker of the St. Petersburg Police Homicide Division." He waved a palm at Officer Williams. "This is Officer Williams." He looked at the name plate on her desk. "Miss Hamilton, we're here to search the room of Mrs. Blake." He handed her a document. "This is our search warrant. Read it over. It gives us the right to search her possessions."

Miss Hamilton took the stapled sheaf of papers and quickly skimmed through the document. "Fine. Let me show you her room." She briskly stepped around the desk and motioned for them to follow her.

At the nurses' station inside the doors to the lobby, she spoke to the first nurse who looked up. "These police officers are here to search Mrs. Blake's room. Please inform the rest of the staff to cooperate fully. I'll take them down to her room. Please send an aide to help move Mrs. Blake to the dining hall."

She looked back at Detective Parker. "If you don't mind, I would rather not agitate her. She's recovering from pneumonia, and I am sure you don't want to effect a relapse." She turned down the left corridor and didn't look back to see if they followed.

At the end of the corridor, she turned into the room on her left. Detective Parker and Officer Williams silently followed. The room was decorated like an old-fashioned schoolroom. There were maps, corkboards, whiteboards, photographs that had been enlarged to poster size of a house and a backyard, and, finally, a portrait of Amanda. These were obviously memory cues for the resident.

Mrs. Blake was sitting upright in a narrow hospital bed, with an oxygen cannula held in place under her nostrils with flexible tape. Miss Hamilton stood beside her. "Good morning, Mrs. Blake. You have some visitors." She took a moment to tuck the soft yellow blanket around the patient, nodded to Detective Parker and Officer Williams, and briskly left the room.

The room was furnished as much like a home as a hospital room could be. Several pieces of furniture had obviously come from Mrs. Blake's home: a tan recliner with white doilies fastened to the back and arms, an armoire with a mirror on the door and hat boxes stacked on top, and a matching long dresser that had nine drawers and more than a dozen jewelry boxes arranged on top.

Detective Parker leaned over the small white-haired resident. "Good morning, Mrs. Blake. I'm Detective David Parker, and this is my associate, Officer Williams. We're here to have a look around. We won't be long, and we'll be as quiet as we can." He nodded toward Williams, and she reached into her pocket and pulled out a pair of plastic gloves. She stepped over to the door and began searching the room clockwise, looking through every cupboard, shelf, drawer, box, and closet.

Looking around the crowded but cozy room, Parker found a folding chair and placed it as close to Mrs. Blake as he could manage. He sat down, leaned in, and spoke in a low and soothing tone. "Mrs. Blake, have you seen your daughter today?"

Mrs. Blake turned her head from the muted television that was hanging from the ceiling on a movable crane-like arm. "Amanda? Amanda is here every morning and every evening. Sometimes when I'm having a bad time, she'll stay with me and sleep on the recliner. You missed her. She's such a good daughter."

"Yes, I'm sure she is, but—"

"What is the nurse bringing me? Is this my birthday, and is she hiding my present?"

"She's not a nurse. This is my associate, Officer Williams. She's helping me gather up some of Amanda's things. Do you know where Amanda stores her things?"

"Sir, Amanda leaves her things at home. She's living there now and taking care of my plants. I have some beautiful roses. You can see them in the picture over there." Mrs. Blake pointed to one of large posters.

Detective Parker looked at the roses. "Very beautiful, Mrs. Blake. I don't have a yard. I live in a condo."

"How terrible. I have only a single African violet with me for my visit. Amanda brought it so I would have something to cheer up this room. She's done a lovely job, don't you think?"

"I think you are lucky to have such a devoted daughter. When did she stay overnight last?"

Mrs. Blake frowned and rubbed the top of her head. "Oh, dear. I get very muddled with what day it is." She looked directly ahead at a large calendar mounted on the wall, one showing the day, month, and date in large bold letters. "It's Friday, isn't it?"

While Detective Parker and Mrs. Blake continued their conversation, Williams worked her way over to the only closet in the small room. Clothes were stuffed on the rack, purses were crammed on the upper shelf, and boxes of shoes on the floor were stacked two deep and six high. She started on the upper shelf by removing each purse and searching through it and piling them on the floor.

"Yes, Mrs. Blake. Today is Friday. Can you tell me the last time Amanda stayed the night?"

"I think it was a few days ago. Either Monday or Tuesday." She turned her face to Parker and smiled sweetly. "She's such a good daughter."

Detective Parker caught Officer Williams's attention and mouthed, "Hurry up," in her direction before returning his attention to Mrs. Blake. "It would help us if you could remember which night she stayed with you."

"Oh, now I remember. She has been staying every night. She stays with me when I have to be on oxygen. She's such a good daughter." Her smile was aimed at the large picture of Amanda tacked on the center of the corkboard.

Officer Williams worked her way through the hanging clothes by removing each garment, searching it, then replacing it in the closet. Then she sat cross-legged on the floor and reached for a stack of shoe boxes. One of them tumbled to the floor and spilled open, causing a pair of elegant teal silk kitten heels to slide under the hospital bed.

Detective Parker glared at Williams, but the noise didn't register with Mrs. Blake. In fact, the crinkled lids over her faded blue eyes seemed to be closing slowly. Parker stood and walked around the bed to the closet. He whispered, "She's asleep for now. Hurry as best you can."

Williams nodded and continued to search each shoe box. She had worked her way to the back row when she straightened up, rose from the floor, and stood next to Detective Parker. "Is this what you're looking for?" She held open a shoe box to reveal an old bottle resting comfortably inside a pair of black stiletto heels.

"This looks like the bottle we found in Martin's dive bag." He tilted his head to get a better look at it. "There's a dark stain near the bottom, and it has a crack from the base to the tip. Bag this up for forensics. This could be the bit of evidence that allows me to arrest Amanda for the murder of her boyfriend."

Chapter 24

Why would Amanda take off? It makes her look guilty. She knows that!

Savannah stood with her hands on her hips, trying to control the flash of anger that swept through her. There was no way to help Amanda if she ran away. What was she thinking?

Gone was gone, however, and today's workshop needed to be completed. Luckily, they had worked on the lesson plan together. The final day of class included learning to build a clock with a flattened bottle and cleaning up the projects left in the kiln overnight.

After she had finished opening up the shop properly, Savannah called Jacob and told him she wouldn't be arriving at the studio until late in the afternoon. Staffing two sites was always going to be a challenge, so she needed to think about another assistant as a backup resource for both the shop and the studio.

I didn't think I needed to worry about Amanda. I was wrong, she thought.

The front door jangled, signaling the start of the last day of the workshop.

Everything progressed smoothly, and in what seemed like minutes, it was time for the class to pack up and leave with their work.

"Thanks, Miss. Webb," said Patty Kelner. "This has been the best class I've taken ever, ever, ever. You and Amanda are fantastic."

"Yeah, we need to do this every summer," Yvonne Whittaker said, piping up. "I'm going to talk to my counselor and tell her what a great class this is. Maybe you can work up a class for our school." She looked over at Patty. "Wouldn't it be super awesome?"

"Yep. I'll go with you. We can take in our projects. That will clinch the deal."

"Thanks, girls. I'll give your counselor a call in a couple of weeks and see what we can come up with for Christmas break."

They left the shop, still chattering about who they would invite to a class.

"Thank you for persevering through such difficult times." SueAnn reached out and took Savannah's hands in hers. "It's such a shame your instructor is so unreliable. She seemed like such a generous soul, but you never know about people until you give them responsibilities." Squeezing her hands for emphasis, she added, "You must learn not to trust so easily, dear. The world is a harsh classroom."

Savannah bit back the words flashing through her mind in defense of Amanda. She realized that from SueAnn's perspective, things looked haphazard. It was unlikely that Webb's would ever see SueAnn back as a student.

After SueAnn left the shop, the twins converged on Savannah. Rachel started. "Okay, tell us what's happening. We know Amanda would never miss class for anything but her mother's death. What's going on?"

Faith circled an arm around Savannah's waist. "Come on. We're practically family. What's the matter with Amanda?"

Savannah smiled down at these two absurd-looking elders and felt warmth spreading in her chest. They were right. They felt like family—her family.

"Ladies, I wish I knew. She seemed to be handling everything fairly well. I mean, the new class was a slam dunk. But then, after Martin was murdered, she was distant and distracted. I misunderstood and thought her mother was ill again. Unfortunately, the case is much more complicated. She was secretly engaged to Martin and is under investigation by our very own Detective Parker."

Faith spoke. "Where is she now?"

"I don't know. She ran out the back when Officer Williams came by to notify her that a search warrant had been issued. I haven't heard from her. She's too smart to be at her apartment. I've been leaving voice mails and text messages on her phone. She's got to surface soon. Her mother needs her."

The twins looked at each other and said in unison, "What can we do?"

"I don't know, but I sincerely appreciate the offer."

Rachel looked up into Savannah's eyes. "We are serious about helping. We know you are consulting with Detective Parker and—"

"It looks like this is going to get serious for Amanda," Faith said, finishing Rachel's statement. "We want to help with the investigation."

Rachel nodded. "We think this is much more serious than a simple 'Amanda under stress' problem."

"We think Amanda is going to be arrested for Martin's murder," Faith said.

Savannah stepped back. "Ridiculous. Amanda wouldn't hurt anyone."

"That's not what it looks like from Detective Parker's point of view," said Rachel.

"From their point of view"—Faith pointed a finger at Savannah—"she has fled to avoid a warrant. That must elevate her to the rank of their prime suspect."

They gathered their bags and projects and made their way toward the front door. "Remember," said Faith.

"Call us when she gets arrested," said Rachel.

They left a huge silence behind when they left and closed the door.

Savannah had begun cleaning up, in preparation for closing the shop, when the bell jangled on the front door.

"Hey, love. I brought some iced tea and lemon cookies. Are you ready for a little break?" Edward set the tray on the sales counter and folded Savannah into his arms. "I heard from Jacob that you were finishing up the workshop today, because Amanda's gone missing. He thought I should know."

Her voice muffled by his embrace, she said, "I can't understand why she ran away. She knows how bad that looks. She also knows we're her friends and we would do anything to help her if she's in trouble."

Edward released her and grabbed her hand in both of his. "Pet, this is a serious situation. It's quite possible the next thing that happens to Amanda will be her arrest."

"What do you mean, my arrest?" Amanda walked in from the back office and stood with her hands on her hips. "I haven't done anything."

"Amanda!" Savannah nearly squashed her in a bear hug. "What is going on? You have to tell us."

Amanda looked up with tear-filled eyes. "You're right, of course." She poured herself a glass of tea. "I need to tell you guys everything. Let's go back to the classroom." She walked over to the front door, locked it, then turned the hanging sign around from OPEN to CLOSED. She led them into the classroom, motioned for Edward to bring the iced tea tray, and settled herself on the nearest student work stool. "I don't know how to start. It's all been so horrible . . . keeping everything a secret from you guys."

"Start from the beginning." Savannah wiggled onto a stool next to Amanda. "You need help."

"Okay. From the beginning, then." Amanda took a huge drink of the iced tea. "Okay, like I told you guys before, I met Martin about four weeks ago on one of those dating sites." She cupped her hands around the glass and looked down. "I don't know why I signed up. I think it was because Mother was getting more and more distant and . . ."

Savannah reached over to rub Amanda's arm. "It's all right." She looked over at Edward. "We know this is a difficult time. That's one of the reasons I thought teaching the new workshop would be good for you." She tilted her head and gave Edward a look that meant "Say something."

Edward blurted, "Yep, we did. We thought it would be good for you." He glanced at Savannah and gave his shoulders a tiny shrug.

"I know, but still I wanted something . . . someone. So I signed up, and there was a bunch of trolls, so I was convinced I had made a terrible mistake. But then there was Martin. We clicked right away." She smiled and fell silent, with a faraway look.

Savannah reached over to touch Amanda's shoulder. "Keep going."

Startled, Amanda said, "Oh, right. We met for coffee at first. We chattered like chipmunks for three hours. Then we tried a lunch." She looked at Savannah and Edward in turn. "Just to make sure. You know lots of guys survive the coffee but not the lunch. Martin was terrific at lunch, as well. We laughed so much, my jaw ached for hours." Amanda fell silent again.

"Then what?" Savannah asked.

"Well, after that, things went pretty fast—too fast— so fast I was embarrassed to tell you." She held up both hands. "I know. I know you would have been supportive, but I got it into my head that if anyone else knew about us, the magic would disappear and he would be gone."

Edward shook his head. "That's crazy. We would have been happy for you."

"Crazy is exactly what I was afraid of. If I thought I was crazy, what would others think of me?"

"Your friends wouldn't think such things. That's why we're your friends." Savannah stood. "Even so, you should have told us everything you knew on the day Martin's body was found."

"When was the last time you saw Martin? Did you meet him on Monday after class?" Edward poured more iced tea all around.

"Amanda, we've been to Martin's trailer. We've talked to Martin's neighbors. The old guy next door saw his girlfriend that night. You have to stop keeping secrets. We know you were there," Savannah revealed.

Amanda took a deep breath, and then her shoulders seemed to collapse. "You're right. You deserve to know." She cupped her iced tea for a long moment. "My last words with Martin were ugly. I'm so ashamed. I didn't mean it."

"What happened?" Savannah dropped her voice low.

"On our last night, I spent the evening at Martin's trailer. After we made love, he got very quiet and serious. He said he had been thinking about us, our future." She smiled a distant, dreamy smile. "Our future, he said, needed to be based on something more than a few art pieces sold online." She fell silent.

"That was sweet," Savannah said.

Amanda started and continued. "Yes, but he wouldn't tell me what he thought should change. He said only that things had to change, and right now."

Edward spread his hands. "So, not horrible, then."

"That wasn't the end of the argument. That was the start of the argument. I told him that I was working at Webb's and that I expected a small inheritance from my mother's estate. I mean, she's pretty frail, and she's already far exceeded the normal life span for someone with vascular dementia. He got mad. He said he wasn't the kind of man who lived off his wife. He expected our family to be able to support itself without needing a lot of money."

"Your family? That must have made you feel wonderful," Savannah said.

"It did indeed. For a minute." Amanda downed the rest of her iced tea. "Then, I suppose, my independent spirit kicked in. I told him I could support us very nicely. The next thing I knew, we were fighting like rabid dogs. He said he wouldn't be a boy toy on the arm of a cougar. That really hurt. Then I told him that his art alone wouldn't support diddly-squat. He said that engagements were nothing. He said that he was also engaged to Vicki. I lost it completely, and I don't know what I said, but it wasn't nice. He said something more about the bottles, but I stomped my way out of the trailer and spun gravel as I drove away. It was our first fight—and our last fight."

Silence.

After a few seconds, Savannah touched Amanda's arm. "He was engaged to Vicki at the same time?"

Amanda nodded her head in misery.

"What time was it?" asked Savanah.

"I kinda, sorta lost track of time at that point. I think it was close to midnight, but I can't be sure."

"Where did you go?" asked Edward.

"I tore off down the road and drove down Gulf Boulevard for a while, until I calmed down. Then I parked at Pass-a-Grille Beach, just thinking things over. Then I tried calling Martin to apologize. When he didn't answer, I got mad again. Then I drove over to see my mom. She was still at the Abbey. I still have my key from when I worked there, so I slipped in the back door and sat in the room with my mother. It calmed me down. Anyway, I texted Martin all night, asking him to explain."

"But, Amanda, why didn't you tell us what was going on after it was clear the unidentified diver was Martin? Help me understand," Savannah said.

"I was afraid you wouldn't want to help me. I mean, I had already been keeping our relationship a secret for several weeks." She reached into her hobo bag and drew out an old-fashioned flower-printed cotton hankie. She blew her nose, ending with a small trumpet noise. "He was so much younger than me. It all seemed very wrong. He was ten years younger, and I could hear my mother in my head, telling me that I was robbing the cradle."

"That's ridiculous. You know how liberal this community is. It's not quite as diverse as deliberately quirky Gulfport, but we're a close second. None of that would have mattered."

Amanda bit her lip and swallowed hard. "I know that now, but at the time I was so worried about what you all would think of me that I didn't want to tell you. Then, after he admitted that he was also engaged to Vicki, it was clear that I meant nothing to him."

"What was your reason for running out of here and away from the police?"

She held the hankie up to her nose and blew again. "I don't have an alibi. They know about me and Martin. I didn't want to be arrested. Sometimes they arrest the wrong person."

"We've got to get on the right side of Detective Parker with this. You need to call Officer Williams and give her your apologies," Savannah urged. "You didn't actually come face-to-face with her and the warrant, but you need to make this right. Understand?"

Amanda sniffed noisily and nodded her understanding.

"Now, get yourself off to see your mother, and stay out of trouble until we get this figured out."

Amanda nodded quietly and gathered her things to leave. "I'm sorry. I won't keep secrets anymore." With that said, she headed to the display room and walked out the front door. She left a large silence behind.

Chapter 25

Friday Afternoon

"I've decided we must continue running our investigation without Amanda," Savannah announced to the rest of the group. "She's too emotionally involved to help right now. There is also the distinct possibility that she may be picked up for questioning at any moment. I sent her to spend some time with her mother."

After Amanda's revealing confession, Savannah and Edward had left Webb's and had driven over to the studio to bring Jacob up to speed. They now sat around the conference table, feeling Amanda's absence.

Jacob pulled Suzy onto his lap and began to stroke her head. "We can investigate without her. It will not be as quick, because she is wicked fast on the computer."

Edward grimaced. "True. None of us are as quick"—he smiled at the others—"but we are wicked persistent. Let's get on with it."

"Great lecture." Savannah stood with her hands on her hips. "Let's review and regroup. Wow!" Savannah ran a hand through her hair. "We've basically worked almost all these leads with not a lot to show for it. This is discouraging. One new element is that Vicki and Martin were also secretly engaged. That means we must find out where Vicki was on Monday night. Since Vicki was the social media partner in the craft business, Amanda would have been a great help. I can also ask Detective Parker not only about Amanda but about Vicki, too."

"Another avenue is Captain Collins," said Edward. "We didn't get much from our first visit. We can follow up on that."

"I can go to the main library and investigate where the bottles were found on the sea floor. Suzie is allowed in there. One of the librarians likes to help me with research," said Jacob. "There's a bus stop right in front of the library."

"Good idea. I don't know when I'm going to hear from the experts. It will be a big help to have information now rather than later. Edward and I have visited Martin's trailer and talked to two of his neighbors. They didn't mention anything about an argument between Martin and Amanda, but maybe they didn't want to say anything to strangers."

"Which means they might have reported it to the police," said Edward.

"Another subject for Detective Parker. I can also tell him that we've talked to Captain Collins. That didn't pan out, but he might not know about his connection to Martin."

Jacob chimed in. "That Vicki person might also know. She worked with Martin on his art projects."

"This is a lot harder than I thought. It seems like all our investigations are leading us around in circles." Savannah sat at the end of the table and folded her arms across her chest.

Edward reached over and tapped her on the elbow. "You're forgetting about what happened in our prior investigations. We got to a point like this, when everything seemed to be mired in tail chasing. Then we got a break, and things worked out very quickly afterward."

"I remember. So we're in the middle muddle?"

"I prefer to believe we're about to get the resolving lead."

"You're such an optimist."

Jacob frowned and held Suzy a little tighter. "I'm going to the library before they close." Rather than make an exit, Jacob lingered, concern etched on his face.

"Let's meet back here in the morning and see what we've got. Thanks, Jacob."

Edward pulled the conference room telephone toward him after Jacob left the room. "Let's call the captain first. He'll be the most difficult."

Savannah pulled a card out of her backpack. "Here's the number." She sat in the chair next to Edward, letting their thighs touch for a moment.

He smiled at her as he dialed the number. "I'll put it on speaker."

After seven rings, the call rolled over to voice mail. Edward left a message, asking the captain to call him back at the studio number, and hung up.

"I'm confused," Savannah said. "Why didn't you leave your cell number?"

"I don't know. It didn't feel right to give him so much information about me. I bottled out."

"What?"

"Oh, sorry. It's an expression we use in England when someone chickens out."

"Weirdly appropriate." She reached for the telephone. "Let's try Vicki. Be ready to cover your ears. She curses like a sailor." She dialed Vicki's number.

"Vicki's Treasures. How can I help you?"

"Hi, Vicki. This is Savannah Webb. You're on speakerphone. Remember me? My friend Amanda Blake and I asked you some questions about Martin."

"Are you really such an idiot? I told you not to harass me."

"I merely want to ask if you know where Martin got his bottles."

"If you call me again, I'm going to file a formal complaint and get you thrown in jail. Don't call me again." The dial tone followed immediately.

Edward frowned. "She can't do that, can she?"

"She can certainly call Detective Parker and complicate my life by complaining to him. That could jeopardize my consulting status."

"He'll ignore her."

"I hope so. But it still doesn't give us anything to go on for finding the buried treasure location of the bottles." Savannah jotted a few lines in the notebook she had placed on the table at the beginning of the meeting.

A sharp knock on the conference-room door made

both Savannah and Edward turn their heads. Arthur poked his head in the room.

"Sorry, Savannah, but can you show me where you keep your supplies?" His neck turned pink, and the color raced up to his hairline. "The bathroom needs more . . . supplies."

Savannah pressed her lips into a tight line. "I'll be right back."

Arthur backed away from the door. "Sorry to interrupt your meeting."

"It's no trouble. I should have shown you where everything was kept on your first day," she said as she headed in the direction of the bathroom.

"Are you guys investigating another murder?"

"Well, yes, in a minor way. I'm helping Detective Parker as a consultant with a glass bottle that was found with a murder victim. How are you doing with your studio space? Is it helping you at all?"

She opened a small metal cabinet next to the bathroom. It was stocked with paper towels, tissue boxes, and toilet paper, along with an assortment of cleaning supplies and rags.

"Wow. G-good." Arthur stared. "This is great."

Savannah sensed his hesitation. "Just find what you need. I'm going back to my meeting."

When she returned to the conference room, Jacob had also returned. He and Edward were discussing the logistics of going to the library. She stood in the doorway and let them come to the inevitable conclusion when Jacob was involved. He was not going to get on Edward's motorcycle and leave Suzy in the shop.

"I am not allowed to be without Suzy. There is no room on your motorcycle, and it would not be safe for me to hold her." His voice was strong and it had the low range of a teenager transitioning to adulthood.

She leaned against the doorknob and waited until they both looked at her. "Jacob has an excellent point. Take my Mini. I'm going to be working in here." She pulled the car keys out of her pocket and tossed them to Edward.

Edward and Jacob left, and Savannah returned to her office and tackled the stack of papers that grew into a mountain every time she turned her back. After a tedious hour, she heard Jacob and Edward return.

Back in the conference room, they were leaning over a pile of maps that completely covered the surface of the table.

"What's this?" Savannah asked as she entered the room.

Jacob's face beamed. "My librarian helped me find some old maps that were available during the time the bottle was made. She likes to help me and Suzy."

"That's great, but—" Her cell phone rang. "It's the museum. Hi, Dr. Smithfield. I'm putting you on speaker for my friends who are helping me research these bottles." She pressed a key and placed her cell on the conference table.

"My colleague in Bristol got back to me on the bottle he received from your Detective Parker."

"Oh? He didn't tell me the bottle had been sent over to Scotland Yard." Savannah turned and mouthed to Edward, "He's not *my* Detective Parker." Savannah turned back around and said, "What's the story?"

"It is an authentic, original Bristol Blue bottle manufactured for patent medications. It was a popular export to the new colonists of North America. The tiny maker's mark on the bottom actually identifies the glass factory and the glassblower."

"Jacob was right about that one being an original. What's the value?"

"It's not extraordinarily valuable. It usually sells at auction for under fifty dollars."

"Thanks, Dr. Smithfield. I don't know how or if it fits into the motive for Martin's death, but I appreciate the efforts of you and your Bristol colleague." Savannah ended the call and shrugged her shoulders. "Another dead end. The bottle is old, but why is it important? It doesn't add up."

Jacob pointed to a section on one of the old maps. "This appears to be very close to where Martin was found."

"We've nothing to lose." Edward started gathering up the maps. "Let's go to the discovery site and see what we can find out by comparing today's shoreline with these maps."

"Don't touch them." Jacob pulled the maps toward him. "I'll take care of the maps. My librarian friend said I must be in charge of the maps all the time." He looked at Savannah and lowered his head in a challenge. "All the time."

Edward held his hands up. "Don't get your knickers in a twist."

"What does that mean?" Jacob carefully rolled up the maps and put them in a cardboard shipping tube.

Savannah gave Edward a warning look. "It means don't get worried over something unimportant. We will let you take care of the maps exclusively, won't we, Edward?"

"Of course." He nodded.

They loaded into the Mini and drove straight down Central Avenue.

Chapter 26

"I think this is the spot." Jacob had Suzy's leash slipped over his wrist. The tube of maps was tucked under the other arm, and one of the maps was spread between his hands. "Yes." He twisted the map slightly. "This is the spot."

They had parked the Mini on Park Street and had walked along the seawall to the place where the newspaper stated Martin's body had been found.

Savannah looked at the large Mediterranean Revival–style homes that backed onto this small bit of Intracoastal Waterway. "What we need to find is the young couple and their dog who found the body. They were taking their dog for a walk."

She had barely gotten the words out of her mouth when a great, lumbering hulk of a chocolate lab came galloping down the narrow beach.

"Charlie! Stay!" The command came from a young couple about twenty yards away. The man held a leash in his hand. He ran up to them, with the woman a few feet behind.

Charlie skidded to a tumbling halt and wound up lying on his side, looking up at Suzy with adoring eyes.

"Don't panic. He's a real softie." The man snapped the leash onto Charlie's collar. "We don't often find other dogs out here."

"Suzy is a service dog." Jacob backed away, still holding the map.

"No problem. Charlie is curious about her vest."

The young woman stepped forward, with her hand outstretched. "Hi. I'm Julie Wedlake, and this is my husband, Paul. We live a few houses over on Park Street."

Savannah and Edward shook her hand and Paul's and introduced themselves to the couple, but Jacob kept a tight grip on the maps.

"What are you looking for?" Julie looked at her husband. "Maybe we can help."

Savannah didn't hesitate a second. "We're looking for a cache of old bottles turned up by one of my students. I own Webb's Glass Shop on Central Avenue, and this week we taught a glass recycling class, which started on Monday. Martin brought in an old bottle that he said came from the water along here."

"Do you mean the diver who was found here on Tuesday morning?" Paul asked.

Savannah nodded. "Yes. He was in class on Monday and brought a Bristol blue bottle that he said he had salvaged."

The couple looked at each other.

Paul said, "We're the ones who found him. The bottle found with him was broken, but you could still see the cobalt blue through the mesh of his dive bag."

"I'm consulting with the police department as

their glass expert, and I would like to ask you some questions, if you've got a few minutes."

"Definitely," said Julie. "Our house is a few doors away. Please follow us so we can be more comfortable and can get these dogs out of the heat. I'm sure Suzy would appreciate a little water, as well as everyone else."

"Thanks," said Edward. "We're happy to take you up on it."

After Savannah and Edward helped Jacob stow the borrowed maps in the tube, the little troupe followed the couple down the beach to the back entrance of an early 1920s stucco and clay-tiled mansion. They entered through the back door and found themselves in a screened-in area with an Olympic-sized pool, which could easily have hosted a swim meet. They followed Paul and Julie inside through the door to the kitchen.

"Let me get some water for the dogs first." Julie picked up a large bowl from the floor and grabbed another one from a cupboard in the enormous granite-topped island. After she filled the bowls with water and placed them down several feet apart, she said, "I don't know about Suzy, but Charlie doesn't like to share either food or water." Charlie practically inhaled the liquid in noisy, sloppy slurps.

"Suzy is a polite dog." Jacob led her to the smaller bowl. "She's had lots of training to prepare for all situations." Suzy lapped some water, then sat.

"Good," said Julie. "I'll get us some iced tea, and we can chat in the living room. Paul, get everyone settled, and I'll be right in with a tray."

They followed Paul and were soon settled in a casual, comfortable way, so that it felt like they had all known each other for much longer than the few minutes that had passed.

After Julie served the iced tea and sat, she said, "Now, what do you want to know?"

Edward nodded over at Savannah, and she cleared her throat. "We want to know where Martin found the bottle. We think it is the key to solving his death."

Paul and Julie looked at each other with eyebrows raised.

Paul nodded slightly. "This is weird, but we actually might be able to help you."

"Fantastic, but how?" Savannah asked.

"We have a marine science business," said Paul.

"And it fits in with your questions very well," said Julie. "It combines a remotely operated vehicle, called an ROV, with bottom-sensing instrumentation. It is possible for us to—"

"Scan the bottom of the Intracoastal Waterway to search for the bottles," Jacob said, finishing the statement.

"Right," said Paul. "We're in the process of collecting data right now in support of a grant application to map sections of the gulf to document sea grass destruction. We're also going to measure the effectivity of different methods of sea grass restoration."

Edward frowned. "I'm sorry. A grant? I'm not familiar with funding for science in the States."

Julie smiled. "I'm not sure anyone is, but basically, Paul and I are applying for funding to prove that our ROV is more effective at documenting sea grass damage caused by boats that run aground and tear up the bottom." She nodded at Paul.

"The grant will fund a feasibility study for using high-definition cameras tethered to our vehicle for not only providing proof of damage but also for estimating the fines levied on the boat owners for the restoration of the sea grass." Paul lifted his eyebrows. "If this gets approved, we can offer our services to the restoration companies for damage assessment and proof that the damage has been repaired."

"Currently, the sea grass is counted by hand, a tedious and error-prone estimation method," Julie added.

Savannah spread her hands. "How does this help us locate the area where Martin found the bottles?"

Julie looked at Edward. "I see where you're confused. We haven't selected the areas where we're going to collect baseline data. It means we can use our ROV to search in the most likely places Martin would have been able to access. It's a win-win."

Jacob tapped the tube of maps. "That's why I have these old maps. We can figure out what would have been a good place to bury the bottles on the old maps, and then we can match where they might be in the Intracoastal. Then the ROV can scan those areas for us to see if there have been disturbances on the bottom."

"You've got it, young man," said Paul. "We have to accumulate a significant amount of data regardless to accompany our proposal. We might as well make it interesting."

"You know, this sounds like a very thinly disguised treasure hunt." Julie tilted her head sideways.

"No," protested Paul. "This is actually aiding in a murder investigation." He grinned wide. "Even better."

Edward stood. "How do we start?"

Paul also stood. "Jacob, I'm going to get my set of modern charts, and let's determine some target areas for the ROV scans based on your maps. Then we'll start scanning tomorrow afternoon. Good? Let's go into the workshop and plot this out." He looked at Julie, Savannah, and Edward. "You don't mind, do you?"

"Mind? You don't think you're doing this without us, do you?" Julie waved at the entire group. "It's this way. It was originally a billiards room, but we've found it to be the perfect laboratory for our business."

Jacob could hardly contain his excitement. He followed Julie and Paul into a large room outfitted with all the work space and instruments that could be found in any university laboratory. He unrolled one of the maps onto a long table near the end of the room and pointed to an island in the middle of the Intracoastal. "This is one of the possible locations where I think the treasure cache should be."

Paul rummaged through his collection of charts stored in a flat set of drawers and pulled out a chart of the same area, which was a modern update. "This is still a shallow area of the Intracoastal. Let me plug this into our application and see what parameters we will need to enter into the ROV navigation program."

Jacob sorted through his maps and pulled out another location, which Paul located on one of his charts as a final possibility. After the coordinates were plugged into the ROV and Paul had taken pictures of Jacob's maps, everyone fell silent.

Savannah looked at Paul. "When are you going to perform the data scans?"

"It will have to be during low tide tomorrow, which will be at about three in the afternoon. This will give us the best chance of detecting any kind of disturbance on the bottom. The water is so murky that the less water there is, the easier it will be for the cameras to analyze for anomalies."

"Can we come along?" Jacob scooped up Suzy, who had been about to remind Charlie that she was a service dog. "I won't be any trouble."

Edward spoke up. "I think we should all be involved. This is serious business, and not merely a lark for the scientific fun of it. Even though it does look like this ROV of yours could shortcut the efforts of salvage divers across the world."

It was Jacob who voiced the thought foremost in everyone's mind. "We might finally find Gaspar's treasure."

Chapter 27

Saturday Morning

"I'm at the hospital with my mother. She's got pneumonia, and it's very serious. I can't come into the shop today."

Savannah had answered the early morning call a few minutes after opening Webb's Glass Shop. "Oh, I'm so sorry. What can I do to help?"

There was a long loud sigh from Amanda. "Thanks, but they've got her in an oxygen tent and have pumped her with enough antibiotics to cure leprosy. She's doing very well, but I can tell she doesn't understand what's happening. Whenever I get near, she grabs onto my hand like she's drowning. At this point, I'm her life preserver."

"Then, of course, you must stay with her."

"When I got the call from her nursing home, they also said that the police had searched her room."

"Your mother's room? That's crazy!" Savannah could hear the anger in her voice.

"Not so crazy. In her closet, they found a cracked blue bottle with blood on it."

Savannah cleared her throat and spoke softly. "That's not good. Was your mom upset?"

"I don't think so. She's been sleeping pretty much all the time."

"Why don't I come over, and we can both sit with your mother?"

"Oh, thanks. I would appreciate it. This is so hard to do by myself. Mom looks so scared, and I—" There was a great gulping sob, followed by "Mother! Stop! Stop that!" and then the phone went silent.

"Amanda? Are you there? Amanda!"

There was a commotion, and loud voices were telling Mrs. Blake to remain calm. Several more long seconds, maybe even minutes, went by.

"Savannah?"

"I'm here."

"Thanks. Mom deliberately pulled off the oxygen tent, and everyone is upset and frustrated. They're talking about giving her even more medication to sedate her. I need to go talk to the doctor and make sure they understand about her dementia."

"I'll be there as quick as I can."

Savannah locked up the shop and drove the short distance down to the hospital. She asked at the desk for Mrs. Blake's room and was soon walking into a room jam-packed with monitors, respirators, IV lines, and an even paler than usual Amanda, who was wringing her hands like an automaton.

"Savannah!" Amanda grabbed her and crushed her slim frame into a bear hug, showing the desperation she felt. "I'm so glad you're here. There's a real possibility Mother is dying."

After she extracted herself from Amanda's desperate clutches, Savannah led her to one of the two visitor's chairs in the hospital room. "Sit down and, even more important, calm down. This is not helping. Now, take a deep breath and let it out slow."

"But—"

"I mean it. Deep breath."

Amanda inhaled a short breath and released it quickly. "I have more—"

"No talking until we have your emotions under better control. Your mother can sense it, and she'll take longer to recover, because she's reacting to your anxiety. Now, deep breath." Savannah took a deep breath, and Amanda followed suit. They breathed in time for several minutes, until Amanda's color returned.

"Thanks." Amanda looked over at her mother, who seemed to relax and breathe easier. "You're right. I need to be calm when I'm here. Just because she can't remember my name doesn't mean she doesn't know who I am."

"That must be horribly upsetting." Savannah leaned back in her chair. "What do the doctors say?"

"Ugh. It's a lot of mumbo jumbo, but it boils down to 'She's old,' as usual. I've got a call into the primary care physician who used to be her favorite until she went into the Abbey. If he can, he says he will stop by and review her condition. That will make us both feel better. Thanks for being here."

"That's what friends are for."

They both looked over at Mrs. Blake, who was now sleeping peacefully, although her breathing was still labored.

Chapter 28

Saturday Morning

Sandra Grey walked into Detective Parker's office, placed a folder on his desk, then sat in one of his guest chairs. She crossed her legs and tugged at her black pencil skirt. "My office has just received the results for the blood on the bottle you found at the Abbey. We can confirm that the blood is from Martin Lane."

Parker raised his eyes from her smart red pumps to her equally red lips. "I'm not surprised. This will make for an interesting conversation with Amanda Blake. We should be able to pick her up for questioning this afternoon."

"Amanda? You mean Savannah's friend? You're sure?"

"I'm not going to have any choice. The evidence pointing to her is piling up, and I can't ignore the facts." He ticked them off on his fingers. "One, she had opportunity. Since she was Martin's girlfriend, he would have let her get close enough to him to strike the fatal blow. Two, she had access to his bottles. That's the method."

"I'll give you that, but what is the motive?"

"I believe that's why she ducked out on our officer Williams. Something happened. An argument or maybe even the realization that those bottles could be worth thousands as part of Gaspar's treasure. In any case, I have enough to pick her up for questioning, and I can start the arrest process." He picked up the receiver on his desk phone and dialed. "Officer Williams, do you have the warrant processed? When do you expect it to be completed?" He glanced over at Sandra. "It's still in the signature chain." Returning to the phone, he said, "Regardless, we can pick her up for questioning. Pick me up out front in about five minutes. We should find her at Webb's Glass Shop."

Sandra stood. "I know the evidence looks overwhelming, but my gut is telling me that it's not Amanda."

"I've arrested and gotten a conviction on less. Virtually anyone can be driven to violence, given enough stress."

Glancing back at him as she walked through the door, she said, "I think you're wrong on this."

Detective Parker scooped up his cell phone and made his way to the front of the station. Williams was waiting in one of the distinctive green-and-gold-striped St. Petersburg Police Department patrol cars. Her small form was overwhelmed by the large sedan, but her fierce expression and alert posture demanded that she be treated like a cop.

He got in the passenger seat and buckled up. "It's Webb's Glass Shop. Straight down Central to about Twenty-Third Street, on the right."

Williams nodded and a few minutes later pulled

into the shop's parking lot. The shop was locked, and the sign was turned to the CLOSED side. Detective Parker looked at a poster taped to the window, announcing the opening of Webb's Studio.

"They must be at the studio. The location is a few blocks down on Twenty-Second Street South. Let's check there."

Minutes later, they pulled into the gravel parking lot and walked into the studio, Williams first.

"Is Amanda Blake here?" Her voice was loud and authoritative. "We need to speak to Amanda Blake."

The reaction was immediate. Jacob, Arthur, and Helen all came out of their work areas.

Helen challenged them immediately. "Why are you looking for Amanda? She's not here. She's the manager over at Webb's Glass Shop."

Officer Williams responded in a calm tone. "We were just there. It's closed. Do you know where she might be?"

Jacob stood in the doorway of Savannah's workshop with Suzy standing beside him. "She's not here. She might be with her mother at the Abbey. Her mother has been very sick. You should check." He turned around and closed the door.

Officer Williams looked over at Detective Parker and raised her eyebrows.

"Jacob is right. She's more likely to be there, but let's call first," Parker said.

After getting the news that Mrs. Blake had been sent to the hospital in the middle of the night, Williams drove them back downtown and parked in front of the hospital's main entrance.

"Stay here. I'll bring her down."

"But, sir. Won't you need help? I—"

"I can manage. She won't be able to escape this time."

Detective Parker asked for Mrs. Blake's room and soon walked into a flurry of activity surrounding a frail form being reconnected to a breathing mask and tent.

"Why does she do it?" cried a tearful Amanda. "It's there to help her."

"She doesn't know," said a middle-aged physician who was watching the bank of signals on a monitor over the hospital bed. "It startles her when she wakes up, and she thinks her bad breathing is due to the oxygen tent. Not surprising when you combine pneumonia and vascular dementia."

The nurse finally finished connecting Mrs. Blake to all her sensor disks, then tidied her bedclothes and adjusted the pillows.

Mrs. Blake looked up at her and said, "Are you my daughter? My daughter is supposed to be here."

"Here I am, Mother." Amanda stepped close to the bed. "I'm right over here. I'm right here with you."

Savannah moved to stand beside Amanda and looked down at the frail creature who was looking calmly at them both through the plastic tent. "She's better now. See? She's calm."

Amanda turned her head. "But only until the next time she goes to sleep and wakes up in a panic. This is horrible. Thanks for being here with me, but you need to get back to the shop. I'm good to stay here for the duration."

"The next few hours will tell us if she will improve or decline," said the physician. "I'm sorry to be so blunt, but it is something you need to know since she has 'do not resuscitate' status officially established. If she stops breathing, we're going to let her go."

"*Can* she recover?" Amanda asked in a tiny voice.

"Absolutely. If she makes it through the next twenty-four hours, she should return to her usual self."

Parker realized that no one had noticed he was in the room. He cleared his throat. "Miss Amanda Blake, I'm here to take you in for questioning about the murder of Martin Lane. Please accompany me down to the station."

Amanda and Savannah turned in unison to stand openmouthed before Detective Parker. Savannah recovered first.

"What are you talking about? This is no time for Amanda to leave this room. Her mother is critically ill. Besides, she didn't kill Martin."

Parker looked at them. With a very quiet voice, he said, "I understand this is terrible timing, but nevertheless, Amanda, you need to come with me for questioning about your relationship with Martin Lane."

"But . . . ," Amanda protested weakly.

"Please don't make me summon my officer to take you out of here in handcuffs, Amanda. That isn't going to help the situation at all."

"But, David," pleaded Savannah. "She's innocent. You know Amanda. You can't believe she would kill Martin."

Parker shook his head. "This wouldn't be the first time I've arrested someone I considered to be a friend. But the evidence is compelling, and, of course, I won't be sharing it with you, Savannah. Your consultancy is suspended."

"Suspended! I haven't given you my results."

Amanda's shoulders slumped. "Guys, it's all right.

I am innocent, you know. The quicker we get this straightened out, the quicker I can be back here with Mother."

Savannah nodded. "We'll be looking into the case and doing everything we can to disprove any assertion of your guilt. I promise."

Amanda nodded absently. "I would rather have your promise that someone will be here with Mom while she's still in danger."

"I'm not sure we can do both," Savannah mused.

Detective Parker stepped closer to Amanda. He took her gently by the elbow. "We have to go now."

Amanda looked at Savannah. "Promise me you won't allow her to be alone. One more panic attack and she won't recover. Promise."

"Okay, I promise that one of us will be with her at all times. Now go. We'll manage."

Amanda walked alongside Detective Parker with her head bowed very low. At the door she turned to give her mother a teary look. "'Bye, Mom. I'll be back soon."

The room was ominously quiet, the only sound the hum of the oxygen.

Chapter 29

Saturday Morning

Savannah sat in the intensive-care visitor's chair, staring at her clenched hands. She was reeling from what had happened. Reluctantly, she agreed with Detective Parker's assessment of the evidence against Amanda. The combination of Martin and Amanda's lovers' argument, the bloodstained bottle hidden in her mother's closet, and Amanda's lack of an alibi would require serious examination. The fact that she had withheld information and had also evaded a warrant made it a dire situation.

There must be additional evidence for Parker to take steps to question Amanda downtown. Of course, he had probably searched her home. *I wonder what else he has found.*

Mrs. Blake was sleeping peacefully. Her labored breathing had calmed and was less noisy. As soon as they had arrived in the intensive-care ward, Savannah had recognized a high school friend of hers whom she had kept in touch with during her glassblowing scholarship in Seattle. That her friend had turned out to be the head nurse was a distinct advantage. After a conspiratorial chat, they had agreed that Savannah would be known as Amanda's long-lost cousin and would be permitted access to the room at any time. There were certainly benefits to returning home, where everyone knew you.

Sitting here is not going to get Amanda cleared. I know I promised to take care of Mrs. Blake, but I can't do it at the expense of Amanda's life.

Reviewing her options, she considered having Jacob or Edward come to Mrs. Blake's bedside, but she didn't think it would be an effective use of their time, either. Now that Amanda had been taken in for questioning, they had to work together quickly to find out what Martin had discovered when he found those bottles and to figure out who would kill him for that knowledge. It was the only way to stop Parker from arresting Amanda. Martin's death had to be connected to the bottles.

Rachel and Faith had told Savannah to call them once Amanda got arrested, but she needed their help now in a different way. The twins would be perfect as Mrs. Blake's advocates in the hospital. They were energetic, socially engaging, and willing to take on new adventures. Another advantage was that since there were two of them, they could take turns sitting with Mrs. Blake if one or the other needed a break.

Savannah immediately phoned them, and as expected, they were more than willing to help and promised to come right away to relieve Savannah. And sure enough, within fifteen minutes, the twins were sitting comfortably in two visitor's chairs. On the walk to the hospital parking garage, Savannah phoned Edward and Jacob to arrange for them to meet her at the studio to formulate a plan for clearing Amanda.

As soon as everyone had assembled in the conference room, Savannah spoke. "We have to clear Amanda, but since Detective Parker is busy with her, we are severely limited. How can we work around it?"

Jacob and Suzy were in their usual places at the end of the table. "Does she have a lawyer? They have to be given any evidence."

"You've been learning from your mother. Simply brilliant." She looked at Edward. "I don't think she has enough money for a lawyer. I may have to help."

"I don't know. I haven't got my head around the basics of your legal system. It's so different from the British, I find it impossible to follow."

"My mother can find out who her lawyer is," said Jacob. "She's a judge, you know."

Savannah smiled. "Points for Jacob again. Could you ask her for us? She knows Amanda."

"Would I have to call her?" Jacob's voice rose an octave. "I'm not good on the phone."

"You have a cell phone, right?"

Jacob nodded and pulled it out of the back pocket of his jeans. "Mother insists that I keep it fully charged and with me at all times."

"Do you know how to use it?"

"Mother taught me how to call her, but I haven't needed to."

Savannah sighed deeply and softened her voice. "We need you to call your mother and find out about Amanda's lawyer. This is part of being a team. Each

of us contributes important things in order for us all
to work best."

Edward turned to Jacob. "Please, mate. We need
you to do this."

Jacob pressed his lips into a thin line and placed
the phone on the table, then reached over to take
Suzy into his lap. He pressed the redial button. "Mom?
This is Jacob."

An alarmed voice answered. Edward looked at
Savannah, who closed her eyes and crossed her
fingers on both hands.

"This is not an emergency. My friend Amanda
needs help to get out of jail. Detective Parker is questioning her for the murder of Martin Lane. I told you
about my research for this investigation. Savannah
asks if you will find out who Amanda's lawyer is. We
need to know." Jacob nodded his head. "No, I won't."

He pushed a button to end the call and put the
phone back in his pocket without releasing Suzy.
"Amanda's lawyer's name is Lindsey Gardner, one of
my mom's former interns. She's had lots and lots of
interns."

Edward walked over and gave Jacob a high five.
"Great job, mate."

"Perfect. Thank you, Jacob. I know how difficult
it is to overcome a fear." Savannah stood up and
looked directly at Edward. "I'm still afraid of heights."

"We need to get cracking." Edward returned the
gaze as he took a seat.

Hands on her hips, Savannah circled the conference-room table. "We're running out of time. Let's
cut to the chase here and ask Amanda's lawyer for a
summary of the evidence against her. Edward, use
your fancy phone and find out where the lawyer's

office is. We need to bring her up to date on our investigations."

"Sure, sure." Edward bent over his phone and thumbed in the search. "She works at an office quite near where Martin washed ashore."

"Great. As soon as we're done here, we'll go see her." Savannah stared at the table. "It looks like we've completed almost every investigation we had going. I got my information from Dr. Smithfield. Jacob found those old maps at the library, and we've got an appointment with Paul and Julie to investigate possible sites for the bottles."

Edward stood and followed Savannah as she paced around the table. "Okay, we need to talk to Amanda's lawyer and then—"

Savannah returned to her seat. "Let's meet with Amanda's lawyer as quickly as she can see us. Jacob, I'd like for you to come with us to the lawyer's. You pick up on things everyone else misses. We shouldn't be long."

The wide grin on Jacob's face reminded Savannah that her teenage years had been full of adventure, as well. *This is precisely what he needs—a little adventure.*

Edward spoke forcefully. "Wait a tick. We also need to do some serious checking into Captain Collins. We stopped by his place that one time. Since then I've driven by twice, but he's making himself scarce. We need to run that to ground."

"Yes, yes," said Savannah. "We'll tackle him after talking to Amanda's lawyer."

After confirming that they could meet immediately with Attorney Gardner, they drove to the lawyer's office. It was obviously a former residence and blended into the Park Street neighborhood.

Only a small wooden sign next to the double front doors revealed that it was a professional office.

They opened the door and entered the waiting area, which had probably been the living room. A few seconds later a pale red-haired young woman entered the waiting area from an adjacent office. She stretched out her hand to Savannah.

"Hi. I'm Lindsey Gardner. Amanda told me I could count on you for information that might clear her completely. You must be Savannah."

Savannah nodded. "Nice to meet you, Ms. Gardner."

"Please call me Lindsey." She turned. "You must be Edward." She shook his hand, giving it a quick pump. "You must be Jacob and Suzy." She didn't offer her hand when Jacob nodded and picked up Suzy. "Take a seat in my office, and I'll let you know what's going on downtown."

They sat at a small, round conference table in her office.

"First, let me tell you right up front, I recently graduated from Stetson University College of Law— this past May, in fact—and this is my first solo case."

Savannah's eyes grew wide, and she looked at Edward and Jacob.

"Before you panic, let me assure you I think Amanda is wrongly accused. I also graduated in the top five percent of my class. I was appointed by the court as her defense attorney, and I intend to get her cleared as quickly as possible. First things first. If we can't come up with enough information to secure her release in the next"—she looked at her watch—"eighteen hours, she will be transferred to the county jail."

"We can't let that happen," said Savannah. "She needs to be with her mother, who is in the hospital."

"I know that. But if we can't clear her quickly enough, we can at least post bail."

Edward, Jacob, and Savannah looked at each other. Savannah turned to Lindsey. "I think I'm the only one who could post bond."

"No, you can't. You have already put yourself in debt to purchase the warehouse for the new studio," said Edward.

"*You* most certainly can't finance her bail. Your business is barely in the black, and you rent a condo. I can still mortgage my house," countered Savannah.

Lindsey tapped on the table. "We don't have to decide this minute. Let's hope it doesn't get to that. However, I'm relieved to know that you are willing to go so far for Amanda's sake."

Jacob looked directly at Lindsey and patted Suzy on the head. "Amanda is our friend. We want to help her."

He's beginning to handle stress much better, thought Savannah. He didn't pick Suzy up.

"I understand, but in order to do that, I need to know everything you know about the case. I understand that as a group of amateur investigators, you have had some successes in the past."

Savannah cleared her throat. "You must also realize that Amanda may have exaggerated about our expertise."

"Oh, it wasn't Amanda who told me about your successes. It was Detective Parker."

Chapter 30

Savannah stumbled into her house and plopped down directly onto the couch. Rooney decided she needed to be welcomed with a full body press and sloppy kisses as insurance.

"Rooney, please." She gave him a halfhearted shove, but it was a great joy to have him so excited to see her.

Her confidence in her ability to act as a consultant for Detective Parker had surged after Lindsey had revealed that he had told her about their prior successes as investigators. His regard was important to her. If she didn't act ethically in this investigation, he would close that door forever. That was something she wasn't willing to give up.

Savannah, Edward, and Jacob, who had held Suzy tightly, had all been expertly cross-examined by Lindsey on every point in the investigation. Savannah felt confident in Lindsey's ability to defend Amanda in court, if it came down to that. They had agreed, again, that the best solution would be to clear

Amanda before her defense attorney's skills were needed.

"Rooney, this heat saps the will out of me. You've been inside this air-conditioned bungalow, all cool and comfortable. I've been in and out of the car all day." She cuddled his gray head and scratched behind his droopy ears and finally said the words he was waiting for. "Do you want to go outside?"

He leaped up and turned around in a happy circle, dancing. Savannah smiled and grabbed his leash. She was halfway into their normal thirty-minute walk when she remembered she should have called the twins to ask about Amanda's mother. Her cell was inside the house, in her backpack.

"Okay, Rooney. You've succeeded in distracting me once again. Remind me to make sure I call Rachel and Faith."

Rooney looked up at her and cocked his head to the side.

"Of course you will."

As soon as she had fed and watered Rooney, she sat at the kitchen table, called the main hospital number, and asked for Mrs. Blake's room.

"Hello. This is Mrs. Blake's room. Faith Rosenberg speaking."

"This is Savannah. How's Mrs. Blake?"

"Hi, Savannah. I'm so glad you asked us to stay with her. She woke up about thirty minutes ago and had a panic attack. The nurses settled her down, but her breathing is now a bit worse. They've increased the oxygen level, but there's no change."

"Good grief. This keeps getting worse and worse. Can you stay awhile longer?"

"You just try to make us leave. This lady needs someone to watch over her every minute. Leave this to us. We'll let you know when there's a change, good or bad."

Savannah placed the receiver back on the wall-mounted phone and walked back into the living room. The old-fashioned message machine on the main phone blinked a numeral two, indicating two voice messages were waiting. She pressed the PLAY button.

"Savannah, this is Julie Wedlake calling. We've been exploring the sites Jacob identified this morning. I know we should have waited for you, but it turns out our new cameras are so powerful that we no longer need to wait for low tide. Anyway, the even better news is—"

The message stopped. Savannah rolled her eyes. It served her right for not replacing her dad's phone with one that included digital message recording. His still used a cassette tape. She pressed the message PLAY button again.

"Savannah, your machine cut me off. Anyway, reviewing the recordings, we've found two areas of bottom disturbance that might be what you're looking for. I've sent you a short video of them. If you want to be with us when we go back out to dive, give us a call. If so, we're launching at about four. Wear a swimsuit under casual clothes. It will be hot."

Savannah dialed Edward's cell. He picked up immediately.

"Paul and Julie have found two possible sites with their ROV. They want to know if we want to be with them when they dive there before it gets dark today. Do you want to go?"

"Absolutely! Come by the condo and pick me up. I'll be ready."

* * *

Savannah and Edward pulled into Julie and Paul's long driveway, got out, and then helped them load up their small dive boat with water, beer, and diving gear. They had a long dock that stretched out to water deep enough to launch a boat even during low tide.

After the fifth load, Edward questioned Paul. "Will there be enough room for passengers? This is a lot of stuff."

Paul smiled. "Yep, we tend to overpack the boat, just in case. Even though the boat is small, there should be enough room for the four of us. We're going to become close friends or new enemies." He laughed. "We won't be going fast, though. This is a lot of weight."

"How far are we going?" Savannah handed a picnic basket down to Julie, who magically found room for it.

"The areas of disturbance are at the second and third sites Jacob identified. Unfortunately, neither one is very close, so it will be about a twenty-minute ride. We'll be having a picnic supper after our first dive. If that one is a bust, then we'll check out the second."

By the time everything was loaded and they launched, they were all hot and had worked up a sweat. But the breeze of the moving boat cooled them down quickly. Julie passed beers around, and they gulped them down. Talking over the noise of the engine entailed a pattern of shouting something, followed by saying, "What did you say?" which ultimately forced them to travel in silence until Paul cut back the engine and dropped the anchor.

"This is the first site we found on the ROV camera. It's definitely an anomaly on the bottom of the bay, as it's not a natural disturbance. Biological bottom effects don't normally have sharp, regular edges, but we couldn't tell what caused this. Anyway, we'll know in a few minutes." Paul looked at Julie. "Do you want to take this one or wait for the second dive, if we need to go there?"

"Go ahead, dear. This might be as far as we have to go today." She smiled and began pulling various bits of gear out.

It was certainly a precarious process to get Paul outfitted with his scuba gear in such a confined space. They appeared to be used to the space crunch, and in no time Paul was over the side, with a bright yellow line attached to him.

With the boat still, the heat attacked them. Not a breath of air stirred to keep the swelter at bay. They watched Julie dole out the yellow line more and more, and then it stopped. They watched the bubbles on the water, mostly because there was nothing else to watch. The bubbles moved in a ten-foot radius and started another ten-foot circle when the bubbles stayed stationary.

Three sharp tugs on the yellow line was the signal for Julie to begin hauling it in to support Paul's return. In a few minutes, he was at the surface, and then he handed most of his gear to her while he removed it at the side of the boat.

"It was nothing. It looks like someone decided to clean out their garage and dump the contents here. Mostly old motors, car parts, a lawn mower, and other garden tools. It was done years ago, I think, because it was a push mower, and everything is covered in a thick layer of barnacles."

Julie helped him into the boat. He didn't bother drying off.

"Thanks, honey. Let's have our picnic supper, and then we'll push off to the second site."

They devoured the contents of the picnic basket, then weighed anchor. Several miles northward, Paul dropped anchor again in a wide channel of the Intra-coastal Waterway. He helped Julie put on her diving gear, and this time he belayed the yellow line. The heat found them again, their only company as they watched Julie's bubbles make circular searches on the bottom.

In the warm shimmer of the sea, Savannah ran through her list of worries. She was afraid they might not find anything on this expedition. What would happen if she couldn't clear Amanda? Would Amanda's mother fade away without seeing her daughter again?

The bubbles stopped moving, and everyone tensed to await whatever would be next. Savannah gasped when the bubbles stopped completely.

"What's wrong! Is she in trouble?"

"Hang on a second," Paul answered calmly. "She's holding her breath for a second. She does it when she finds something."

A large group of bubbles broke the surface, quickly followed by three tugs on the yellow line. Savannah and Edward looked at each other with raised eye-brows. Savannah showed Edward her crossed fingers on both hands.

Julie broke the surface and removed her scuba mask. "We found it. There's a whole load of blue bottles down there." Then she paddled her way to the boat. "I pulled one out of the bottom for you. It's in my dive bag."

By the time she had handed her gear to Paul and

had awkwardly made it into the boat, Savannah thought she would burst from wanting to handle the bottle. Finally, Julie removed the bottle and gave it over.

Nearly dropping it, Savannah removed the loose debris with her fingers and cleaned off the bottom of the bottle. After confirming her suspicions with a magnifying glass, she looked at Edward.

"This is a duplicate. We've found the dump site for the fake bottles."

Chapter 31

Savannah dropped Edward back at Queen's Head before returning to the hospital. He walked in and waved to his assistant manager and best bartender, Nicole Borawski.

"Good. Another update. I love following your detective adventures. Did you have any luck?" She grinned and tucked a pen behind her ear. Her good looks and her wicked smart sense of humor were major reasons why his new pub was becoming an area favorite.

"I don't think so, but it's hard to tell. We found a pile of fake bottles that had been dumped in one of Jacob's prospective treasure sites." Edward slipped in behind the counter. "Not sure how it helps or hurts the investigation."

"Have faith. You guys always find the bad guy."

"Well, I feel like we're spinning our wheels on this one. This is not the way to get Amanda out of the frame for Martin's murder."

"There was a guy here earlier. He was talking about bottles. Blue bottles, right?" said Nicole.

"Yes, they're called Bristol blue, from the type of cobalt used in their manufacture. The earliest version of that type of glass was first recorded in the late eighteenth century. These bottles were made in about seventeen eighty and could be part of José Gaspar's buried treasure. Who was talking about it?"

"He isn't a regular, but he's been here a few times. He drinks Guinness—unusual at this time of year. Most people switch to something a bit lighter for the dog days of summer, but not him."

"Talked about blue bottles? Was he a sandy-haired guy who looks like he's spent a lot of time outdoors?"

"Not very helpful. You've just described half the male population here in St. Petersburg." She laughed. "I'm not too observant about what men look like. What they drink? That's a different story. Remembering their drinks is how I get good tips."

"Was he with anyone?" Edward asked.

"Yes. His friend drank Jack Daniel's and Coke with a twist of lime. Yeah, that sounds right. He called Guinness guy Captain."

"I know him. He's Captain Collins. We've been trying to find him to get some information about Martin's diving activities. This could be important. What did he say?"

"He was saying he was in here last week, celebrating a new salvage site that appeared to be associated with Gaspar the Pirate. He said they had the specific blue bottles to prove it. I don't think he meant to say so much. He shut up after that and left right after he slammed his drink."

"Which way did he go? Did you see what kind of car he drove?" Edward quizzed.

"Hang on. I was handling the bar by myself, you know."

"Sorry. I know, but this is pretty serious. Amanda is still downtown, being questioned by who knows who for who knows what."

"I know. But I can still tell you only what I saw. Calm down."

Edward took several deep, slow breaths. "You're right. Did he happen to say he was going somewhere?"

"No, but he kept checking his watch. He must have had an appointment somewhere else."

"There are tons of places around here. But if I don't search, we don't have a chance at all. I need to tell Savannah. Thanks, Nicole." He kissed her on the cheek and left the pub.

He dialed Savannah from the parking lot. "Love, a bit of luck. Captain Collins stopped by the pub earlier and appeared to have an appointment. He told Nicole he had found some blue bottles that were dated from Gaspar the Pirate days. I'm going to try to find him."

"That's a great lead. Let me know if you track him down."

Edward rode his Indian motorcycle toward downtown and dropped in at the Amsterdam on the off chance that Captain Collins was repeating his stops from the celebratory bar crawl. Across the traffic circle and down a side street, he found the Captain's beat-up truck with the monster boat hitch mounted on the back.

He parked the Indian and considered the options. Captain Collins could be in the Amsterdam, the Burg, or the Flying Pig. All three bars were on the same street, half a block apart. All were well within reasonable walking distance of the truck and boat. If he selected the wrong one, chances were good Captain Collins would slip away. Nervously twirling his keys, he headed for the Amsterdam first. It was so small, probably less than five hundred square feet. It would take him only a second to ascertain if Captain Collins was there.

It did take only a second, even accounting for the vast difference between outside sunshine and inside darkness, to determine that Captain Collins wasn't there. He checked the Flying Pig next, since although it was larger, you could scan the entire bar in one glance. Not there, either.

Ferg's was an institution in St. Petersburg. It had opened in the late eighties and had grown in fits and starts from a small café with a bar into a three-stories-tall spread over an entire city block. If Captain Collins was there, there would be no quick way to find him.

Luck can favor the virtuous, thought Edward. *I need to have faith I will find him.*

He scanned the outside areas and then headed up a flight to one of the sports-focused rooms. There on a bar stool, with a full pint of beer in front of him, was Captain Collins, staring at one of the television screens with a raised fist and yelling, "The referee is blind. Throw *him* out of the game." He was sitting with a group of weather-beaten men who, Edward assumed, were pals in the salvage business.

Edward sat a few tables away. Far enough away not to be noticed, but close enough to hear their conversation. A waitress came by, and Edward ordered a Harp Lager. He settled in to spy on the captain.

Most of the group's conversation concerned a soccer game between the Tampa Bay Rowdies and the Atlanta Silverbacks that was being played in

Atlanta. Although primarily a rugby fan, Edward had to admit that the game was being expertly played. The fans seemed to be as passionate, but there weren't as many yobs as he had encountered back home in the UK. He still wasn't ready to embrace the sport over here.

During a break in the action, Captain Collins told his companions, "Don't forget. We need to get everything we can before word gets out."

Several of them nodded their heads.

"We know. Meet at five at your place. We'll be there," one of them said.

"You bet you will. If you don't show, no share in the treasure. It's final. No excuses, no negotiation. If you're not at my place at five in the morning, you're out your share, no matter how much you helped up to this point. Understood?"

They all raised their drinks and looked at each other one by one.

Edward signaled his waitress for the bill and quietly left Ferg's without being noticed by Captain Collins. He rode back down Central Avenue to Queen's Head and called Savannah's cell.

"I found Captain Collins at Ferg's, and I basically overheard him say he's taking his salvage crew out to retrieve more bottles tomorrow morning at five."

"He's running the salvage for the bottles?"

"Apparently. I think it's suspicious. Don't you?"

Savannah paused a few seconds. "I think we have to check it out. We would kick ourselves if we didn't run down everything we can think of."

"I'm afraid we've already thought of everything."

"If he killed Martin, there must be something we can find to help clear Amanda. Something."

"I feel the same."

"So, he'll be gone for several hours at least."

"Yeah, but we don't have a boat."

"We don't need a boat to look around his house trailer. Evidence that he's Martin's killer won't be in the gulf. It will be somewhere near Captain Collins. We've had a look around his warehouse. Now we need to search his home."

"Right. Knock me up at five, and we'll go have a look around."

Savannah looked puzzled. "Knock you up?"

"Sorry. I mean, stop by here at five." He shook his head slowly.

Chapter 32

Sunday Morning

Savannah turned off her cell phone alarm as quickly as she could to avoid waking Mrs. Blake. She had sent the Rosenberg twins home and had taken over the watch for the night. Mrs. Webberly had promised to take in Rooney, so she had covered that worry. The nursing staff had brought her bedding to use with the visitor's chair, which could be converted into a bed. It was uncomfortable, but it was better than trying to sit and sleep.

Mrs. Blake woke up twice in the night but didn't panic and tear her way out of the oxygen tent. Plus, her breathing seemed easier. The nurses felt this was a good sign.

After folding her chair bed back into its daytime configuration, Savannah folded the sheets and blankets into a neat package and placed them in the closet. She was convinced at least another night at the hospital would be in the cards.

She told the head nurse to expect Rachel and

Faith at any minute, then picked Edward up at his condo. It was five o'clock on the dot.

"I grabbed us some scones from Queen's Head." Edward handed one to Savannah after he had settled into the Mini. "I've also got a thermos of coffee."

"Thanks. This seems like the kind of morning when even my coffee needs coffee."

"Funny. Any word on Amanda?"

"I called Lindsey last night, and they had held Amanda in custody. If she hadn't fled, I think she would have been able to come back to the hospital."

They drove slowly by Captain Collins's small concrete-block house, which was not far from Park Street but was definitely in a small working-class neighborhood. There was no one around. There were several cars parked in his driveway, but his truck was gone from the carport.

"I think we'll park on the next block and walk down the alleyway. It's our best chance at looking around without the neighbors finding out and telling him," Savannah said.

"Is this wise?" Edward looked sideways at her. "No one walks in America. We'll stick out like tourists."

"Good point. Let's see what I can find."

She circled a few blocks and happened upon a nearby neighborhood park. "This will do. We can be early morning walkers, and then we'll veer off to get a good look at Captain Collins's place."

After making a show of power walking around the small park, they arrived at the back of the house. Savannah walked into the screened-in lanai in the back and opened the back door.

"This is just plain wrong. No one leaves their house unlocked these days," she said.

"Look at this." Edward pointed to the metal doorjamb. "It's been bent by something, like a screwdriver. Someone has broken into his house."

"Do you think they're still in there?"

"I don't think so. Listen. It's too quiet."

"Lucky for us and Amanda, as well."

The back door opened directly into a kitchen that hadn't been updated since the house was built in the 1950s. A terrazzo floor, popcorn ceilings, painted kitchen cabinets over square-tile countertops with ancient grouting screaming for a good cleaning. Coffee cups were sitting in the sink, but all was reasonably neat. The living room was open to the kitchen and was furnished with a sectional, a side chair, and a large flat-screen television mounted on the far wall.

"Nothing much here." Savannah put her hands on her hips. "We need to find something to help Amanda."

"Let's see what's in the bedrooms. It looks like there are only two."

They walked down the hall and peeked into a small bathroom with mint-green fixtures.

"Ugh," grunted Savannah. "If he keeps all this original, this will be worth something in about twenty more years."

The bedroom facing the street was obviously used by Captain Collins. There was a bed with only one bedside table, which held a lamp and a tall stack of books. The only other furniture in the room was a chest of drawers.

"Nothing here. One last room, and then we're done." Edward opened the door to the second bedroom. "Ha! Here's where he's cleaning them."

The open door revealed three tables set along the perimeter of the small bedroom, with a chair in front of each table. All were stacked with uncleaned blue bottles on the right, and a towel sat in the center, surrounded by brushes, scrubbing pads, and cleaning liquids. The left side was obviously reserved for the cleaned bottles, but there weren't any.

"No wonder they're out getting more bottles today," said Savannah as she picked up one of the uncleaned bottles. "These are originals—not the copies. I wish I knew what it means. There's what? Only seven bottles ready for cleaning?" She pulled out her cell and began taking pictures of everything in the room.

Edward moved over to another table, which was set up for packaging. There was a flat stack of boxes ready to be assembled, along with a small roll of bubble wrap. Pens, labels, and two kinds of packing tape were lined up, ready to use.

Savannah stood beside him and snapped a few pictures of that table, as well.

"Hey, we'd better get out of here." He looked at his watch. "It looks like people should be coming in to work on these last few bottles and then to start on the ones they bring up today."

"Right," said Savannah. "One last picture." She took a wide shot of the entire room.

They had reached the back door when they heard a key unlocking the front door. They ran like deer but froze in their tracks at the sound of a pump-action shotgun racking and a loud "Stop right where you are!"

Edward and Savannah instinctively raised their hands.

"Turn around slowly."

They carefully faced a very large shotgun barrel that was being pointed at them by Captain Collins.

"What's going on? What are you doing in my house?"

"Sorry. We tried to call, but there was no answer," said Savannah. She swallowed hard to calm her shaky voice. "The door was already busted open, and we thought you might be hurt. We wanted only to talk to you about Martin and his salvage dives."

"You two are messing around in something you don't understand. It can get you killed." He waved the shotgun alternately between the two of them. "Martin has already paid the price for being too curious. Is that what you want, as well?"

Edward slowly lowered one hand and grabbed Savannah by the upper arm. "No! We don't want to bother you at all. Now that we see you're fine, we'll just be getting along. No worries at all, mate."

They watched as Captain Collins lowered the shotgun and waved them away with his other hand.

They scooted out the door like the scared rabbits they were.

Back in the Mini, they put some distance between themselves and the captain's house before pulling into a drugstore parking lot. Edward poured good strong coffee into the cup of the thermos and handed it over to Savannah.

She sipped the brew down to the bottom of the cup and sighed, "Heaven. I feel nearly human."

Edward smiled. "I definitely prefer you in the human state." He leaned over and gave her a soft kiss. "Good morning."

"It's been an awful week, hasn't it? We haven't had a minute alone since . . . since this business with Martin began. I'm sorry."

"Why are you sorry? This is what we do. We help friends in trouble."

"I don't feel like we're helping Amanda at the moment. I can't seem to figure out what the bottles have to do with Martin's death. Why are there copies? Who is making copies? What could Martin have discovered to make Captain Collins kill him?"

"It's not coming together, is it?" Edward reached for her cup and refilled it.

"We've never collected the clues in a sensible order. We always have to figure out what all the disjointed facts mean when viewed from the killer's perspective. I've never felt so inept."

"This isn't helping. What next?"

Savannah gulped down the second cup of coffee. "Right now I don't have a clue how to point Detective Parker to Captain Collins. Although very scary, pointing a shotgun at us will not be enough to clear Amanda." She drained the cup and handed it back to Edward. "I think I'll take a long run with Rooney. I do my best thinking when we're running. Let's meet at the studio in about an hour. I'll call Jacob and see if he can help us figure out what to do next."

Chapter 33

Sunday Morning

Savannah stood in front of the corkboard, pinning up a picture of Captain Collins next to the blue bottles. "Let's go back to square one and see if there's anything else we can discover. Let's think about what we've done. Have we exhausted everything?"

Jacob sat straight in his chair. "We haven't found the bottles."

Savannah bit the corner of her lip. "We've talked to Amanda's lawyer. Is there anything else we can learn?"

"What about researching the ship that carried the bottles?" Edward asked. "Did it reach its port?"

"We don't think it did, but we don't have solid evidence. Jacob, do you think your librarian friend could help with the history of the ship?"

"Yes."

Savannah pinned up a picture of a period merchant ship. "One of the things it can lead to is a more likely location for the genuine Bristol blue bottles. Then we can have Paul and Julie help us find where Captain Collins is salvaging them."

"It's frustrating," Edward said.

"Why don't we all talk to Jacob's librarian." Savannah grabbed her keys.

They drove down to the main library on Ninth Avenue and got there a few minutes after it opened at noon. Savannah and Edward followed Jacob and Suzy into the mid-century-style building. It had recently been remodeled to return it to its original look after an unfortunate eighties update. It was the first time Savannah had been in the building since she'd used it for high school research papers.

"Oh, wow! This is nice. It looks more fifties than the original fifties," she noted.

Savannah and Edward followed Jacob and Suzy as they turned left at the first corner and walked into a large room with generously sized worktables surrounded by cases and cabinets with every type, size, and flavor of reference materials. Behind a row of desks sat the librarian. She was a young, fresh-faced hipster who wore her red hair in a topknot decorated with number two yellow pencils. The nameplate in front of her desk read BETSY KING.

"Good morning, Jacob." Ms. King came out from behind her desk to lift up Suzy and give her cuddles. "Good morning, Suzy. Thanks for bringing my favorite patron in this morning. He always brings me a research challenge that makes my day. Who is with you, Jacob?"

Jacob stood taller. "Good morning, Miss Betsy. Miss Betsy, this is Miss Savannah Webb. She owns the glass shop where I work. This is my friend Edward Morris. He owns Queen's Head Pub, and he helps when we investigate cases for the police. We're here to ask more questions about the case of the cracked bottle."

Savannah and Edward looked at each other. They were impressed with Jacob's longest speech ever.

Jacob beamed at Savannah and then turned back to Betsy. "We have another research task. The blue bottles I asked about earlier this week could have been cargo on a ship leaving Bristol, England, and travelling to America sometime between the years seventeen eighty and eighteen thirty." He smiled at her. "We need to know the name of any ship captured by Gaspar the Pirate."

Betsy lit up like a Christmas tree. "Fantastic! I have my notes on the Bristol blue bottles, so I'll expand the search to include known cargo shipments to America that were insured and lost at sea."

"Yes, ma'am. That is the exact information we need," Jacob said.

"This will take a little time, however. If you would like to have a little walk around the place, I should have something to report in about thirty minutes." She looked at her watch. "Be back about twelve thirty."

Savannah jerked her head back. "Are you sure?"

The librarian nodded. "I have some friends I can contact who will be able to tell me quickly if the records exist. Then it's a matter of getting them to send them to me. Easy!"

"Suzy and I will be looking at the DVDs."

Savannah watched Jacob lead Suzy into the main stacks in the next large room. She turned to Edward. "I'm so frustrated. Each bit of information leads only to more questions. Nothing is leading to answers."

"It will." Edward looked at her. He reached out and took her hand. "We're doing the best we can."

"It's not good enough. Amanda has been taken in for questioning, and we have only hours before she is

charged, then transferred over to the county jail."
She looked at her watch. "They'll probably do it on
Monday."

"Let's walk in the back garden."

Edward turned, led Savannah back the way they
had come, and pulled her outside, and they walked
along a winding path that ended up at a lake's edge.
A short bench faced the lake, and Edward sat and
pulled Savannah down next to him. "Just relax. We're
doing everything we can at the moment."

"I know. I know." Savannah lifted her feet onto
the bench and leaned into Edward's shoulder. They
sat there in the shade, a faint breeze rustling the
leaves. In a few more minutes, the sound of birds
was the only conversation. It felt perfectly natural.

Savannah drifted off and awoke to Edward's
jostling.

"It's been a half hour. Let's see what she has found,"
he said.

Betsy was standing at the desk, waving at them
to come over when Savannah, Edward, and Jacob
rounded the corner. Jacob picked up Suzy, and they
stood like children awaiting the call to lunch.

"There was indeed a ship carrying a large cargo
of freshly manufactured Bristol blue bottles in eighteen thirty-eight. The name of the vessel was the *Blue
Lady.* Her last known location was St. Augustine, but
she never reached the Port of Galveston and was
reported as captured by pirates, with all souls lost."
She paused and looked up from her notes. "Sadly, it
was the way of it. The entire crew would have been
killed or conscripted at threat of death."

Savannah turned to Jacob. "This is what we're
trying to find. Let's go back and look at your maps

and see if we can target more sites for Paul and Julie to examine."

Back at the studio, they stood around the conference table, and even Suzy was sniffing the papers, looking for a likely place on the old maps but one that was out of the way on the new charts.

Edward and Savannah mainly stood back while Jacob's fingers traced incomprehensible paths on both the old maps and the new charts that Savannah bought at the marine store. After a long wait, he pointed at one of the new charts. "This is the best place to look."

"Why?" asked Savannah. "I don't see the logic of your choice."

Jacob pointed to a large sheet of paper on the conference table. It was a hand-drawn marine chart of the inlets and channels near the beach where Martin's body was found. He adjusted it until it lined up perfectly with the edge of the conference table.

"This chart is a compilation of all the charts available during the time of Gaspar the Pirate's raids. I used all the versions that the library could get to draw a composite. Although they look similar, there are details that point to locations from the old maps that would have been in protected inlets but are now out in the middle of the waterway. I have the five most likely spots circled in red on my maps. But I think this one is the best choice. It would have been a small, protected harbor where the pirates could have destroyed the ship and buried the valuables. The other ones are still possible, but in diminishing order of likelihood. Still, I think all five are probable."

He looked at both Edward and Savannah, then sat down and waited.

"I'm bowled over," said Edward. "We need to get these checked out right now."

Savannah reached for her cell. "Absolutely. Let's see if we can use the ROV." She called the couple. "Hi, Paul. We've gotten more information from the library, and Jacob has identified several more sites we would like to investigate. Are you still interested?"

"We were hoping you would call. Having a real objective is so much more interesting than yet another anonymous data trip."

Savannah nodded in the affirmative for Edward and Jacob. "Great. Is it possible for us to go out this afternoon?"

There was a long wait. Savannah put the phone against her chest and whispered, "He's asking Julie. Apparently, they had another location in mind for this afternoon." She put the cell phone back to her ear. "Yes, we'd like to ride along. Okay. We'll be there in about fifteen minutes."

Chapter 34

Sunday Morning

Savannah and Edward dropped Jacob off at his house. Frowning, Jacob pointed out that the old maps and new charts were especially difficult to correlate, and for the sake of efficiency, he should be allowed to ride in the boat.

"Please, I'm the one who found the site. Besides, I want to see how they operate the robot."

"I promise to arrange a demonstration." Savannah waved him along. "They have an Olympic-sized swimming pool they use for camera evaluation and robot calibration."

He still frowned and picked up Suzy. "It's not fair."

Savannah smiled. "What if I ask them if you can steer the robot using the remote control joystick? It's a lot like a video-game controller. A little more sophisticated, but very similar. Deal?"

Jacob nodded. "It's a deal."

In a bare ten minutes, Savannah and Edward were helping load the boat and then casting off from the dock. Edward was showing Paul the new location for their bottle search when Julie swerved the boat around a floating obstacle.

"Hey," yelled Paul. "What's the idea?"

Savannah had grabbed onto Edward and had caused him to fall on her, creating a tangle of knees and elbows.

"Love, this is not the time and place." He laughed at her expression.

Savannah slugged him in the arm.

"Sorry," said Julie. "I almost plowed us right into the submerged trunk of a palm tree. You know how dense they are. It could have punched a hole in the boat."

Over Edward's shoulder, Savannah caught a glimpse of a shiny orange flash in the mangrove bushes along the shore. "Julie, can you circle back? I think I saw something hidden back there."

Edward twisted around to scan the shore, while Julie made a large circle and then dropped the anchor on the spot. "There shouldn't be anyone in this area. There aren't any homes nearby, and this is not a good fishing spot. Let's launch Red Rover to see if we can figure out what's going on without alarming anyone."

Paul and Julie checked the battery charges on both the vehicle and the controller, then ensured that the display application was working on the ruggedized laptop, before they slipped the ROV over the side. Paul double-checked that the umbilical cord was feeding out smoothly. Red Rover sank and was under powered control in a mere few seconds. The laptop displayed images of a white sandy bottom crisscrossed with mangrove roots. Then the screen showed the bottom of a scratched and scraped boat, anchored at both bow and stern.

Paul looked up from the display. "Someone meant for this to stay right here."

"Can we tell if anyone is aboard?" Savannah asked.

"Not from using Red Rover. Unless someone is peering over the side. Even if I bring Red Rover to the surface, there's no way to verify that the occupants aren't on the other side or ducking down to hide."

Savannah squinted at the image. "Can you bring it back a little distance so we can see the colors just above the surface?"

"Hmm." Paul fiddled with the controls. "I can rock the motors so the camera is tilted upward for a second." He stared at the display and managed to get a quick flash of the topside of the boat.

"It looks like Captain Collins's salvage boat." Savannah squinted again at the display. "Can you rewind and freeze on a frame?"

"Absolutely. Let me park Red Rover out of harm's way, and we can search for an image." Paul manipulated the ROV controls and set it to pause. He tapped a few keys on the laptop, and the screen filled with a sequence of images. He stopped on one that showed the whole side of the boat.

Edward pointed to the screen. "The boat belongs to Captain Collins for certain. It looks abandoned."

"No, it's not abandoned. It's hidden," Paul said. "Look, there are lines tied to several sturdy mangroves, and two anchors are set. I wonder why he decided to hide it here. It looks like whoever was on board might have used a small dinghy to leave." He pointed to the back of the boat. "You can see where something was usually tied back there on the stern." He grinned. "One aspect of having a dirty boat is you can easily tell how it's been used."

"Is that blood?" Savannah pointed to a large spot near the stern. It had dried, but the drips were a shade of red brown and looked fresh. She grabbed her phone from her backpack. "I'm calling Detective Parker." She placed the call, and the detective picked up before the second ring.

"Detective Parker, this is Savannah. You're on speaker. We're out in the Intracoastal Waterway, near Jungle Prada Park, with Paul and Julie Wedlake, using their underwater robotic camera. Captain Collin's salvage boat is hidden here, with no one on board that we can see, and there's fresh blood on the boat."

"It could be fish blood," the detective replied.

"Except that Captain Collins never fishes. He's strictly a dive and salvage operation."

She waited through a long moment of silence.

"I'm sending a marine patrol boat to investigate. Give me the coordinates."

She shrugged her shoulders at Paul. "I'll text them to you."

"Thanks. Savannah. Stay away from the site. Let the patrol boat have clear access."

"Absolutely." Savannah ended the call and cleared her throat. "Okay, you heard him. We need to get cracking. Remember where Amanda is while we're out here."

"Absolutely." Edward sat back next to Savannah. "Let's find the bottles."

Paul retrieved Red Rover, stowed it and the controller, then snapped the laptop back in its case, and they were soon on their way. It proved to be exactly as difficult as Jacob had predicted to find the right spot. After the fifth trial Red Rover launch and recalculation of the coordinates, Savannah regretted not letting him come along to interpret the disparities between the old maps and the new charts.

"Okay, I think this is it," Paul said. "Well, I think it's a possible site. I've stopped being sure we're over the equivalent site on Jacob's old maps. Anyway, let's look here." He set the anchor and launched Red Rover with a low toss into the waterway.

The display revealed the Red Rover's slow dive to the bottom.

"This new camera is giving us a clearer image than a human diver would see. It's so much quicker to drive this around than for us to do the same fully suited," Paul observed.

Paul clicked on the keyboard and brought up the chart in another window. In the center was a little red square. "That's where Red Rover is at the moment. With this feature"—he clicked on another selection from a pull-down menu—"we can leave a search trail on the display, so we know where it's been and we don't backtrack. Well, at least we will know *when* we backtrack. The bottom terrain sometimes foils the best search algorithms."

Julie piped up. "You like driving it, anyway. Don't blame the algorithms. If you gave them more time to learn, those algorithms would be better."

Paul frowned but kept his concentration focused on the controls. "This is where I think Jacob indicated the wreckage is most likely to be." He slowed the motors down a notch and started a systematic search of the area in larger and larger circles from the center point.

At the beginning of the fourth circuit around

Jacob's coordinates, Julie tapped Paul on the shoulder. "Wait, wait. I saw something on the edge of the screen."

Paul paused the Red Rover. "Which way? Show me on the screen which corner."

Julie pointed to the lower left-hand corner. "There it was. Just a glimpse."

Paul returned his attention to the controls and manipulated Red Rover to replicate Julie's sighting. He slowed the ROV's speed and began a new small grid search. Within a few seconds, a funny-looking lump appeared on the bottom.

"There," Julie said. "That's the shape I saw."

Savannah peered at the screen. "It could be a bottle that's been buried neck down."

"I've saved the precise GPS location so we can return here. I'm going to raise Red Rover to expand the viewing area." Paul guided Red Rover up a few feet, and the screen filled with single lumps similar to the first one. "Yes! Yes! This is it." He pointed to one of the shapes. "What do you think, Savannah?"

"It is definitely a bottle. Can you go down and bring some up?"

"Absolutely." He turned and revealed a huge smile. "Julie, keep Red Rover steady, and I'll follow the tether to the bottles." He passed the controller to Julie, and as quickly as he could, he put on his dive gear. In only a few minutes, he was over the side.

Julie was concentrating on keeping Red Rover steady, while Savannah and Edward were staring at the display. It wasn't long before they saw Paul. He gave a wave to them and dropped down to the lumpy bottom. He picked up the first bottle they had located. It was a few feet from the rest. He shook the loose sand from it and held it in front of the camera.

"Look." Savannah pointed at the screen. "You can see the blue. It's either a copy or an original. It's too dirty to tell."

They watched as Paul put the bottle in his dive bag, then moved over to the area where the other items were clustered. He picked up something small, and he waved it in front of the camera in agitated excitement.

"What has he found?" Savannah asked Julie. "I can't tell, because he's not keeping it still."

"I don't know, either. He won't be still."

They watched in silence while he stowed the small object in his dive bag and retrieved several more bottles.

Julie yelled at the screen. "For heaven's sake, Paul. Bring them up here so we can see them."

Savannah laughed. "Look. He must have heard you."

Paul looked into the camera and showed them a thumbs-up.

"It's works that way with us sometimes. Watch for him and help him get in the boat."

Paul surfaced, holding a small disk in one hand. He pulled off his face mask. "It's a piece of stamped gold. I think we've found Gaspar's treasure."

Chapter 35

Sunday Morning

Everyone cheered and helped Paul get on board and out of his tank and flippers.

"The bottles are mixed in with coins." He was breathless with excitement. "The whole site is only about two foot square. Without Red Rover, we could have been diving for years and missing it by inches."

Julie tapped Paul on the shoulder. When he turned, she gave him an enthusiastic kiss and a high five. "Wonderful find. Are you forgetting something?"

"Forgetting? Oh, right. Let's get Red Rover back on board."

They turned to the task of retrieving Red Rover, performing the smooth actions of a practiced routine. After all the retrieval, the rinsing, the shutdowns, and the checks were completed, they turned to the contents of Paul's dive bag. He pulled out six bottles and three clumps of coins.

"I took everything that was visible from the surface. We can use one of my other cameras to search the area for more artifacts. This is more than enough to get grant funding for a thorough scientific study."

Paul and Julie high-fived again.

Edward turned to Savannah to say something, but a whizzing sound passed between them. Edward yelped, grabbed his arm, overbalanced himself, and tipped over the side of the boat. Savannah stepped on the gunwale and dove in after him. She grabbed his shirt and hauled him to the surface.

He spluttered, coughed, and looked totally confused. "What was that?"

"It sounded like a bullet."

Edward looked at his upper arm. It was bleeding, the blood running in a wide stream from a narrow gash. "Someone's shooting at us!"

Paul and Julie appeared at the side of the boat. "Hey, this is no time for a swim. We need to get back—"

"Duck!" yelled Savannah. "Edward's been shot. Someone is out there shooting at the boat."

"What! Is he okay?" Paul turned around and scanned the far horizon. "There's a small boat about fifty yards away. That has to be it. Hurry back on board!"

"For heaven's sake, get down! You're giving the shooter a perfect target," Savannah said.

Savannah and Edward swam back to the side of the boat. Paul and Julie helped them back on board, and they all crouched low among all the equipment. Savannah looked at Edward's arm. The furrow wasn't deep, but blood was running down his arm in a stream.

"Julie, can you get to the first-aid kit? Edward's bleeding needs to be stopped quickly. Paul, can you call the Coast Guard?"

Julie scrambled on all fours to grab a small first-aid kit, while Paul reached up to grab the radio mic.

Zinggg!

"Hey! That was close." Paul dropped down below the gunwales again. "I can't reach the radio."

"Where's my backpack? I'm calling Detective Parker."

Julie made her way to the pile of personal stuff and tossed Savannah's backpack to her. Savannah pulled out her cell and dialed Parker.

"Hi, Savannah. No, we have not released Amanda. She is—"

"David, it's not about Amanda. Edward has been shot. We're out in the Intracoastal Waterway, near Jungle Prada Park, and we're being attacked."

"How bad is Edward? Can you get away?"

"Edward's good. It's a shallow crease on his upper arm. The big problem is the shooter has us pinned down."

"I'll divert the marine police to you. Keep out of range if you can. If the shooter is alone, he can't shoot and drive the boat. Use the time to escape. Over and out."

"You heard him." Savannah stowed the phone. Although they had crouched down as low as they could, it wasn't enough for them to avoid being a target.

Paul eyed their profiles. "Let's pile some of this gear higher so we have more shelter."

"Brilliant idea," said Edward. He started to reach for a box to stack.

Savannah pulled him back down by the tail of his shirt. "Not so fast. Let me get a compress on this wound, or you're going to pass out."

"Fine, but hurry."

Savannah pressed the wound with wadding until the bleeding slowed. Then she placed a large gauze pad over the furrow and taped it on tight enough to keep the wound compressed.

They all stacked equipment and coolers in the center of the boat. The pile added a foot to the silhouette of the boat and made it easier to hide from the shooter.

"Paul, can you see the boat?" Savannah whispered. "It was way out there when he shot at Edward."

Paul poked his head above the equipment barrier and ducked down again. "The boat is coming at us full throttle. We've got to move quickly, or we're going to get shot. I'm going to raise the anchor. I can do it without being seen. Julie, break out the emergency paddles."

"Good," said Savannah. "If we can get to the mangroves, we can slip away."

"One of the paddles is on this side." Julie scooted down toward the stern and unhooked a short paddle. She handed it to Savannah and crawled to the other side of the boat. Savannah heard her curse. "It's stuck. One of the clips that holds it is bent."

Edward peered over the top of the equipment barrier. "There's a small boat right on top of us. Wait! The boat has run aground."

Savannah looked at the boat. It was a small, low-riding johnboat with a loud engine. It was less than twenty yards from them.

Julie pointed to just beyond the grounded johnboat. "There's Captain Collins in a rubber dinghy."

"The shooter is Captain Collins. Oh, crap!" Savannah yelled. "He's aiming at us. Get in the water. Bullets are completely useless at depths more than two feet. Hide under the boat!" She grabbed Edward's good hand, and as they all jumped overboard, the crack of a rifle struck cold fear in Savannah's heart. They were sitting ducks.

As soon they surfaced, they heard a blaring siren, quickly followed by "Put down the weapon," shouted through a bullhorn. "Put down the weapon and raise your hands now!"

Savannah and Edward swam to the stern of the boat and hung on to the rear anchor chain. She had a clear view of the person standing in the grounded boat and swinging a rifle toward the police launch.

"That's Vicki! She's going to shoot," said Savannah.

Vicki screamed at the top of her lungs, "That treasure is mine! No one is taking it away from me. I've killed for it!"

About twenty yards away, Captain Collins motored his rubber dinghy directly toward her. Vicki fired. The police officers returned fire. Vicki dropped the rifle overboard and fell back into the boat. Captain Collins cut back the throttle, and the dinghy slowed and finally bumped into the johnboat. He looked down into Vicki's boat and shook his head from side to side. He yelled, "She's dead." Then he put his rifle down in the bottom of his dinghy and raised his hands high.

The sudden silence was crushing.

The police launch anchored behind Captain Collins, and the officers swarmed over both boats, securing the scene.

Savannah grabbed Edward. "Hold me. Hold me very tight." She buried her face in his chest.

It seemed like they were held there by the police for a hundred years, but Savannah realized it was probably only a little over an hour, and then everyone traipsed downtown to give signed statements.

While they stood outside the station, Captain Collins explained that he became suspicious of Vicki's erratic behavior after he and Martin found a small cache of bottles. He discovered that she had arranged to get copies of the bottles made by a glass artist downtown who specialized in molded objects. She was going to take those few bottles and sell them for three thousand dollars each.

"We found your boat and couldn't figure out what had happened," Edward said.

"Little did she know that the original bottles are now worth about thirty thousand dollars, if not more," said Savannah.

"Apparently, Martin disagreed about selling the forgeries, and she flew into a rage and struck him." The captain shook his head. "I would like to think she didn't mean to kill him."

"Why was she on the Intracostal?" asked Edward.

"She was convinced that I had found the main treasure trove. I hid my salvage boat and took the dinghy to throw her off my trail." Captain Collins shrugged his shoulders. "I am a salvage expert. I had to try to find Martin's cache."

"It's sad, but Gaspar's treasure is now in the hands of the scientists. That's where it should be," said Savannah.

Chapter 36

The afternoon sun was still blazing white heat through the heavily tinted windows of the Queen's Head dining room. The large ceiling fans helped the struggling air conditioner keep the blistering heat at bay, but it was the company that was cool. Edward had reconfigured the two tables on the east side of the pub to accommodate those Savannah had invited to celebrate Amanda's release as a murder suspect.

Edward entered from behind the bar with a flight of new draft brews to try. He stood next to Savannah and placed the small box filled with four small glasses in front of her. "I've been experimenting with different beers lately, so I have a full selection, from a light wheat ale to the boldest stout. I have a box like this for everyone—except Jacob, of course. This will be fun."

Bartender Nicole helped him place a box of beer samples at every setting.

"I borrowed these from 3 Daughters Brewing. I think I counted correctly, but we'll see," Edward noted.

A quiet Jacob arrived with Suzy. He sat across from Savannah. He smiled hello to Nicole and ordered a root beer.

The Rosenberg sisters arrived in eye-piercing head-to-toe silver garb. "We're here!" they said in unison.

Rachel smiled at Faith, then said, "Mrs. Blake is recovering so nicely that the hospital—"

"Scooted us away earlier this afternoon," Faith said, finishing her sister's statement. "They've taken her back to the Abbey, and she's all settled by now."

Savannah leapt up and gave them each a big hug. "You two were absolutely fabulous with Mrs. Blake. I'm sure Amanda is immensely grateful." She guided them to a pair of seats, and Edward tried to give them each a beer sampler.

"Oh no, Edward. We are cosmopolitan girls," said Rachel.

"Yes. Nicole knows what we like," said Faith.

"Coming right up. Two cosmopolitans—shaken, not stirred." Nicole reached for the large Belvedere Vodka bottle behind the bar and started to make their cocktails.

Paul and Julie arrived just then.

"We have something to show you," Paul said as he placed a shiny coin down on the surface of the table. "It's from the right time period, but not unique in any way. It's the bottles that identify the treasure as belonging to José Gaspar, but it's not yet a verified discovery. I've started the horrendous paperwork to claim it." He nodded at Jacob and Suzy. "We're including Jacob as a principle. Without his analysis . . . Well, it would still be undiscovered. Even so, it may take years of scholarly research."

Nicole placed their sampler boxes in front of them after they sat.

Julie turned to the group. "We were disappointed at first, but then we realized this would be valuable for attracting funding for our robotic bottom-mapping project. A little pirate mystique will put us at the top of the allocation lists." She smiled at Paul, lifted one of her beer samples. "Here's to grant funding. May it never end."

Paul clinked her glass, sipped deeply, and followed that with an enthusiastic kiss. "I agree completely."

Julie blushed, then raised up a finger. "But here's the even better news. It has already gotten out that we found the treasure with Red Rover. We've been getting e-mails from serious treasure hunters, asking to buy our system. We may not even need grant money if even ten percent of these orders come through."

Tracy stood at the door. Halfway in and halfway out. "Is this the party for Amanda?"

Savannah walked over to her. "Yes, Tracy. I'm so glad you could come. I'm so sorry that we barged in on you at the university. That was not one of my better decisions this week."

"No. Don't apologize. I'm glad. This has shaken me out of my shell. I made a terrible mistake by not getting in touch with Martin. Now it's too late."

"Don't be so harsh. Families don't always make sense. He should have tried harder to stay connected. You're welcome here."

She smiled weakly. "Thanks."

Savannah turned at the sound of the door opening. "Here's our guest of honor."

Amanda walked through the door, dressed for a celebration in a pink paisley midi dress and rhinestone flip-flops, her hair tinged violet. She and Savannah hugged for a long moment.

Savannah waved her hand. "Sit here at the head of the table, next to me."

Lindsey followed Amanda and smiled at everyone at the table. She sat next to Amanda and thanked Edward for the beer sampler.

The door opened again, and Captain Collins entered. He sat at the far end and waved a friendly hand. "Hey, guys. Thanks for inviting me. I'm very happy things are set straight."

Later Amanda ordered her favorite pint. "It wasn't obvious, to me at least, that Vicki was incensed by my relationship with Martin. When he began talking about meeting his sister and getting married, Vicki must have stalked him to his favorite dive spot and killed him with one of their creations. She put a bottle in Martin's dive bag to lead the murder investigation to me, because she knew he took the bottles to the workshop. When that wasn't effective enough, she planted the bottle used to murder Martin in my mother's room at the Abbey. She just walked in there, bold as brass, and no one even glanced her way. I'm afraid that's the way with most nursing homes. There are so many visitors and so little staff. If you walk in like you belong there, no one will bat an eye."

"That one worked," Jacob said in a clear voice. "I'm glad you're out of jail." He leaned over and gave Amanda a side hug.

She froze during the hug. "Thank you, Jacob. I appreciate it very much. I missed everyone a lot." A big tear ran down her cheek. "I've checked out a support group recommended by my mom's nursing staff. They have convinced me it will help with the stress of being a caregiver and will boost my self-confidence, as well. I've been a terrible person to the best friends in the world. I'm truly sorry. Anyway, I'm going to give it a try."

Jacob straightened up in his chair. "I am going to assist with more map locations for Red Rover."

Paul nodded. "Oh yes! He's our newest consultant in the ROV business."

Edward stood and waved a hand at Nicole. She approached their table with a tray laden with fresh pints of golden ale. "What our server is placing in front of each of you, except Jacob, of course, is a new ale I helped the brewer create for this special occasion. I've named it Tall Trouble, and I dedicate it to Savannah." He turned to her, and they all lifted their pints and saluted her.

Savannah blushed but tasted the brew. "Oh, my goodness. This is perfect! Everything I like in a craft beer is in this delicious brew." She looked around the table. "In light of our experience over the past few days, I have a new appreciation for the terrible effect that secrets can have on friendships and also relationships." She looked over at Edward. "This is the perfect time to tell you that Edward and I are well and truly friends . . ." She let a long moment pass. "And lovers." She lifted her glass. "Cheers to Edward, the new man in my life."

GLOSSARY OF TERMS

Kiln A kiln is a thermally insulated chamber, a type of oven, that produces temperatures sufficient to process a substance, such as by hardening, drying, or altering it chemically. Various industries and trades use kilns to harden clay objects and transform them into pottery, tiles, and bricks. The earliest known kiln dates to around 6000 BC and was found at the Yarim Tepe site in modern Iraq. Neolithic kilns were able to produce temperatures greater than 1600 degrees Fahrenheit. Their uses include annealing, fusing and deforming glass, and fusing metallic oxide paints with the surface of glass. Kilns operated by electricity were developed in the twentieth century, primarily for smaller-scale use, such as in schools, universities, and hobby centers.

Slumping This process involves heating glass in a kiln from room temperature to a temperature high enough to cause it to soften and slump (sag) into or over a mold. The finished item takes the shape of the mold.

Upcycling Also known as creative reuse, upcycling is the process of transforming by-products, waste materials, and useless and/or unwanted products into new materials or products of a better quality or a better environmental value. Upcycling is the opposite of downcycling, which is another aspect of the recycling process. Downcycling involves converting useless materials and products into new materials of greater quality. Most recycling involves converting useless material into reusable material or extracting useful materials from a product and creating a different, useful product. Upcycling has been increasing due to its current marketability and the lower cost of reused materials.

INFORMATION ABOUT
STAINED GLASS INSTRUCTION

Signing up for a class that teaches you how to recycle your excess bottles is an excellent way to save the environment. Webb's Glass Shop is based on Grand Central Stained Glass & Graphics, a business owned by our friends Eloyne and Bradley Erickson. The Web site for the business is www.grandcentralstainedglass.com. I'm very lucky to live in St. Petersburg, Florida, where there are multiple instructional glass shops all within a short driving time.

Find a class by searching the Internet for "stained glass classes" within your town, city, or state. Most classes have six to eight sessions and meet for a few hours each week. There are usually also various classes geared toward single-session or short-term projects specially designed to help you create a specific item or try your hand at a particular glass method. Many upcycle/DIY projects can be undertaken in this type of class.

If you have no glass shops near you, there are Web-based tutorials available that can teach some of the basics necessary to complete a simple project. I find these most helpful when I need to review a technique that I haven't used for a while. The instructions are usually step-by-step, with pictures and videos with an accompanying narrative. The best online classes offer a trial period, so you pay for the class only when you commit to it.

Chapter 1

Savannah fingered the key ring her late father had used only a week ago. She knew each key by memory, having used them from babyhood up through borrowing his car with her newly issued driver's license. She clenched them in her fist and took a deep shaky breath. *Dad will never twirl them barely out of my reach again.*

Paint flaked off the heavy, fireproofed and double-bolted back door. *It's like Dad,* she thought, *well-worn, but strong and solid.*

How could her smart, funny, marathon running dad die of a heart attack?

Savannah unlocked the shop, stepped into his office, and keyed the alarm code. With walls built of salvaged barn wood, the tiny space awakened a vision of his shoulders hunched over a mountain of paperwork. The sharp smoky scent of his aftershave clutched her heart.

Stop thinking about him. The students will be here soon.

Forcing a slow breath, she dropped the keys onto the rolltop desk that had once been her grandfather's. Small pilings of papers, files, bills, and Post-it notes covered every available flat surface and all the pigeon holes were stuffed like magpie nests. Grandpa Roy had used the sturdy desk for the motorcycle business he'd started after World War I. In continuous use by her family since the 1920s, it looked at her with serious expectations.

I guess you're mine now. I'll do my best.

She ran her hand over the top and smiled when her fingers reached the dent caused by a wildly thrown toy rocket when she was five. Her dad had yelled at her.

He seldom yelled.

Startled by the ringing of the black wall-mounted phone, she cleared her throat and picked up the receiver. "Webb's Glass Shop. May I help you?"

"Oh my. I wasn't expecting a real person. I meant to leave a message."

Good guess. I don't feel like a real person today. "It's okay. I'm opening up. May I help you?"

"I wanted to know if class has been cancelled. I would completely understand, you know, because the funeral was on Saturday. It was so awesome—all those young men in military uniforms."

Savannah flinched, recalling the haunting echo of *Taps* floating behind the gravestone that marked the final rejoining of her parents. She swallowed quickly. "Classes are being held as scheduled beginning today. Which one are you taking?"

"I'm in Beginning Stained Glass."

"It starts in half an hour. What's your name?"

"Amanda Blake. I signed up for more classes with

John, I mean with Mr. Webb, last month, but I thought the shop might close."

"Hugh Trevor is taking over the classes for Dad. I mean Mr. Webb. I'll see you in—"

"Oh my goodness. Are you Savannah?"

"Yes, I'm—"

"I am so, so sorry. I saw you at the funeral. You must be devastated. Mr. Webb was so proud of you. He talked about you all the time."

"Thank you. I have to—"

"He was so proud that you were studying at Pilchuck Glass School on a special scholarship. He told every class about how you won the Spinnaker Art Festival on your first entry when you were only seventeen."

"How embarrassing. Every class?"

"Yes, it was always in his first lecture."

Savannah struggled to keep her voice from breaking. "It's going to be difficult to—"

"Your dad looked so strong, so healthy, and so positively vital . . . if you know what I mean."

"Yes, it was a shock."

"He was such an excellent teacher and mentor. How are you going to manage everything?"

"I'm not sure yet." Savannah's stomach fluttered. "Sorry, but I've got to go. I'll see you in class." Savannah clicked the receiver down before Amanda could continue.

You're not the only one who is confused about why he died.

Savannah finger combed her short black hair, tugged up the waistband of her skinny jeans, and rolled up the cuffs of her classic white shirt. It was her basic teaching uniform. Calm, she focused on getting the shop ready for the day's business.

Shoving the key ring into her back pocket and

picking up the waiting stack of student handouts, she walked into the classroom. Situated between the office and the retail area, the large classroom contained six sturdy worktables for students, each with a tall wooden stool. As she placed a large brown manila envelope on each of the worktables, she remembered how her dad had experimented with various table sizes, table heights, stool types, and the number of students per table.

He'd tried to rope in Hugh to help, but his long-time assistant had no empathy for a student's environment. However, the crusty Hugh could teach a mule about the beauty, art, and mystic nature of always-liquid glass. Her dad's meticulous research had resulted in the current configuration of three rows of two worktables facing a whiteboard on the front wall and an instructor worktable facing the class. He'd practically wiggled with joy after he'd found the perfect environment for his students to create great glass art.

She switched on the overhead natural lighting that illuminated the projects of former students displayed around the walls. Her heart wrenched when she noticed her dad had placed her first piece, the traditional green turtle sun catcher panel, on the narrow shelf of the whiteboard. He had been planning to use it for the first demonstration project. Tears immediately formed and she pulled a tissue from her back pocket to press them away.

In her mind's eye, she saw her nail-bitten child's fingers struggling with the pieces of green glass. She had desperately willed them to be nimble and sure as she assembled the little turtle under her dad's watchful guidance. It must have pleased him to no end to use it as an example for the class.

After switching on the task lighting lamp for each worktable, she walked to the room at the front of the shop facing the street. It served as the student display gallery and retail section. It was neat and orderly as he'd always kept it.

Off to her right, she looked at the closed door of her dad's custom workshop. They had spent many, many hours working on delicate restorations, complicated repairs, and amazing consignments from almost every church in the city.

Deliberately delaying opening up the workspace that held her oldest and strongest memories, she found the right key and unlocked the front door. *If I don't open the workshop door, I can imagine that he's still in there working on his latest project. I know it's childish, but I don't have to be a grown up all the time.*

At twenty minutes before ten, it was a little early to open the shop, but some students preferred to arrive early so they could lay claim to their work area. She looked out the floor-to-ceiling windows that ran the length of the storefront to see a short man with an elaborate comb-over getting out of a red BMW then striding up to the door.

"Rats," she muttered. It was the owner of Lattimer's Glass Shop, her dad's competitor. She pushed down a rush of panic and put on her face reserved for welcoming customers. Savannah opened the door. "Hi Frank. What brings you down here to the Grand Central District? Your shop is still downtown, right?"

Frank pursed his soft lips into a thin line. "Good morning, Savannah. I see you're opening up. I thought we could talk about my offer to buy Webb's Glass Shop." He stepped closer, but she blocked him from entering.

"I'm not ready."

"What's to get ready? Why are you torturing yourself when you could accept my offer and be on your way back to Seattle?"

Not slamming the door in his face took willpower. "I'm on bereavement leave. My scholarship will still be there when I get back. Besides, I haven't worked out all the finances yet."

"You can trust me on this. It's a generous offer."

Savannah started closing the door, "Yours is not the only offer, you know.

"Oh sure, that land shark Smythe can mention a tempting figure," he said, putting a name to the corporate real estate tycoon who wanted to buy the block to build a Big Value Store. "But he has to work through his corporate office *and* get the other stores to sell along with you. I'm only trying to save you time and trouble. Come on, Vanna. Your dad would have signed in a heartbeat."

Savannah snapped, "That's a bald-faced lie. The two of you hadn't spoken in ten years."

"You know he was a good businessman. That doesn't necessarily mean he wouldn't approve."

"Approve? You didn't even come to the funeral. He would expect me to have thrown you out on your ear."

Frank was quiet and the silence between them grew large and heavy. He looked down. "I'm sorry. I was busy. We did have some pretty wide differences. But that's only natural between teacher and student. He really was a wonderful teacher. I never thanked him for all he taught me. Now it's too late."

Savannah looked at the floor and took a calming breath. "Look. I need to check the books. I'm not turning it down. Quite the opposite. I need to make sure everything is ready and that there are no financial surprises."

"No one was a better businessman. John would have approved."

"He sounded stressed the last few . . . Never mind. Let's meet downtown for lunch, say Wednesday at the Casita Taqueria just down the street. I promise I'll give you either an answer or a counteroffer."

"Fair enough." Frank nodded his head. "I'll see you then. Vanna, trust me. John would have approved."

She leaned out the door. "Don't call me Vanna," she yelled as an afterthought, watching him scrunch back into his sleek status symbol, screeching tires as he drove away.

She had been lying. She had no intention of selling to Frank. If all went well, she would leave for Seattle the next day and let Hugh handle everything else. *I should have told Frank,* she mused. *A little suffering would do him good.*

Closing the door gently enough not to jangle the bell at the top, Savannah slipped behind the retail counter facing the entry door and tentatively pushed the power ON button to the point-of-sale PC. She watched it nervously, her fingers crossed that it would start up. Pushing the button was all she knew how to do.

I hope Hugh is on his way. It's more than strange for him not to be here already. I better call again. We need to finalize the transition plan of ownership of Webb's. I also need him to teach this class.

Savannah picked up the phone beside the screen and ran her finger down the tattered list of contacts taped to the counter top, stopping at *Hugh Trevor*. She dialed the number and heard his answering machine message. "I'm out. You know the drill." *Beep*.

"Hugh, are you there? It's Savannah. I need your help to open the shop. I hope you're on the way. Please be on the way. Please. See you soon."

As she spoke, the doorbell jangled fiercely and a tall man dressed in black western boots, black jeans, and a French blue oxford shirt topped with a black string tie bolted through. "Don't touch it," he cautioned in a BBC-newscaster accent. "If the cash register starts up wonky, it'll be ages before it sorts itself out."

Savannah looked into his seriously green eyes and caught a faint whiff of Polo Black. He crowded her to the side and peered at the PC screen. As she was six-foot in stocking feet, not many men looked down on her.

She stretched around his back to hang up the phone. "I didn't want to start it, but I couldn't wait for Hugh any longer. Who are you?"

He peered into the monitor. "Good. Coming online and"—he looked for a certain sign from the monitor—"brilliant. It's happy." He pulled back then turned to her. "I have the same system next door and I had a meltdown with mine this morning."

"Right, but who—"

The tinkle of the door opening interrupted Savannah's question. A plump young woman with wildly spiked pink and yellow hair entered the shop. Wearing a white peasant blouse and patchwork midi skirt, she shouldered through the door balancing a huge purse, a canvas bag of tools, a briefcase overfilled with glass remnants, and a large plywood square for mounting stained glass work.

Green-eyed man lunged to hold open the door. "Amanda, you shouldn't try to carry everything at once."

Savannah's eyebrows lifted.

Puffing like an espresso machine, Amanda said, "It's all right. Two trips would take too much energy. My aura has been weak since I heard the terrible news about Mr. Webb." She made a beeline for the classroom.

Savannah scurried over to push the classroom door out of the way. She nudged a doorstop in place to keep it open.

Amanda grunted and plopped her bundles on the worktable in the first row. "I want to sit where I can see." She nudged her bold orange glasses back onto her nose. "Savannah! Oh my goodness. You're just as beautiful as John said." She clamped Savannah in a round tight tug, stepped back, and looked into her face. "And you have his cobalt blue eyes. I'm so happy to meet you."

"Thank you, Amanda. Welcome to class."

Savannah turned to stare pointedly at the green-eyed man.

Again, the doorbell jangled and two slender elderly women entered, wearing matching gray ruffled blouses with gray polyester pants over gray ballet flat shoes. They carried large gray tote bags. One carried hers over the left shoulder. The other twin carried hers over the right shoulder. Even their round black glasses were identical.

Savannah gulped. *I'll never be able to tell these two apart.*

"Let's sit in the back. I don't like others to overlook my work," said one twin.

"Silly. Everyone walks around and looks at each

other's projects. It's how we learn. Let's go for the front so we can hear properly," said the other twin.

The first twin put her materials on the far back worktable. "It's my turn to pick the seats. You chose for the pottery class."

"Very well. But don't whine if you can't hear the instructions."

"It's my turn."

Savannah turned to Green Eyes and whispered, "Have they been here before?"

His eyes crinkled, and he leaned closer and whispered, "The Rosenberg twins, Rachel and Faith, are addicted to craft classes."

"So, they're good?"

"Let's just say they make everyone else feel above average. They take classes for the sheer joy of criticizing each other. And they lie. About the quality of each other's work, about who made what mistake. They lie when there's no need to lie. They're the biggest liars in the district."

The bell announced the arrival of a deeply tanned couple. He was brown-haired with brown eyes wearing khaki cargo shorts, a closely tailored navy golf shirt, and Topsiders without socks. She was blonde with sky blue eyes wearing a perfectly tailored khaki skirt with a teal sweater set accented by a single strand of pearls. They were perfectly on trend and looked more like they should be boarding a cruise ship rather than attending an art class. They slipped into the remaining open row of worktables.

The early-forties trying to look late-twenties woman looked around as though welcoming them into her living room. She smiled at each person until she caught their eye, and when she had everyone's attention, she said, "Good morning, y'all. We're Mr. and

Mrs. Young. I'm Nancy and this is my groom, Arthur. I've called him my groom since the day Daddy announced our engagement. I'm the Director of Programs at the Museum of Fine Arts and my groom plays third chair cello for the Florida Orchestra. We're so happy to be here taking this wonderful class with y'all."

Green Eyes grinned a wide smile and turned to Savannah. He caught himself and the smirk disappeared behind an uncomfortable cough. He shifted his weight slightly foot to foot. "Look. I wanted to offer my sincere condolences. I think the loss of your father is one of life's most devastating events."

"That's very kind, but who—"

"Most of us along this street were at his funeral. I stayed behind to run the pub so most of my staff could attend. John made such a difference in standing up for the small businesses on this block. We'll miss his advice and experience in negotiating with the mayor and city council."

"Thank you so much. I appreciate it."

"I've got to get back to the pub." He walked out then turned to lean back through the front door. "If you need anything, I'm right next door or you can call. My number is on the list under Edward, Edward Morris. I own the Queen's Head Pub. Welcome to the Grand Central District." He quietly closed the door with a small click.

Savannah smiled and let out a sigh of relief. She was glad he was right next door. It looked like she might have more on her plate than she originally expected, especially if Hugh made a habit of running late. She checked the list of contact numbers and there was Edward's number standing out clearly on the smudged list. She plugged it into her cell.

Checking her dad's roster, the five registered class members had all arrived. She frowned. Where was the sixth and even more worrying, where was Hugh? She glanced at the large plain clock on the wall. It said 10:00 sharp as did her watch.

I'm going to have to start teaching his class until he gets here. I haven't taught beginning stained glass since I left for Seattle. Yikes, that's over five years ago. I hope it's like riding a bicycle.

She softly stepped behind the instructor's workstation and cleared her throat. "Good morning. I'm Savannah, Mr. Webb's daughter." Her voice shook at the mention of her dad. Ducking her head, she covered her mouth with her fist to clear her voice and stabilize it to a lower tone. "Welcome to Beginning Stained Glass. Each class will be structured roughly the same. First, a short lecture followed by a skill demonstration. Then you'll practice on a small piece to reinforce the skill. Hugh Trevor will be your instructor. He's a master glass craftsman who—"

Amanda's hand shot up into the air. "What's the project?"

"A small sun catcher panel." Savannah picked up her little green turtle sun catcher and held it high. "It's a simple design, but looks complicated. You will learn the skills of cutting glass, applying copper foil, soldering, and bending zinc came."

"What's that zinc cane stuff? I thought we were learning to make proper leaded stained glass," said Nancy.

"Good question." Savannah turned and wrote *C A M E* on the whiteboard. "Lead is a heavy metal that can, over time, leach into your skin. The new came is a preformed miniature U-shaped channel of zinc that can be bent to follow the edges of the panel. Modern knowledge sometimes overtakes tradition."

She looked at the door once again. *Hugh better have a damn good excuse for not coming in today.*

"Now, for a quick history lesson. Honest, I do mean quick. As a material, stained glass is colored by adding metallic salts during its manufacture. In ancient time, the colored glass was crafted into windows held together by strips of lead and supported by a rigid frame. The oldest known—"

A scraping shuffle and the jangle of the doorbell turned all heads to the front of the shop.

Thank goodness. That must be Hugh.

A gangly blue-jeaned young man with a black backpack over his shoulder rushed through the display room and into the classroom. He stopped cold in front of Savannah. "Sorry, I signed up for this class," blurted the pale-faced teen. He looked down at the floor. "Mr. Webb told me I could attend this class. He promised me his apprentices don't have to pay."

Okay, here's the last student. How on earth could I forget about the apprentice? This must be Jacob. Dad was wildly enthusiastic about his talent, raving in fact. He said Jacob reminded him of me at eighteen. But, really, where is Hugh?

Savannah pointed to the remaining vacant work space. "It's no problem. You see we have plenty of room."

"I've been working with Mr. Webb and Mr. Trevor." The young man's eyes widened to owl-sized intensity.

"You must be Jacob. Mr. Webb told me so much about you, I feel like we're already friends." She pressed her hand over her heart. It was so like her dad to take this awkward fledgling under his wing as an apprentice. "My name is Savannah Webb. I'm Mr. Webb's daughter."

He gulped and nodded vigorously, then stepped forward to solemnly shake her hand. "My name is Jacob Underwood. Pleased to meet you."

She smiled. "Dad's apprentices are always invited to classes. Go ahead and get yourself settled." Savannah guided him to the remaining worktable.

"Where's Mr. Trevor?" Jacob perched on the work stool with his feet resting on the bottom rung and placed his backpack on his lap without letting go of the straps.

She moved back to the instructor station. "Mr. Trevor is delayed and I'm filling in until he arrives. Now, where was I?"

Amanda launched her plump hand into the air like a rocket. "You were telling us about the origins of stained glass."

"Yes. As I said, they crafted the colored glass into windows or objects held together by strips of lead and then supported by a rigid frame. The oldest known stained glass window was pieced together using ancient glass from an archaeological dig."

"What did she say?" One of the twins leaned into the other's ear, whispering loud enough for everyone to look back at them.

Faith flushed from her throat to the roots of her white hair and whispered even louder, "Turn on your hearing aid, Rachel. You've forgotten again."

"Oops," muttered Rachel, turning the tiny volume control up with her polished blood red fingernail until there was a high-pitched squeal.

Gotcha! Rachel wears nail polish. Faith doesn't.

"Now, it's too loud!" Faith frowned. "Turn it down and be quiet."

Rachel adjusted the volume and ducked her head in a sheepish grin to everyone. "I'm ready now."

Savannah started again. "First things first. Before we start learning to cut glass, make sure your work surface is clean and clear of debris. If even the smallest glass chip is under your work, it will break in the wrong place and ruin your day. The best thing is to use a very soft brush on the entire work surface before you start anything. A well-worn paint brush works great, but Dad always used an old drafting table brush."

He gave me mine when I took my first class. It's back in Seattle. She swept her worktable clear and spread newspaper on the work surface.

"I want everyone to take out their clear window-pane glass for scoring and breaking practice." She held up a small nine by nine-inch square piece for everyone to see. "The green piece of glass is for your project. Just put that aside."

"Ouch!" Arthur dropped his practice pane onto the worktable in a shattering crash. "I cut myself." He squeezed his thumb until a large drop formed, stuck it in his mouth, and began to suck the blood.

"Don't, honey bunny. It'll get infected. You have to be ready for the next concert." Nancy dived a hand into her purse, hopped off her stool, pulled Arthur's thumb out of his mouth with a soft *pop,* and pressed a tissue onto the cut. She looked around and eyed Savannah. "Is there a first aid kit?"

Savannah crossed the room to the large Red Cross first aid kit attached to the wall. A quick rummage produced a square compress pad and some ointment. She handed them to Nancy who was right behind her.

"Let me see," said Amanda, leaning over Arthur's hand. "I'm a trained caregiver, you know. I work in a nursing home."

Ah, she must liven up that atmosphere considerably. Savannah edged in between the women to get to Arthur. "I've got this, ladies. I can't even begin to tell you how many cuts I've dressed here and in Seattle. I've a finely tuned judgment for stitch count." She gently removed the sodden tissue, refolded it to expose a clean section, and then pressed it firmly onto the cut. "Good, it's small. No stitches."

Nancy fanned her face. "Thank our lucky stars, Arthur. You know that second chair cello player is unreliable." She mimed that he was a drinker. "You must be prepared to step into first chair at any performance."

Amanda peered over Savannah's shoulder. "It is quite small, but glass cuts are the evil older brother of paper cuts—so much blood for such a tiny nick."

"Miss Savannah, Miss Savannah." Jacob hugged his arms around his chest and rocked his weight from side to side. "I need to get my tools."

"Of course." She softened her voice and tilted her head. "Where are they?"

"Mr. Webb let me keep 'em in the workshop."

"No problem." Savannah pulled the key ring from her back pocket and handed them over to Jacob. "Go fetch them, please. It's the blue key." She turned back to deal with the Arthur situation.

"No need, Miss Savannah," he returned the key ring. "I have a set of my own."

Nancy wedged her body between Arthur and Savannah. "Excuse me. I can take care of my Arthur, thank you. Just hand over everything I need."

Amanda flushed a bright hot pink and returned to her seat, struggling to control her trembling lip.

Savannah used her teacher voice. "I'm sorry, ma'am. I'm the only one present who is authorized to give first aid in this shop. If you want to treat him yourself, that's fine, but you'll have to leave the class." She looked from Nancy to Arthur's bleeding finger then back to Nancy. "Both of you."

The woman pressed her lips into a thin scarlet line. "Very well. Of course, I didn't understand that. We have similar rules at the Museum of Fine Arts."

The class watched silently as Savannah removed the tissue, applied an ointment, and taped the sturdy bandage to Arthur's wound.

As one, the class looked up at Savannah.

"Okay, first blood goes to Arthur. Well done. Amanda is right. Glass cuts bleed like fury, but by their nature, the cuts are clean and normally heal quickly."

"Miss Savannah," shrieked Jacob, his voice breaking. "Miss Savannah, please come quick!"

Savannah nearly jumped out of her skin, then bolted through the door of the classroom, ran through the gallery and into her dad's workshop. Amanda was on her heels.

Jacob was pointing to the far wall of the custom workshop behind a long workbench. "Mr. Trevor won't wake up."

Savannah saw Hugh lying on his side with his face toward the wall. "Uncle Hugh, Uncle Hugh!" She could hear her voice shriek as she struggled to roll him over onto his back. His kind face was ash gray and he had been sick on his clothes. The sour smell was sharp and fresh. His chest was still and he wasn't breathing.

"Amanda, call 911!"

She was aware of Amanda's sharp gasp and heard her feet pound steps toward the phone. Savannah straightened him as much as possible in the tight space. Making a fist with one hand and the other hand wrapped around it, she started chest compressions to the rhythm of "Staying Alive" as her CPR coach had taught her. She didn't know that she was crying until the tears dropped one by one onto her forearms.

No way was she stopping. Uncle Hugh was all the home she had left. He needed to stay alive.

She dimly heard the ambulance arrive and numbly got to her feet when the paramedic gently lifted her up from the floor by her elbow.

Uncle Hugh can't be dead, too.

Catch up with Savannah in

Shards of Murder

On sale now wherever books and ebooks are sold!

Chapter 1

"You're going to love the Beach Blonde." Savannah raised her glistening pint of straw-colored beer to clink her former mentor Keith Irving's glass. "It reminds me of my favorite ale back in Seattle."

"You had a favorite? I seem to recall that you were determined to try a different beer every time we walked into a brewery."

Is he saying that I was flighty? When she had been Keith's student back in Seattle, she *had* been a little prone to fancy. She was always exploring new glass-working techniques before she had completely mastered the old ones. That must have been frustrating for him—he drew on an unlimited reserve of patience with her erratic experimentation.

Keith sipped the ale and his dark bushy eyebrows raised over his iris blue eyes. Putting his pint back on the beer mat, he looked around the 3 Daughters Brewing tasting room. "You have a point, though. This is as good as anything back home."

"Damn straight," Savannah grinned wide. It was a

warm reminder of how much she desired his approval. She and Keith were sitting at a high top near the back of the tasting room. The noisy after-work happy hour crowd had gone and the Friday night date crowd hadn't yet arrived. That meant that the modern industrial décor felt cozy and intimate rather than raucous and celebratory.

Keith looked down into his beer. "My condolences on the death of your father. He was a significant loss to the stained glass world. I'm very sorry."

"Thank you, I appreciate that. I didn't realize how well respected he was until after he was gone."

"How are you coping?"

"Not as well as I would like. It was a—" She was startled by the tightening of her throat. It had already been a couple of months. "It was a difficult time. It still is, for that matter. But now, I've got some great help. My office manager, Amanda Blake, is an outrageously cheerful person and I've taken on Dad's apprentice, Jacob Underwood. He's incredibly talented, and the deep concentration required for the craft helps him manage life with Asperger's syndrome. Jacob is flourishing to the real benefit of Webb's."

"Is it true what I heard?" He tilted his head slightly with a gentle smile. "That you were involved in the investigation of your father's death?"

Savannah wiped a hand across her forehead, then cupped her pint. "Yes, it turned out that both Dad and his longtime assistant were murdered. I arrived here planning to sell up and return to Seattle, but I was driven to decode the messages my father left behind. Dad had been a cryptographer for the government. The result of the adventure was that it helped the police catch the murderer.

Everyone helped and I felt like I found my forever home."

"So, you not only dealt with the death of your father, but helped catch his murderer—I just can't imagine the emotional toll."

Savannah looked around the brewing house, taking a long moment to clarify her feelings. "It was a horrible experience, but oddly satisfying in the end. I learned some valuable lessons. First, I have some incredible friends who care about me. Second, the local business community has supported Webb's from the time my grandfather had a motorcycle business here in the twenties until my dad started the glass shop. My family inspired that."

Keith nodded slowly and sat silent for a few moments. "Speaking of Webb's, what's it like to go from student to business owner in a heartbeat?"

Savannah looked up at the ceiling, "Wow, you are literally correct with that one. I'm still struggling with the abrupt change of focus. There are so many things that Dad took care of that I'm discovering surprise by surprise."

"It requires a totally different skill set from a carefree creative artist. The transition from student to master requires tremendous personal growth. Some can't do it. You appear to be doing fine."

Squirming in her seat, Savannah replied, "Carefree artist is a good description of my former self. I'm having difficulty with the role of community leader within the Grand Central District of St. Petersburg, Florida. I don't have a background in politics and it's all about relationships and history and things that I don't know about."

Keith leaned over, a conspiratorial glint in his eyes.

"I'll tell you a secret. No one understands small-town politics."

Savannah laughed. "I'm so glad you're here. I've been tossed a huge speed bump. My dad's friends appointed me as the judge in the glass category for the Spinnaker Art Festival this weekend."

Keith was in town for the festival to support one of his current protégés in entering the competition. He already knew all about Savannah's appointment as a judge—and her nerves surrounding the job.

Keith chuckled. "As my former star pupil, I expect it won't take very much advice to bring you up to speed."

"Judging was not a part of your curriculum back at the studio." She sipped her beer. "Seriously, how do I choose?"

"I've never found it difficult to choose a winner. My challenge has always been to keep from alienating the chief judge and the other artists. Innovation in the glass arts is not always of interest to the mainstream art collectors or appreciated by the organizational committee. Did they give you some guidelines to follow?"

"They didn't have time to give me anything. The original judge was going to be my dad. He was famous for his widely popular choices—he wouldn't have needed them. Their first replacement had a family emergency, so they turned on the charm and I accepted. I'm simply a last-minute solution."

"Do you think the reason they called on you as a judge was solely due to your dad's reputation?"

"Frankly, I think it was the safe thing to do. They could give it to me as a tribute to my dad's memory and give the snub to Frank Lattimer once again."

She named the owner of Webb's rival glass shop.

Frank was not well loved in town, and his failed attempt to buy out Webb's during a vulnerable time was well known. Even though she was nervous about judging a competition, she was privately pleased that the festival committee had given their support to her over Frank.

Keith looked surprised. "Oh, come on now, you can't believe that. Surely they wouldn't go that far to insult him. He has a business right downtown with a huge display gallery."

"I don't know who in particular he has annoyed on the committee, but Frank can annoy even the most amiable of supporters." She paused, then admitted, "Honestly, in all practicality, they should have given him the job this year. I don't have very many qualifications other than being John Webb's poor orphan daughter."

"Don't sell yourself short. I can give you enough practical guidance to get you through the Spinnaker Art Festival—I've been judging for more years than I care to admit. But, in reality, all I can do is tell you how I approach judging." He grinned. "Judge for yourself what makes sense to you. Your instincts are good."

"If you say so." Savannah sipped her beer.

"I say so. Remember what I used to say?"

"Oh no, not a test! You were a fountain of inspirational quotes."

Keith chuckled. "Okay, but this one is true. 'Life begins at the end of your comfort zone.'" He paused and poked a finger into her upper arm. "You know that."

Savannah leaned away and nodded. "I remember that one. I've been living it."

"Anyway, first I walk around and get a quick look at

each exhibit booth and see if any of them hit me emotionally without analyzing or thinking about it. That gives me a chance to see if there are any works that immediately stand out from the rest, and it has been my experience that the winner is usually among them. Later, I stop in front of each booth and analyze what I see in design, color, and mastery of technique."

"That's easy enough."

"Also, if the technique is traditional, such as a Tiffany-style stained glass lamp, it should be a new approach. I always look for something unique showing me a deep understanding of the underlying principles, or a completely different twist on the ordinary."

"That sounds pretty straightforward."

"It should be—and that's the secret. A truly unique approach to glass should stand out like a flame in the darkness."

"Ugh, I'm terrified that I won't live up to Dad's reputation."

"Understandable, but no one would have more faith in your judgment." Keith covered her hand with his and gave it a light squeeze before letting go. "He was a great judge, but you're his daughter, and I have to tell you, the apple didn't fall far from the tree." He grinned widely, and Savannah smiled as well.

Maybe I have a natural instinct. That would be awesome.

"The timing couldn't be much worse." She ran a hand through her closely cropped curly black hair. "I'm starting a new weeklong workshop on Monday."

"Timing will never be right. What type of class?"

"This one teaches the major aspects of fused glass. I've got a monstrous new kiln installed along with one that Dad already had and we're almost ready to go. I haven't even tested the big one yet, but I'll do that this weekend. It has an electronic control panel to automate the timing and temperature changes for the firings. That makes the process less math intensive. Even better, we can let it run overnight and increase our production.

"That's good for both students and clients. The ones we use for teaching in the studio require hand calculations for glass size and a timer for changing the manual temperature settings. It's tedious, but the real purpose is to teach a thorough understanding of the principles of fusing."

"That's exactly the right approach." He touched her arm softly. "How about dinner?"

"Sorry, I'd like that but I'm totally distracted by everything that's swirling around right now. How about after the festival is over? I'll be in a much better mood."

She sensed a movement behind her.

"So, this is your mentor?" Edward pulled up a bar stool between Savannah and Keith. His posh British accent oozed smoothly from a thin frame in a black shirt over tight jeans tucked into tan rattlesnake Western boots. He extended a hand. "Hi, I'm Edward Morris, owner of the Queen's Head Pub, right next door to Webb's Glass Shop. I hear that you're the best hot glass teacher in the world."

Savannah widened her eyes. Edward must have stopped by to arrange for more beer for his pub. She didn't specifically invite him to meet Keith here. Edward was not yet a lover—but definitely a strong candidate. Savannah's reticence was mostly because her feelings were still a mess of unresolved ex-boyfriend angst. Plus there was the complication that Edward had been a principal suspect in the murder of her father.

Keith stood and shook hands with the very tall man. "Keith Irving. I've heard about you, too."

They stood looking eye to eye. Savannah felt the tension sizzle while also realizing in a flash that both men were the same height.

Savannah patted Edward's stool. He took the hint and sat.

Keith sat and looked sideways at Edward. "Glad to hear the nice part of my reputation precedes me."

"There's a not nice part?"

Savannah smothered a huge cough with her hand, then rearranged her face to disguise the surprise and slight annoyance at Edward's comment. "Keith has the well-deserved reputation for destroying glasswork that doesn't meet his exacting artistic standards. I've left the studio shattered in every sense of the word more than once."

Keith stiffened his back a bit taller. "In truth, there's no room for the merely ordinary at Pilchuck Glass School. It's not helpful for the growth of a student to condone mediocrity. Remarkably, the threat of immediate destruction brings out their best work. For the naturally gifted"—he eyed Savannah—"it gives them amazing confidence to start a successful career as a true artisan."

Savannah grimaced over at Edward. "A lecture I've heard more than once."

Keith sipped his beer and looked at Edward over the rim. "I've heard about your escapades with Savannah, as well. Helping her find the man who murdered her father is a task most would not have accepted."

"It was a team effort. We're a very close community here in the Grand Central District. Besides, an actual third-generation St. Petersburg native is as rare as bluebells in July. She deserves to be safe from harm."

Edward waved a hand to the bartender. "Hi, Mike. My regular pint of Brown Pelican, please." He turned to Keith. "So, other than the lovely Savannah, what brings you to town?"

Savannah looked sharply at Edward. *What's wrong with you?*

"Good question," said Keith. "I am a long way from home."

Savannah smiled and propped her chin into both hands.

Keith raised both hands in surrender. "I confess I'm here for more than just a visit to see a former student. Two of our students from Pilchuck have taken jobs with the local Chihuly Museum as interns to learn the business end of art."

"But I thought there was a program for that in Seattle," said Savannah.

"There is, but there aren't enough positions for each student to have an opportunity to rotate through the program. It's not just learning about the various methods and history of the glassworks; they also learn to care for the exhibits and discover the harsh realities of an invisible monster named 'cash flow.' "

Edward squinted. "What do you mean by caring for the exhibits? They're all glass. They don't need to be fed or watered or anything."

Savannah and Keith looked at each other for a second. Keith motioned for Savannah to answer.

"It's extremely important that the glassworks in the museum stay dust free. It's not such an issue in Seattle, but here in hot, sandy Florida, it's quite a challenge. Each visitor brings in a bit of the outside and it's impossible to control that. So someone needs to dust the priceless and very fragile exhibits without breaking them. That's what students learn to do."

"Oh." Edward looked sheepish. "Duh."

"Don't feel bad." Savannah squeezed Edward's arm. "It's not particularly obvious."

"Anyway," said Keith, "I'm here to check up on the program and also to help one of them with setting up an exhibit booth tomorrow at Spinnaker."

"You have a student in the show?"

"Yes, he was admitted in good time so that we could arrange the intern position with the Chihuly Museum. Another of my former students, Megan Loyola, has also been accepted into the festival. She reminds me very much of you." Keith nodded toward Savannah.

"How so?"

"She's wicked smart and has a genius for inventing glass techniques to form something completely different and spectacular. I can't wait for you to see her work."

"Hey, you're not trying to influence a judge are you?"

Keith shook his head. "No chance. You are your father's daughter; he was unbelievably ethical. The interns are Vincent O'Neil and Leon Price. Vincent is a good craftsman with broad technical and mechanical knowledge. Leon, however, is a bit of an uptight urbanite and that rigidly controlled approach comes out in his work. They're sharing living and travel expenses. Leon is the one who has an exhibit booth at the Spinnaker Art Festival. Vincent applied, but didn't make the cut."

Edward shifted a bit and signaled the bartender for another round. He turned to Savannah. "Have you told Keith about your new project?"

"Not yet." She looked crossly at Edward. "I'm still in the investigation stage."

"What new project?" Keith drained the last of his beer.

"I'm going to open a new glass studio in this area. It will be the largest in the South once I've got it up and running."

"Wow, that's the kind of success we hope our students will achieve after they leave. Will it be in this area of town?"

"Only a few blocks south of here in an up-and-coming new industrial park district. It will be an artist's loft space with reasonable rental rates on a month-by-month plan. As an incentive to the eternally cash-strapped prospective client, I'm offering the space without a long-term lease."

"How much square footage?"

"I'm thinking over ten thousand square feet. Part of that will be an exhibit space. That will give my students a transition phase between student and professional artist. There will also be a media room for presentations and tutorials."

Edward shifted in his seat. "But you're keeping the original Webb's as well?"

"Absolutely." She sipped her beer. "That building has been in the family forever and is the anchor store in that block. It's absolutely perfect for beginners—but not for the intermediate- to advanced-level artists."

"Wow, Savannah," said Keith with emotion cracking his voice. "I predicted great things from your skill and talent, but this fantastic news is beyond my expectations. What are you going to call it? Where is it going to be?"

"Webb's Studio is the working title I'm using until

I register it as a business name and have my accountant file the corporation paperwork. He'll organize a name search to make sure it's unique, but I think it is." She smiled. "I've been looking at some available warehouse properties a little south of where we're sitting. I think I've found a candidate location."

Edward lifted his glass. "A toast to the success of Webb's Studio." The three glasses clinked in perfect harmony.

GREAT BOOKS, GREAT SAVINGS!

When You Visit Our Website:
www.kensingtonbooks.com
You Can Save Money Off The Retail Price
Of Any Book You Purchase!

- All Your Favorite Kensington Authors
- New Releases & Timeless Classics
- Overnight Shipping Available
- eBooks Available For Many Titles
- All Major Credit Cards Accepted

Visit Us Today To Start Saving!
www.kensingtonbooks.com

All Orders Are Subject To Availability.
Shipping and Handling Charges Apply.
Offers and Prices Subject To Change Without Notice.